BREATHLESS

"Whoa there, card man! What do you think you're do-ing?"

A challenge darkened his eyes into midnight coals. Nick smiled, a beguiling expression that made her flutter where she wasn't sure she had any ruffles.

"I'm undressing. Getting cleaned up . . . for dinner." He unfastened one button, then another.

"But I thought you'd, I'd, well, we'd—" As the last button unfastened and Nick's broad shoulders were suddenly bared, Alewine stood there with her mouth gaping. His muscles, shiny with perspiration, flexed with the mere effort of folding his shirt and laying it on top of the armoire. Some slender thread of propriety told her she ought to turn around and close her mouth, but he looked too good to stop staring.

His smile broadened, deepening each dimple until her own lips curved in response. When it dawned on her that she was staring ogle-eyed at him, Aly did an abrupt about-face. Once, twice, she blinked, finding it difficult to breathe and trying hard to rid herself of his tempting image. She hadn't felt this winded since getting bucked off Ol' Bone-Buster last spring.

Other *Leisure* books by Dia Hunter:
THE BEHOLDING

THE GENTLE SEASON

DIA HUNTER

LEISURE BOOKS   NEW YORK CITY

A LEISURE BOOK®

April 2000

Published by

Dorchester Publishing Co., Inc.
276 Fifth Avenue
New York, NY 10001

ISBN 0-8439-4705-5

This book is dedicated to
Susan Akers.

Though our roads have often been rough,
we traveled them diligently and discovered
we were headed in the right direction
all along.

Thanks for your friendship,
your wonderful sense of humor
and for seeing around my rough edges
to discover the true me.

Also, a special thanks to Ginny Laut,
founder of the American Domestic Skunk Association,
and
to all the libraries on the Harrington Users Group
for providing the best research material available
.and the service to match it.

THE GENTLE SEASON

Chapter One

May, 1887

"Would ya look at that?" A tall, lanky cowhand swung open the batwing doors of the Lazy Lady Saloon, offering the patrons a better view of the street. "Anybody know what's going on over at the freight office?"

The tinny music banging out on the piano halted its jaunty rhythm. Several heads turned. Eyes peered through the smoky haze that layered the favorite drinking establishment in Valiant, Texas, eager to witness anything that would pump excitement into the uneventful May afternoon.

"Lots of cursing and carrying on?" Nicodemus Turner asked, leaning back to balance on the hind legs of his ladderback chair. His opponents' attention now focused on the commotion out in the street rather than on the poker game at hand. The gambler had tired of the game an hour ago, finding no real challenge with this particular trio.

"Before you answer . . ." He flipped a twenty-dollar gold piece into the air and caught it. "Anyone care to wager that smack dab in the middle of all that hooting and hollering is a bluster of blonde wearing buckskins and a coon cap?"

"Possibly," the cowboy admitted. "That is, if it's under all them feathers."

"Feathers?" The word was echoed as Nick's opponents stuffed their winnings into their pockets and headed into the street to investigate.

"Aly's gonna do it, by gawd!" one of them announced.

"Said she would," another patron confirmed. "Ain't never gone agin her word, that I know of."

The saloon girl standing beside Nick wrinkled her nose and shuddered. "Oooh, it gives me the shivers just thinking about it."

"Hell, everything gives you the shivers, Sadie. Get some hide on them bones or wear a coat." Ophelia Finck, the saloon's proprietress, frowned at her employee.

Nick gathered his winnings. With Aly back in town, his wait was finally over. "What's that cata-mount up to?"

Ophelia stepped from behind the bar, her full figure dressed in white from crown to slipper. She tapped her ivory-handled cane against the sawdust-covered floor planks.

"Don't tell me you forgot! I guess you've had your nose up everybody's petticoat so much the last few days, your brain must of developed flounces. The cradle . . . *remember*?"

"Cradle?" Feathers and a cradle didn't make any

sense. But neither did the past week of investigating every soiled dove in town. From the note Ophelia had found under her office door last week, he was certain one of those doves knew the identification of the man who was threatening to take Aly's freighting business by force. But all had kept silent for fear the stalker would carry through with his threat of cutting whoever talked. At Ophelia's approach, Nick stood without hesitation. Gambling hadn't made him forget he was a gentleman.

She linked her arm through his and stared up at him. "If you'd light in one place for a while instead of gallivanting all over the territory, you might've heard that Ben and Rachel McGuire's newest was born yesterday morning. Sweet little thing, she is. Six pounds of pure joy."

Nick shrugged. "What's that got to do with Aly making a fool out of herself?"

Ophelia's eyes narrowed. "Jar your memory, Nicodemus. Aly promised to have that city-bought cradle back here before the baby was born. Said if she didn't, she'd walk down Main Street in molasses and feathers and she'd—"

"Crow at dawn!" Laughter rumbled deep within Nick as he mulled over the image. Aly would do anything to keep her word—a fact he admired about her.

Ophelia tweaked one of the dimples bracketing his lips. "I'd know that chuckle anywhere, Nicky darlin'. And, if I was a betting woman—and mind you, I am— I'd say Miss Alewine P. Jones is about to be the victim of another one of your pranks."

While it was true he and Aly had each spent the last year trying to outdo the other in practical jokes, they also had become best friends during that time. Pranks were one thing, but he was as serious as an undertaker's measuring stick about this particular plan he had up his sleeve. "Let's just say I have an interesting proposition for Miss Jones."

"Got anything to do with that note I found?" Ophelia's brow knitted with concern.

"Maybe."

"Maybe Aly doesn't want your help, Nick."

He stared out into the street. "If she catches wind of what's going on, she won't be scared off by the threat, you know that. But if she thinks *she's* helping *me*, then I can protect her and won't have to sacrifice that stubborn pride of hers."

"Care to let me in on your plan?"

"I'm going to ask her to go to Prickly Bend with me and help me get Jezlynn. That will keep Aly out of harm's way for a while and give me time to settle *my* problem. Once I finish this issue over my daughter's guardianship, then I can concentrate on solving the freighting threat."

Ophelia's eyes brightened and a smile crept over her lips. "You know, you may have just given me an idea how I can help."

"Care to let me in on it?"

"Oh, I will, Nicodemus. I surely will when I've got it all figured out just the way I want it. In the meantime, do you have any idea how you're going to persuade Aly to go?"

"I'm going to challenge her to a bet." The more Nick thought about using a wager to convince Aly, the better sense it made. Adept at reading poker faces, he'd studied the lady freighter many times as she watched the McGuire family and their children. Nick had noticed on too many occasions the longing in Aly's eyes for a home and family of her own. His stomach knotted with compassion when he saw the rough-and-tumble buckskinned woman hide her tears every time Rachel McGuire showed her a new baby gown.

He also knew Alewine didn't want anyone, least of all him, to be aware of that vulnerability. For that reason, Nick kept his admiration of her secret. He'd known that one day, she would either warm to him romantically, or he could somehow stack the deck in his favor without destroying their friendship. That day had finally arrived.

"Looks like you're about to tempt the devil, Nicodemus Turner." Ophelia tapped her cane and motioned them forward.

"Close, 'Phel." Nick escorted the woman into the midst of the moving crowd, taking long strides to catch up with the vision marching down the thoroughfare, feathers flying. "I'm about to seduce Satan's taskmistress herself, and God help me if I lose."

Nick called out to Alewine, but couldn't be heard over the crowd. Sinking two fingers into his mouth, he produced a shrill whistle that elicited groans from nearby passersby. Still, he couldn't draw her attention. "Guess there's no other way but to . . . 'Phel, are you carrying your derringer?"

"I always go heeled." She raised her hem and unstrapped it from her thigh, never missing a step. "One of these days, you're going to wish you did, too."

"Me and guns, we don't even belong in the same territory." Nick nodded for her to fire the weapon. He'd vowed never to touch another gun in his life, and he meant it. Someone usually died when one was pointed, and innocents were left behind to survive and suffer, long after the victim lay in his grave. "Remind me never to ruffle your petticoats."

"Your brother's the only one who can get away with that."

"Lucky man."

When Ophelia fired a shot into the air, the whole crowd spun on its heels, facing her. Suddenly, one person sidestepped, then another as the vision pushed its way through the midst. Alewine Jones approached and a barrier of on-lookers parted to give room.

The lady freighter's hands balled immediately on her hips as her legs settled in a wide stance and challenge darkened her eyes to harvest gold. The fringe on her buckskin swayed, staining the ground with loosened feathers and dripping molasses. "Hellfire, snake piss, and cow turds, 'Phel! You nearly scared the hair off my scalp! Why'n thunder are you making such a spectacle of yerself?"

Silently, Nick thanked fate for the opportunity to set his challenge in motion. "Make a spectacle of herself? What about you?"

When Nick saw Aly's right eye narrow the way it always did when she was about to lash into somebody, he knew he had her right where he wanted her. "I believe that's about the silliest I've ever seen anyone look," he sneered.

Snickers rippled through the gathering. Alewine brushed back a wisp of white-blonde hair and retaliated. "I can think of something that'll look a wad worse."

"Oh?" Nick's hopes raised. Was she taking the bait?

Alewine's fists buried under her armpits, and she winged them like she was in flight. "Yeah, *your* sorry hide a-flapping with molasses and feathers." She cock-a-doodle-doo'ed, fanning her knees back and forth in rhythm with her arms.

Nick might have laughed with everyone, but the sight of her drenched from head to toe with feathers sticking out at all angles from her body and clucking like a chicken made him question his sanity. Why in the name of Bill Hickok did he find her so much more appealing than most women?

The real reason was no stranger to him. No amount of feathers and molasses could stave off the image Nick had secretly hoarded away in his thoughts. Aly had surprised him a year ago when she'd dressed in feminine finery at Rachel's tea party. It was the only time he'd ever seen the lady freighter in women's attire, but the image rose so vividly—and at the strangest times—it never seemed to leave him. Until now.

Nick blinked, wishing he could bring it back into focus. Aly would have to look first-rate if his plan to convince Madeline that the freighter was his woman had any hope of success. This mess of molasses and feathers had a petticoat or two to go before looking even remotely female.

"Nick, honey, this particular taskmistress has horns, thorns, and a bullwhip to boot," Ophelia warned. "You sure you wanna do what I think you're fixing to do?"

Bridling Alewine Jones would be like attempting to lasso a dust devil, but it was the only way to protect her *and* convince Madeline to let him raise his daughter. Deciding it was time to throw down the gauntlet, Nick prayed she could clean up as well as he remembered. "Seeing me crow just might be possible, Aly."

Her mouth slimmed into a grim line. "What's up your sleeve?"

"Nothing. I'm bored. We haven't had time to best each other in a week or so. Thought I'd make it worth your while. Don't want to crow at dawn, do you?"

Alewine walked away, complaining over her shoulder, "Honest-to-hellfire, Turner. You think I like lookin' like a hooved-over hen? I thought you's gonna find me a way I could shed this chicken skin. But I gave my word and I mean to keep—"

"Sure you do. I was only offering an honest way out."

She halted, giving him her attention once again. "First off, you and the word honest don't rightly fit together. And second . . . just what laid it on that scoundrel heart of yours to save my hide?"

"Let's just say I think anyone who'd go to such extremes to keep her word deserves an opportunity to rid herself of the obligation. And we both know, I'm an expert at getting out of messes. Thought I could lend you a hand."

Gratitude softened the glint in her golden eyes. Suddenly, Nick felt every inch the rogue she'd called him. If Aly ever learned the truth about him trying to protect her, she'd never forgive him. She had an independent streak a mile wide. He had to convince her that she would be helping him—not vice versa.

"Here's the deal. We'll play poker. Four of us. If it gets down to just you and me and you win, I'll take your place at dawn, feathers and all."

"That's a deal, Gambler." Alewine offered her hand to seal their pact. When Nick took it, she stared him boldly in the eyes. "And if I lose?"

"You've got to do anything I ask . . . anything . . . one time."

"Well, Chick. It's just you and me."

"Don't call me 'Chick.' " Alewine glanced at the dark-haired gambler and brushed a feather from the tip of her nose. It by-gawd itched, but there was no way she would remove a single, solitary one unless it fell off by its durn self. And she wasn't sure she liked the way Nick's gaze examined her from coonskin cap to boot tip. It made her feel all shivery inside and set her feathers to fluttering.

How many times lately had he roused peculiar feelings within her? They were man and woman kind of feelings. He'd probably laugh himself out of his chair if she ever admitted it. True, she felt a growing attraction to the cardsharp. But Nick was her best friend, her fishing partner, her confidant. He'd told her about his gal troubles in the past, for pistol's sake. He trusted her not to go mushy-eyed over him like the others always did. To succumb to these new feelings might damage their friendship, and she just wasn't willing to risk that for anything or anybody. Especially only to satisfy some new-fangled urge she hadn't quite figured out yet.

"Why don't you take a breather and go wash some of that off? Don't you think you'll win?"

"Hell—heck, yes," Alewine corrected herself, remembering that she'd promised Rachel she would do her best to quit her cussing. If she was going to be godmother to little Amanda McGuire, then she would have to polish up her manners a lot better. The past nine months had made quite a difference already, thanks to Rachel's patience and her lessons. Lessons that surprisingly dug up old habits Aly had thought buried years ago.

"I'm gonna win. You can bet your hat on it," she assured him, wishing she could soak herself in a hot tub. Why was it that Nick always saw her at her worst—dusty from days on the trail, sweaty from brushing down the horses, looking like a molting chicken? "Said I'd wear these dang thangs 'til I crowed, and I meant it. Ain't no way I'm gonna clean up 'til I'm sure you're the rooster taking my place. How do I know you ain't got some of that fancy card-dealing up your sleeves so I'll haveta smear myself up again?"

"You think I'd cheat?" His dimples deepened as a smile filled his dark eyes with mischief.

"Do sinners grin? Hell yes, Nicodemus, you'd cheat me." Truth was, *she* had been toying with the cards all evening, as well, losing just enough to make him think she was nervous. Winning enough to stay in the game. Nick would risk everything if his luck was running strong, or he thought it was.

Though she didn't need the money, Alewine wanted to watch him crow. She hadn't bested him lately, and never at his own game. The week she'd been away delivering that load to Clarendon and Mulberry Creek had given her plenty of time to think of a way to pay him back for those raw eggs in her coffee two Sundays ago. But even that idea wasn't as good as besting him at poker. Besides, talk was Nick had been visiting nearly every dove in town while she was gone. The fact stirred her into a new boil. If he took to spending his time with some new petticoat, their fishing trips would be cut short.

"Ante-up, Chick. Time for the real betting."

The game lingered into the wee hours of the night. Alewine continued to lose for a while, then decided he would question her motive if he won hands too easily. At times, she suspected he was stacking the deck but couldn't be certain. Turner was good with his hands— his skill equal in handling both women and cards. She'd watched him often enough with both.

Finally fortune smiled on Aly. She had Nick right where she wanted him. He now had three-fourths of the winnings stacked in front of him. He'd make a big play, for sure.

"Tell you what . . ." Nick raked all his winnings into the middle of the table. "Five-card draw, winner takes all. You win, you get the money and hear me crow. I win, I get the money, and you've got to do what I ask—but only one time, of course."

For a man who prided himself in being unpredictable, Aly wondered if the fast-fingered finagler had any idea she could read him as easy as a day-old trail. Still, that gleam in his eyes warned her to tread with caution. She'd learned the hard way that, with Nick, things were not always what they seemed.

The fact that he was looking at her like she was the last card needed to hold a royal flush set Aly's skin to crawling. He usually saved that randy expression for one of Ophelia's gals. What was so dadgummed important that he wanted her to do?

Possibilities blazed through her thoughts, but she immediately eliminated them. There hadn't been all that much she and Nick hadn't done together except . . . Her right eye narrowed as she studied him a little closer for signs of insanity. It didn't look like he was any more loco than the last time she seen him.

Aly's throat clenched with a sudden dryness. He wouldn't ask such a thing, would he? He was looking mighty spruced up, though. More so than his usual dandified self. "Need to stretch a mite." A fire lit in her veins, bringing her blood to a heated bubble. "Have me a drink before we get started."

"Fine." Nick waved at two saloon girls to watch the winnings during the delay. Ophelia would run them out of town if either skimmed even a single chip from the table.

Moving to the bar in her best I'm-just-one-of-the-fellas saunter, Alewine leaned over the counter. "Psst, 'Phelia. Got a second?"

The saloon keeper bustled down the long length of the mahogany bar and plunked a shot glass on the countertop. "What'll it be?"

"Sarsp'rilla." Aly's tone lowered. "And some advice."

Fellow patrons shifted at the bar, a long line of them leaning in to listen.

"Ain't y'all got something better to do, like guzzle them suds?" Alewine looked thunderously at the customers. "This here's a private conversation."

"Sure, Aly." The man who answered spit a stream of tobacco at the nearest spittoon and missed.

"Will do." Another man started gulping his beer.

The others grumbled but went about their business.

"This isn't like you, Aly." Ophelia poured the shotglass full of the freighter's favorite drink. "You usually demand everybody's attention. What's so secretive?"

Aly glanced around the room. Satisfied everyone understood the repercussions of listening in, her mouth slanted to one side as she whispered, "It's about female foolery, 'Phel. You know . . . gal goings-on. I feel kinda gangly talking about such things."

"Get to the point, Aly, I've got beer to sell."

Taking no offense because she was a businesswoman herself and knew time was money, Alewine decided just to let the question gush on out. "You reckon I should take Nick up on his bet?"

A smile lifted Ophelia's painted lips. "Any reason not to?"

"Well . . ." Aly hesitated, trying to find the right words to speak her concern. Her cheeks flamed so hot she could have branded them into the countertop.

"Why, Alewine Jones, are you blushing?" Ophelia's odd gray eyes rounded in surprise.

"Heck no, I ain't blushing. All this lollygagging around makes me feel like I'm thirteen and pimply again." Her spine straightened, and her chin jutted forward. "I'll just say it, dadgum it. You think Nick's planning on making me share his bedroll?"

The question exited louder than she expected, and her voice broke right at the crucial last word. Masculine laughter volleyed through the crowd.

Ophelia joined them, adding saucily, "Don't get your hopes up, honey. You're not having that much luck tonight!"

The laughter echoed around her. Aly swung around and realized that Nick had heard the whole thing.

"This one's on the house." The saloon keeper wiped away tears of mirth and poured Aly another sarsaparilla. "Drink up, freighter. There's nothing to worry about. Now, why would he want to buck the tiger with someone clearly unwilling, when any petticoat in town would give her best corset to get such an offer?"

The proprietress propped one elbow on the counter and leaned forward. "True, Nick usually has some scheme up those fancy sleeves, but any gal here can tell ya he's mighty choosey about who gets to shuffle his deck. Aren't ya, Nick, honey?" With a wink, she shooed Aly away from the bar. "But rest assured, Aly-girl, one shuffle with that man is worth the bet."

Ophelia's statement was meant to draw interest from the crowd rather than give Aly encouragement. Beer sales and betting always increased when Aly and the gambler pitted themselves against one another. Alewine deliberately swaggered to the poker table and sat down, refusing to let him or any of these other braying jackasses see her run scared.

Despite her resolve, a wave of uncertainty washed through her. She willed it away, masking it with the bravado that had served her since she was small. "Show me the color of your courage, Gambler."

"You're in luck, Alewine." Nick took the chair opposite hers and offered the two girls who'd watched the table a coin each for their efforts. "I'm feeling particularly generous tonight. I think we need a fresh deck. Ophelia," he called, nodding, "bring us a new one, and *you* deal it. Let's make sure Lady Luck decides our fate tonight, not anyone's sleight of hand."

Aly and Nick's gazes met and locked. If he'd planned to cheat, for some reason he'd decided not to. An urge to thank him ignited within Aly and lingered, but she resisted the impulse.

The shuffling cards sounded like pages of her life being riffled. One pasteboard fell in front of her. Her pulse quickened. A second. Her throat constricted. Another. She swallowed back a gulp. The fourth, her fingertips began to throb, aching to touch. The fifth. Aly sucked in a deep breath.

She closed her eyes and gathered the cards to her feathered chest.

"Well, you gonna look at them," someone asked, "or just sit there and pray over 'em?"

Always one to take her chances no matter what the result, Aly blew out a long stream of breath that rustled the feathers glued to her buckskin. Fanning the cards briefly, she noted the hand dealt her, then closed them and laid them face down on the table. Three tens and two queens! A full house! "You have the biggest ante, Gambler." She willed her eyes to stare at the pile of money rather than Nick. "You go first."

"How many?" Ophelia separated the top card from the rest.

"Two." Nick discarded two and accepted those the saloon keeper dealt.

Every muscle in Aly's face strained to grin, but she kept tight control. Impending victory forced her gaze to meet the gambler's. "I'll stand."

A dark brow tilted over one of Nick's eyes. Was that disappointment she saw written in their depths?

"You're better at this than you led me to believe."

"Hell, both of us have been thinking of cheating all night, and you know it. But all that counts, Gambler, is this last hand. That frock coat's gonna look mighty fine all feathered up and syrupy." She turned her cards face up. "Full house, ten high."

The crowd's cheer rattled the roof, mixing with grumbles from the opposing bettors. Someone congratulated Aly by slapping her on the back, nearly knocking the breath from her. Laughter echoed around the room as the culprit's hand stuck to the molasses and feathers.

"Get your paws offa me!" Aly bolted to her feet, wiggling like a fresh-hooked catfish. The sudden jolt upward yanked the man loose, sending him sprawling backward. She leaned over to rake the winnings to her side of the table but halted as a series of cards sailed atop the pile.

"I believe four threes beat a full house."

The cheers changed, reverberating in Nick's favor. Aly glanced at Ophelia, knowing he hadn't cheated but wondering if he'd had a little help.

The saloon keeper merely shrugged. "Lady Luck has a sense of humor. What can I say?"

"Turkey piss!" Despite her promise to Rachel McGuire, Aly executed a stream of personal obscenities she'd created throughout the years so she could spout off her frustration without actually offending an innocent ear. "I not only gotta wear these here feathers and cluck the dadgummed day in come morning, now I've gotta do whatever dadgummed dang thang you want me to do? Well, I'd just as soon get it over with, Gambler. So don't just sit there with that skunk-eating grin. Name your price. What do I got to do one time?"

Nicodemus looked her straight in the eye and smiled. "Marry me."

Chapter Two

"Marry you?" Alewine skirted the table that separated her and Nick as sighs of disappointment escaped the saloon girls in attendance. She took a swing at him. "Like hell I will!"

Anticipating her reaction, Nick sidestepped Aly's blow and kept moving to stay clear of her aim.

"Don't waste your time with her, honey," one of the soiled doves crooned as she encircled Nick's neck with her boa. "But you can bet that *I'm* in the mood for white lace and room service."

Aly's attention momentarily focused on the brazen woman. "He asked *me*, Mertle Lou. You best curl them snake feathers around somebody else." Aly's sudden lunge forward made Mertle Lou dart for safety.

"Attagirl, Aly. Give her what for!" roared a mule skinner sitting at the next table.

"You stay out of this, Stump! She don't need any

encouragement." Ophelia tapped her cane on the counter as if she were a judge rapping his gavel. "This has been a long time coming. I, for one, want to see if Nick's got enough grit to handle this hellcat."

The mule skinner grinned, his teeth amazingly white compared to the rest of his dirt-encrusted countenance. "Glad it's you, Turner, and not me. I cain't imagine snuggling up to that prickly pear."

"Nobody said nothing about snuggling up to nobody, you old buzzard bone." Aly glared at the instigator. "You best mind your mug there before I empty it upside your head. I don't need any help with the gambler."

"Neither of us need help. I won, Aly. You lost. Marriage is the price, plain and simple." Nick's deception tasted sour in his mouth, but he won the bet fair and square.

When he'd seen vulnerability dart across Alewine's face during the game, he'd suffered a moment of guilt and decided not to play the hand falsely. He *couldn't* do so. He'd left their destiny to fate, and fate had dealt him the winning hand. He pointed upward. "Would you care to discuss this further in private, fiancée?"

"Fi-on-say?"

Aly's fists balled on her hips, and her right eye narrowed. Her fighting stance revealed every feathered angle of her well-honed curves, making Nick very much aware of just how much woman he was dealing with.

"Use my office." Ophelia shot Alewine a warning glance. "And I'd like everything to remain in the same condition you find it . . . unbroken."

"I ain't making no promises." Aly barreled up the stairs ahead of Nick two at a time.

"Looks like I better set her up an account." Ophelia eyed the gambler. "If you two walk out of there without her breaking something, I'll give every man jack in here free drinks for the rest of the night."

"That sure, eh?" While the saloon keeper was extremely generous in sharing her wealth with the children of Valiant, Ophelia was notoriously tight-fisted when dealing with the town's adults. She wouldn't make such an offer if she wasn't sure Aly's temper would get the best of her. "If anything's broken, put it on my account," Nick offered. "Not hers."

"Guess they'll both be yours soon, anyway."

"If she doesn't kill me." Nick's resolve wavered for a moment. He still had time to back out and tell Aly it was all a prank. She wouldn't take kindly to being humiliated, particularly in front of the townsmen from whom she'd won such hard-earned respect. And if he did back out, what would he do about Jezlynn?

Give her time and Aly would get used to the idea, he decided, hurrying upstairs amidst yells of encouragement.

"Make that spitfire pay up, Turner."

" 'Bout time somebody lassoed that burr in buckskins."

"Better go in heeled, Nick. That strip of rawhide's got murder in her eyes!"

The office door loomed ahead like the entrance to a box canyon. Perspiration made his hand slip as he grasped the knob, revealing an uncertainty he hadn't allowed himself since he left Prickly Bend seven years ago. An uncertainty that now would lead him back to the very place he vowed never to step foot again—Arizona. An uncertainty that he was about to drastically alter Alewine's life, and Lord knew if it would be for the better.

The knob turned too easily. He expected there to be resistance. *Whoosh!* Nick ducked as a rush of air whizzed by his head. *Crash!* Something shattered against the bannister behind him.

"Hey, that's my Venetian vase!" Ophelia yelled from below. "Tell her to throw something cheaper, will ya?"

"If I get a chance." Nick ducked again and cautiously approached the hellraiser. "Now, Aly, calm down. I'm just trying to—"

"I know what you're trying to do, you petticoat-plucking speculator. Some best friend you are!" She grabbed a porcelain picture frame from the table, reared back, and threw it with all her might. "Trying to make me believe you and Ophelia didn't have this little scheme already cooked up." Aly spit a feather that had fallen into her mouth. "I know when I've been scammed. I'll be ninety-nine and noodled before I ever keep house for the likes of you, Turner!"

Cushioned Belter furniture filled the office space with white and green floral designs, giving the chamber a mocking air of peacefulness. As Alewine started to grab yet another of Ophelia's prized possessions, Nick decided the only way to regain calm was to dive in head first. He dove. She darted. His body hit the davenport, sending it backward toward a huge window. Feathers flew. The double-seated chair landed with a dull thud.

A loud "Ooof!" reverberated through the room.

Nick tried to stand, but his feet tangled in the curtains.

"Get . . . off . . . me!" the voice beneath him threatened breathlessly.

"I'm trying. Just lie still and I'll—" The davenport jostled once, twice. Aly was strong, he'd give her that. "If you'll hold still for a minute, I can get up from here."

The furniture stopped jostling. "That's better." Nick

27

stood and lifted the large settee upright. Concern gnawed at him as she lay still, her eyes closed, her lips a grim line. "Chick? You all right?"

He leaned closer, bent down to examine her more carefully and found himself once again admiring the feathered curves of her statuesque figure.

Alewine bent her knee, connecting with her target. "Now I am," she clucked and rolled away.

Pain hit Nick in layers, rippling outward from the point of impact. He buckled, cursing himself for being distracted. He should have known she'd do something like this—put him out of commission before the wedding. Best tell her she didn't have to consummate the darned thing, so he wouldn't have to dodge and duck the rest of the day and could sit a stage come morning.

Despite an impulse to yank her over his knee and spank her, Nick held a hand out tentatively to help her up. "Truce? Long enough to hear me out? If you don't think I've got just cause to insist you pretend to marry me, then we'll go downstairs and let you have another go at the game. Deal?"

"Be glad Rachel's teaching me to be nicer or it would have been my fists I threw and not those dust collectors." Aly's eyes widened. "Did you say *pretend* to marry you?"

"That's what I said, Chick. We won't really be married."

She accepted his help.

He grasped her hand and wrinkled his nose as his palm gooed with molasses and feathers. Nick looked for a place Aly's sticky attire wouldn't damage. "Better not sit on the furniture."

"How 'bout straddling this?" Alewine suggested the long table Nick had dived over in his flight to the davenport. "Ain't nothing but cowhide. Ought to clean off good." Her brow furrowed. "Then again, why make it easy for her? You and I both know Ophelia rigged the cards for you."

"Will you sit and listen?" Nick's patience had worn thin. He plopped down on the table, pulling her down with him. Only a couple of hours remained to rouse the preacher and complete the wedding so they could be on their way. The stage to Santa Fe would leave an hour or so after dawn, if it was on schedule, and wouldn't be back for a month. He'd lost plenty of time already.

"What's your all-fired hurry?" Alewine straddled the table like it was a newly busted bronc.

Nick found it hard to look at Aly's comical appearance without laughing. His best friend never failed to amuse and astound him. It was one of the things he admired most about her.

While there had always been sarcastic wit and one-upmanship between them, they'd never been dishonest to each other. Lying to her tasted bad, and he swallowed back the lump of disgust that formed in his throat. He wondered how long he could last without confessing everything to her . . . or worse, how soon she would be able to read it in his expression?

Nick pulled a letter from the pocket of his frock coat and handed it to her. "Read it. Maybe this will help me explain."

She didn't open it. "You know I ain't one much for reading and writing."

"Some folks might think that." Nick opened it for her. "But not me. Why you want people to think you're not as smart you are, Aly, isn't any of my business. But it isn't Pug Rayburn keeping the books straight over at the freight office. So save your secret for somebody else."

Aly held the paper close and squinted.

"Why don't you buy some spectacles?" Nick

admonished. "Or are you too worried how they'll make you look?"

"You're the one who needs your eyesight checked, Gambler. Didn't you notice this here new skin I'm shedding? If I ain't worried about looking this way, why would I worry about—"

"Just read, will you?"

Having won that particular round between them, Aly complied. After a few moments, she glanced up in amazement. "You've got a daughter?"

"Yeah, a seven-year-old I never knew existed. Well, Jezlynn's almost seven. Can you believe it?" He tried to keep the anger from his tone, but couldn't. Rather than let Alewine read further, Nick took the letter. "Her mother, Madeline—Maddy Gilmore—isn't expected to live out the year from what I've been told. And if I want to gain custody of my daughter, then I've got to prove I'm settled down and have steady income. I don't think gambling's going to cut it. Madeline and I talked plenty about what she means by settled down. A marriage, home, family. All that society approves of."

He stared out the window reflecting the encroaching rays of dawn. "All that I've been bucking for seven years."

"Then you want her?"

"Madeline?"

"No, Jezlynn. Do you want your daughter?"

A hint of some kind of emotion Nick wasn't sure he recognized lay hidden in Aly's tone, surprising him. "Of course I want her."

"There's no doubt she's yours?" Golden eyes searched his own.

Nick blinked. Though he'd silently asked himself the same question a thousand times since receiving the letter a week ago, he'd come to only one conclusion—

whether or not the child was his flesh and blood, Madeline had branded her his. That's all that mattered. If Jezlynn was to live life as Nicodemus Turner's daughter, then by all that he held sacred in this world, he'd see to her future. "She's mine."

"Then tell Madeline you work for me," Aly suggested.

"She'll expect a bit more than that, I'm afraid." A hell of a lot more. Madeline had always been big on expectations.

"How much time will we have to stay there?"

Aly had said "we." Nick realized she was considering the idea, at least. In truth, Madeline had set no limit, but he felt six months ought to be reasonable. "She's insisting I spend the next six months in Prickly Bend to get acquainted with my daughter. Otherwise, Jezlynn will be placed in the care of Madeline's oldest sister, Elmertha Bartholomew. That's something I refuse to let happen."

Renewed determination filled Nick. "Elmertha is headmistress at Bartholomew's School for Young Ladies, a strict dream-stealing way of life I'll never allow my daughter to suffer. I want Jez to know she can count on me. With your help, Aly, I believe I can accomplish that."

Alewine's head moved back and forth even before her words refused him. "You're my best friend, Gambler. I wanna help you. But you and I both know I ain't fit to be nobody's mother."

I know differently, Nick silently countered, having no doubt she was the one woman who would love *any* child wholeheartedly. But he couldn't bring up those times he'd watched her watching the McGuires. Those were moments of privacy she would share with him when she was ready to do so and not until then.

"You don't have to mother anyone, Chick," he

31

assured her. "I'll do the parenting. You just pretend to marry me so I can convince Madeline that Jez will have a ready-made family, and that I'm father material. Then in six months when Maddy allows me to bring Jezlynn back here to live, you can resume your old lifestyle."

Watching indecision dart across her face, Nick reassured Aly. "We can tell everyone here in Valiant we had the marriage annulled. I'll make it worth your while. The first big pot I win is yours. Maybe even the first two."

"I don't need your money, Turner."

Would she actually refuse? Fear of having to leave Aly behind unprotected and losing his daughter spurred Nick to use any method necessary to convince his friend. *Dare her*. "What's the matter, Jones? You scared?"

"I ain't afraid of nothing."

Appeal to her business sense. "Then use this to your advantage. You've been wanting to extend your freighting service west. Being ten miles south of the Kearney Trail, Prickly Bend will be a good freighting point."

She laughed. "I can just hear Pug now when I tell him I'm leaving him to run things and taking time off for a honeymoon."

Reassure her. "Not really. Remember, we'll only be pretending to marry. I won't try to claim any husbandly rights."

An unreadable expression darkened her eyes for a moment, then was gone. The desire to reach out and touch Aly engulfed Nick, making him aware of a need that had been growing within him for some time now—a wanting as uncontrollable as the woman who inspired it, an oath his soul had pledged without consulting his mind.

32

She turned away as if she'd read his thoughts and rejected them. "Do I gotta dress in them frilly clothes?"

"Just for a while." Nick exhaled a deep breath. "Long enough to convince Madeline we're married and we're a steady family for Jezlynn. Madeline is the high society sort. She'll want the woman who's going to help raise her daughter to be pure lady."

"Now I know you're blind, Gambler. Have you taken a good look at me?"

"Yes." His gaze swept her from boot tip to feathered crown, remembering that certain tea party that had forever changed the way he viewed Alewine Jones. "I got an extremely close look one day when you were the finest-dressed lady in all of Valiant."

Her lips threatened to grin, and he could tell she was fighting the effort. He hadn't meant the compliment to manipulate her, but it had more of an effect than anything else he'd said so far.

"Why me?"

"Remember that night you confessed about going to one of those finishing schools back East?"

"I say a lot of stupid things when I've been drinking. If you were any kind of friend, you'd forget what I told you that night."

"I haven't told another soul, and you know it. I just hoped your experience there would make you see why I have to do everything possible to keep Jezlynn out of one."

"You're digging up bones I'd like to stay buried, Turner. You sure you're telling me everything? 'Cause if you ain't . . ." Her eyes narrowed. "I'll make your life a misery worse than any hell ol' Lucifer can offer."

"If I'm lying"—*and you catch me at it*, he added silently— "I'll never turn another card at poker."

"Then I accept on account of it seems best for your little girl, and it wouldn't hurt for you to mend your card-shuffling ways." Alewine unstraddled the table and headed for the door, stopping to glance at herself in the oval mirror hanging behind Ophelia's desk. "I guess with it happening somewhere besides here, I won't have to worry none about nobody watching me make a fool of myself."

He felt her staring at him in the mirror, gauging him in some way. Nick waited, wondering if she would back out at the last minute or give her word.

"The thing I ain't figured out is why you had to sucker me into losing a poker game to get me to do this." Aly plucked feathers from off her cheeks. "All you had to do was tell me the why-fors. I'da done it for you."

"I know you would have, but everyone else would expect you to resist marrying me. I had to make it look like you had no choice but to do so."

Approval shone in Aly's eyes as her head nodded. "Smart thinking, Nick. Now that we've convinced them, I only got one stipulation before we get hitched."

"Anything." Nick moved up behind her, staring at their reflection and finding that despite the feathers and molasses, she looked good with him. Cleaned up, they would make a handsome couple. Tow-headed children with honey-colored eyes danced in his imagination, then stopped to throw rocks at him. The man who ever married Alewine Jones would definitely be taking the biggest gamble of his life.

"I ain't wearing none of them fancy do's. I like my hair blowing free."

"That's a deal. Anything else?"

"Yeah, tell Ophelia to fetch the preacher. Tell her to give me a minute or two before she does, though. If you expect me to convince him that I've got enough sense left to know what I'm doing, then this flappery's gonna have to come off. Can't do that, Gambler, until I do this . . ."

Aly walked over to the bannister, looked down at the crowd, then crowed.

The light of dawn, Nick realized, revealed too sharply why his plan had every reason to fail.

Chapter Three

"Would you quit pushing?" a large lady complained
for the hundredth time. The dark-haired child sitting
between her and another man continued to shift on the
coach seat.

"Lose some weight, lady. You're taking up my
half!" the six-year-old boy argued, being tossed first
one way then the other as the stagecoach rattled and
swayed. It bounced along the rutted road at a break-
neck speed toward Prickly Bend. "And you smell like
rotten eggs."

"Your mother should teach you better manners,
young man." The woman fanned herself and pressed a
handkerchief to her forehead and neck, glaring at
Alewine.

She thinks he's mine. Aly was surprised the boy
didn't belong to the woman. Two weeks ago, when the
stage had stopped at Santa Fe, the pair had joined the
passengers. Aly had naturally assumed woman and

child were kin, or at least traveling companions. Was the elderly man sitting on the boy's opposite side his parent? Or maybe the child belonged to the driver. It seemed peculiar for a youngun to be traveling alone.

Alewine pulled back the oilcloth that formed a curtain over the coach's window and watched as prickly pears and saguaros rushed by. Dust kicked up beneath the team's hooves, fogging the view. She closed her eyes against the oppressive heat captured in such close quarters, her teeth rattling with each jostle of the coach. What she wouldn't give to ride atop, feeling the team's powerful pull on the reins. Anything to get away from these boxed-in quarters and ill tempers.

Perspiration dampened her skin and stained this gut-clutcher of a dress Nick had insisted she wear on the journey, making Aly wish for even the slightest breeze. The key fastened to the gold chain around Aly's neck bounced with every rut in the road. Ophelia had given it to her, along with that fancy-looking box stored in Aly's valise. A wedding gift, the saloon keeper had said. For her and Nick. Aly wondered why Ophelia had bought them a present. After all, she knew they weren't really married. Stranger still, was the promise Ophelia demanded from Aly.

"You can't open the box until I say so or you will spoil the surprise. You cannot use the key until you have to yell at Nick how much you love him. Then it'll be the right time. Promise me."

A wasted present as far as Aly was concerned, but if the promise made Ophelia happy, then why not? Aly couldn't imagine a time she'd ever say such a thing to Nick. The worst of it all would be resisting the temptation to open the dang thing anyway.

The only women's clothes available on such short notice were smaller around the breastbone than Aly. At least the rest of the travel suit was shaped like a gunnysack. Some of that other frillery Nick bought wasn't going to be so easy to shinny into, that was for dang sure.

Aly's left arm ached from being squished up against the gambler so long that she was forced to turn. Wrong move. Now her left breast bumped Nick's arm. A heat far greater than any Arizona offered sparked inside Aly, sending a tingling rush of wildfire searing through her.

Nick's dark gaze focused on the point of contact. A smile deepened his dimples. "Uncomfortable, Chick?"

Her temper flared, not so much at him, but at herself for enjoying the spark. In the weeks it had taken to travel the distance from Valiant, Texas, to Prickly Bend, Arizona, she found herself enjoying those strange stirrings he aroused within her much too often. She liked the way she felt when she was near him. He sure was playacting to the hilt, but he didn't have to look *that* interested in her! "Move over, Turner. That ain't no pillar you're propping on."

Clay Driscoll stared at her from across the seat. She'd tolerated the man following her for months acting like a lovestruck bull, but she'd never liked the businessman from Valiant. Though the ladies back home favored his blond, blue-eyed good looks and said he was a good catch for a woman well past her prime, Aly couldn't abide the man. She'd earned the freedom in every single one of her twenty-three years and planned to keep on living them the way she saw fit.

Though Driscoll had never done anything but try to please Aly, there was something in his eagerness that set her teeth to grinding.

Danged if she knew why he'd decided to follow them to Prickly Bend. Aly had seen him in the crowd watching the wedding. The ring Nick had put on her finger ought to have convinced Driscoll there was no hope of her ever marrying him. Hell, the ceremony seemed so genuine, even *she* had a hard time believing it wasn't the real thing. When Nick had placed the gold ring on her finger and Ophelia burst into tears, the strangest sensation had engulfed Aly. She'd felt as if life was blazing a trail for her, and she was simply to follow where it led. But years of freighting warned her that danger could come from the unlikeliest direction.

Maybe Driscoll wasn't planning on dogging her. Maybe all he wanted was to make sure she and the gambler didn't part ways once they left Valiant. There had been plenty of bets placed predicting her and Nick's marriage wouldn't last a month. Driscoll might have bet on the outcome, hoping not only to win money but to resume courting her.

The oddest bet Aly had accepted was when Ophelia wagered that the marriage would last *longer* than the six months. Though Aly gave her word to Nick, she didn't mean for this pretend hitching to last one hour longer than the time agreed.

Still, she had to admit, it had already proved beneficial. Pretending to be Nick's wife kept Driscoll from pestering her. Maybe the businessman needed a bit of reminding so he would quit ogling her in this gutclutcher. "Got me a cramp, Nick darling." Her tone sweetened. "Could you give me some more room?"

Nick shifted.

"Hey, you kicked me!" The child's green eyes narrowed as his foot shot out to retaliate.

The boy had tested everyone's patience all day, squirming and yelling when the grownups would have appreciated dozing. He had asked nine hundred questions, if he'd asked one. Alewine's ears hurt just from listening to him.

"Excuse me, son." Nick wrapped his right arm

around Alewine's shoulder, pulling her close. "There now, that's much better, darling."

Startled, Aly nearly swallowed her tongue as anger mingled with curiosity. He was probably trying to do the same thing she was—convince Driscoll they were loving newlyweds. A good idea, as long as it was hers. But the only time she'd ever been this close to a man before was when she entered the Fourth of July charity wrestle on a bet. For the first time in a long while she felt small, even a little feminine.

Though they had sat side-by-side for weeks, Nick had never once touched her unduly . . . until now. He had kept his word about leaving their marriage in name only, so far.

Allowing her curiosity full rein, Aly turned her face slightly closer to his broad chest and decided he smelled mighty fine for a husband. His scent was sort of like sage in first bloom. Woodsy, male, and . . . the dark stain under his armpit captured her attention . . . well, everybody was a little worse for wear because of the heat.

"Ooooh, lady, that's pitiful. Get it? Pit-i-ful." The dark-haired boy held up his own arms, wrinkling his nose.

Aly jerked around to face the strangers who shared the coach. "What's your name, half-pint?"

"Jessie. Why?"

With one swift movement, Aly held back the curtain and pointed. "See them big ol' cactus there? Those tall ones?"

The boy inched forward and leaned over the man next to him. "Those are called saguaros. Everybody knows *that*."

"Yeah, well, that's what some folks call 'em. Me . . . I know what they really are."

The child's eyes narrowed as he strained harder to see. "They ain't nothing but big ol' cactuses."

"Cacti," the obese lady corrected.

In a hushed tone, Aly whispered, "They're young-uns, just like you. They were too ornery to sit still and be quiet during the stage ride, so the driver made 'em get out and walk. That's when the great Arapa-homanche turned them into sand and burrs for being so prickly with their elders."

The coach jostled, tangling the boy's feet with Nick's. The child kicked at the gambler as if the tangling had occurred on purpose.

"Sit down, son!"

"I didn't do nothing to you, and I ain't your son." The boy's green eyes narrowed. "And I ain't scared of no Arapamanche."

For just a moment, Aly felt ashamed of herself for having initiated the boy's interest in the cacti. "He didn't say you did anything, half-pint."

"Name's Jessie, not 'half-pint.' " He glared at the gambler. "And he better not accuse me of nothing." The boy stood, not having to duck, his body too short to worry about the coach's ceiling. "Somebody switch places with me, 'cause I don't want his legs touching mine."

"Sit down, boy." Nick's patience wore thin. "I've got the longest legs here. Yours are the shortest." Nick scooted his legs up to give the child additional space to stretch. "It's best if we're opposite each other. It gives the rest more room."

"No."

"What did you say?"

"I said no, I ain't gonna sit down. You ain't my pa, and I don't have to mind you."

Nick's eyes darkened to ebony. "It's a good thing,

41

Jessie, because you'd learn to be more considerate of others if I were your father."

"Trying to win him over, are ya?" Aly grinned at Nick, but Nick didn't return the smile. Was he nervous about meeting Jezlynn? He was usually better with children than this. "Hope you ain't got a hellion of a daughter."

"She'll be just like her mother, I assure you. Quiet, dignified, probably versed already in every manner of social etiquette. You can bet she'll be the perfect child. Maddie wouldn't parent any less."

"Amen to perfect children." Clay Driscoll glared at the six-year-old.

"Nobody asked you, mister." The fearless child hiked his leg to step over the obese lady's skirt.

Aly's head swung around fast toward the window. "Will you listen to that?"

Jessie's leg stopped in midair. "What?"

Pretending to listen intently, Aly's tone hushed. "That. Don't you hear it?"

Driscoll caught on and leaned toward Nick, acting as if he heard it, too.

"An Arapahomanche?" Nick winked at her.

"Not for certain," Aly replied. "But it could be. It sounds just like that."

The boy immediately took his seat, wide-eyed and quiet.

Gratitude filled the gazes of each adult passenger as they silently thanked her for this reprieve. She started to thumb up her slouch hat, then remembered she'd packed it away with her buckskins. Maybe she was worrying needlessly about this mothering business. If she could corral this imp with a tall tale, she ought to be able to waltz right in and easily handle a prime piece of priss like Jezlynn Turner.

"Prickly Bend two miles out!" The driver's

announcement whipped through the open-air window, dust billowing the oilcloth curtains that attempted to protect the passengers from the weather. He urged the team to a faster gait.

"Do Indians raid these parts?" The large woman couldn't seem to sit upright well. The jockeying of the coach kept making her slide downward.

The man opposite Aly shook his head. "Haven't for several months. Trade's started up again all over the Gadsen because of it."

His deep sigh of disgust drew everyone's curiosity.

"Isn't that a good thing?" Aly wondered aloud, thinking she'd chosen a good time to extend her freighting business.

"For lots of folks it is, but not for Prickly Bend. We're little more than a trading post between Santa Fe and the Kearney Trail. Most of us make our living supplying water and other goods to nearby outposts and wagontrains headed for the Kearney."

He shrugged. "As long as the Apache were on the loose, no one could rely on the soldiers at Fort Lowell to help bring supplies to the neighboring rancherias. But with Indians becoming less of a threat, the Santa Cruz near Tucson provides a closer water source. We've got three rivers with plenty of water in them, but we're stuck up here practically in the middle of nowhere. Now we've got to stir up more customers or find new ways to make our livelihood."

The horses leaned into their traces, lunging the coach forward. Conversation stopped as everyone listened to the driver compliment the three perfectly-matched pairs, promising them fresh oats and a good brushing when they reached town.

The air took on a sweeter smell, and the heat became less oppressive. Clay Driscoll drew back his curtain and revealed to all the changing vista. The stagecoach traveled a winding road, hugging the Aravaipa River. Paloverde trees flooded the banks with yellow blossoms. The fresh odor of greasewood drifted amidst the flame-colored prickly pears and the red caterpillar-tips of shaggy ocotillos. It was as if the desert had rushed to the riverbank to wash and dress itself for new visitors.

"Home."

The word escaped Nick's lips, but Aly wondered if he realized he'd spoken it. She'd always been curious about the place where he'd been raised. What sort of town spawned such a man? What sort of woman had given him a daughter? Shouldn't *she* be checking herself in at the nearest button factory for considering this crazy playacting?

Well-accustomed to long rides, Alewine thought this one would never end. A month wearing dresses was more than a body had a right to suffer. And to think, she'd promised six!

Finally, the coach seemed to dip backward. The osage wheels groaned as the team's gait slowed from gallop to trot. When the driver reined in and the coach halted in a flurry of dust, leather straps beneath the coach creaked and bowed.

"At last." The obese lady scooted forward in her seat.

Nick straightened, relieving Alewine of the pressure of his arm.

Jessie didn't budge an inch.

Alewine waited while the men disembarked. The obese lady tried to squeeze through the door but got stuck. Alewine lifted her boot to help the woman, but the boy's giggle made her realize what she'd unconsciously intended to do. Aly raised a brow at the child. Jessie nodded vigorously.

The lady broke loose at that moment and swung

around. Alewine jerked her boot down and pretended to look out the opposite window. Jessie's cheeks puffed up like a squirrel's as he tried to swallow back his laughter. Aly winked and moved the curtain aside enough to see the settlement that would be her—their—home for the next five months. Squinting through the cloud of dust that still hovered over the stagecoach, she blinked at the image.

"Wonder if everybody in town meets the stage when it comes in?" She peered harder at the gathered crowd. Time to get down to business. She had to play a full-skirted female. There were at least a hundred people out there. She couldn't fool them all . . . could she?

"They meet every stage now," Jessie informed her.

"Why?"

" 'Cause they hope some people from back East will show up. People with lots of money who'll help us save the bank."

Aly's curiosity spurred further questions. "What's wrong with the bank?"

"Nothing's wrong with it. In fact, it's the best dang bank this side of Tucson. But it's kind of empty right now. There ain't enough business in town to keep it open, the grown-ups say. That's why I keep running away. If there ain't no bank, and there ain't no money, then I can't do what I gotta do."

"And what do you have to do?"

"That ain't none of your business, stranger."

The crowd pointed in the direction of the stage and seemed mighty interested in its passengers.

Jessie closed the curtain and ducked. "Don't let them see me!"

"Why?"

" 'Cause they're looking for me."

"What are you . . . some kind of outlaw?" Aly widened her eyes so he would think she was impressed.

45

"Not yet, but give me time."

She studied the boy. Thin. Wiry. Small for his age, she guessed. A lot like she herself had been years ago—defiant, bullheaded, willing to do anything to gain everyone's attention. Something nagged at her, but Aly couldn't quite put her finger on it. Maybe it was the hair. Looked like somebody had just cropped it off at the collar without any rhyme or reason to the style. She remembered doing that once when she'd wanted to make everyone think she was a— "Why are you pretending you're a boy?"

The child scooted over against the window. "I ain't pretending. It ain't no fun to be a girl."

"Well, Jessie. I agree, but sometimes the Maker has a sense of humor, and He don't see things the same way we do. Best find yourself a way to like being a gal. It ain't all that bad . . . sometimes."

"Name one."

Thankfully, Nick insisted they get out before she had to meet the child's challenge. Aly had a hard time thinking up an answer at the moment.

"Is she really there?" a hysterical voice asked from behind the gambler. "Is she all right?"

"Here goes." Jessie's mouth twisted with sarcasm as she spoke confidentially to Aly. "Wanna buy a ticket for the show?"

It was hard to say what Aly noticed first about the weeping woman who parted the crowd as if she were royalty. Maybe it was the way she grabbed Jessie and started checking her from head to toe for injuries, or the way Jessie kept swatting at the woman's hands. Or perhaps it was the halo of dark hair and the vivid green eyes that revealed what Jessie would probably look like when she aged. This was surely the child's mother.

More than anything, the woman's delicate features

caused Alewine to continue looking. This was a beauty of the first order, and Aly felt as if she were a buffalo comparing herself to a peacock.

"Oh, look what you've done to your hair!" The beauty's hands touched Jessie's shorn curls, but her eyes were not focused on the haircut. Instead, they seemed to be seeking attention from the onlookers. "Have you eaten, love?"

Jessie pointed to Clay Driscoll. "That man there fed me. Thought he was friendly, but I heard him tell the driver it was to keep me from yapping so much."

"Thank you, sir." The woman flashed Clay a disarming smile. "Perhaps I can extend the same hospitality to you."

"I'd be delighted, madam."

"Other than her hair, she looks just fine, Madeline," one of the older gentlemen announced.

"Madeline?" The boots beneath Aly's dress heavied into hooves. Yep, she was definitely a buffalo. Now she had no doubt why Nick had asked her to play his bride instead of anyone else. There would be no temptation to stay married. If he could have a woman like Madeline, what would he find appealing about someone as coarse as herself?

"Seems Jez wasn't kidnapped after all. Driver says he found Jezlynn stowed away in the stage boot. Said she made it clear to Santa Fe this time."

"Jezlynn? My daughter Jezlynn?" Nick's mouth set in a grim line. "If you're too ill to watch her, Madeline, why didn't you hire someone?"

"I ain't your daughter."

"The word is isn't, if you're going to use it." Madeline's eyes frosted like iced emeralds. "But I must disappoint you, dear. This man *is* your father."

"Nick—" Madeline motioned to the child—"this is your daughter, Jezlynn. I have hired many such caretakers, but dear Jezlynn has run them all off with her antics."

Aly's neck knotted with tension. Life was about to get tangled up with the most beautiful woman and the meanest she-devil of a kid this side of Texas. No way would this marriage business work. Attempting to fool these two would be like trying to pull an egg out of a rooster.

Nick's name registered unfavorably upon other faces. Aly noticed a change in the crowd. Many of the men and women glared at him in open disapproval. Nick hadn't told her everything, that was for sure. As soon as they could be on their way to the family home he said he'd kept all these years, she wanted some answers. But for now, an impulse to protect him was greater than any concern she felt for lying about her marriage. She stepped closer to Nick.

Madeline stood and offered a gloved hand to the gambler. When he lightly bowed and kissed it, she cooed, "I thought you changed your mind about coming."

He straightened. "I wrote you I'd be here just as soon as I arranged things."

"That you did. I simply expected you sooner." She grabbed Jezlynn by the shoulders and stood behind her, urging the child to face him. "May I introduce you to your daughter, Jezlynn Theresa Turner? Jezlynn, this is Nicodemus."

Turner? Aly thought Madeline would have given the child the last name of the man she'd married later—Judge Gilmore. For a woman held in such high regard, the lady didn't seem worse for the wear for having had a child out of wedlock. Aly mentally added another question to the growing list of answers she would demand from the gambler before this day ended.

Father and child stared at one another. Nick looked considerably uncomfortable, the girl absolutely unimpressed.

"Well, why don't you two at least shake hands?" Aly suggested, realizing neither knew what to do with the other. "Even strangers do that, for pistol's sake!"

"I don't believe we've been introduced." Curiosity filled Madeline's green eyes.

"We sure ai—haven't." Alewine wiped her hand on her skirt, then held it out, waiting as Madeline tentatively offered hers. *Remember Rachel's lessons,* Aly told herself. *Gotta gussy yourself up for this kind of folk.* "My name's Alewine Jones . . . Turner." *The name's sure having a growth spurt.* "You'll haveta excuse me. It takes some getting used to remembering I just married this fella."

"You're Nick's *wife*?" Madeline noticably paled, swaying as if she might fall.

Nick grabbed her and asked if he could help, eliciting a grumble of complaints from the men nearby.

Madeline blinked rapidly and assured all she would be fine. "The heat must have distressed me momentarily."

"Is there somewhere we can take you to regain your strength?" Clay Driscoll suggested. "I'd be happy to escort you."

Several other men offered to do the same.

"Thank you . . . Mr. Driscoll, did you say? You *will* join me for dinner, won't you? Morgan, will you . . . ?" She motioned to the elderly gentleman who had informed her of Jezlynn's escape. "Please send someone on to the house and inform Bess to set twelve places instead of eight. The invitation includes you, Nick dear, and your lovely wife."

Alewine tugged on his frock coat. "We can clean up at home and take supper with 'em tomorrow."

49

Madeline clutched his arm even tighter, her cheek resting against the gambler's chest. "I won't hear of it, Nicodemus. Your house has been sitting all these years. It will take days to clean it up well enough to move in. I insist you stay with me at least for tonight. It's been a long journey. You need a hot bath and a good night's rest before you tackle such a massive undertaking."

Seemingly genuine concern filled her expression. "Remember that I invited you to Prickly Bend to become better acquainted with Jezlynn before I di—" Her voice broke, and the crowd hushed as she attempted to regain her composure.

Sadness etched each face, clearly defining how well Madeline Gilmore was loved in her hometown.

"After tonight, Jezlynn can stay with you for awhile. Get to know you better. But please allow me to offer the comfort of my home. I have plenty of room . . . though I must admit, I never dreamed you'd be bringing a wife."

Aly fetched her valise. If she'd made the offer to let him have Jezlynn without expecting him to be married, there was no need for this pretending. Guess she'd never get to open Ophelia's gift. "I'm not needed here. I'll take the next stage."

Nick's hand wrapped around her own as it gripped the bag's handle. She stared at it a moment, feeling his closeness, wishing she hadn't grown used to liking his scent, his nearness, being greeted as Mrs. Turner.

"Don't go, Chick. That little girl needs us." The expression in his eyes pleaded as strongly as his words. "I know you think I don't need you now," he whispered. "But Madeline will believe I haven't played my cards straight if she finds we tried to fool her. Jezlynn will be forced to go to her aunt's boarding school."

Why did she feel there was something else he wasn't telling her? Almost as if he were afraid she would leave for some other reason. "Might not be such a bad idea. That kid—and from what I can see, this whole town—hates you."

"Jezlynn doesn't know me yet, and Prickly Bend clearly hasn't forgiven me for leaving Madeline alone and unmarried. I doubt any of them would care to learn that I had no idea I'd left her in such straits. I asked her to leave with me years ago. She said no and never wrote me until recently."

"Jezlynn doesn't *want* to know you."

"You can help me remedy that."

Maybe she could. Maybe she couldn't. But Nick was right about one thing. Jezlynn was too much like Aly when she was that age. From what little she'd seen of the six-year-old, Alewine suspected the imp just wanted to know she mattered.

Alewine allowed him to take the bag and linked her arm through his as she'd seen other women do their menfolk. The arch of his brow said she'd surprised him, and that was good. Best he remember that she could be as predictable or as unpredictable as she wanted to be. "All right, I'll stay. But there's one thing you gotta promise me. Next time that gal fakes a fainting spell, let somebody else catch her."

"She wasn't faking . . ." Nick glanced at Madeline, then back at Aly. "Was she?"

"Wouldn't matter if she was or wasn't. She aced ya. I don't know how you still feel about her, but that black-haired vixen's still hankering after you."

Chapter Four

Not knowing how long the ride to Jezlynn's home would last, Aly was grateful the barouche's top had been folded down and allowed the slight breeze created by their progression.

Some called Texas hot, but in her opinion, Brimstone Alley ought to be Arizona's handle. The land baked and dried the farther it ebbed from the Aravaipa, smothering the air with waves of heat that shimmered on the horizon.

Needing relief from the June sun and the suffocating weight of the layers of clothing she wore, Alewine rolled up her sleeves and unfastened the top two buttons of her high-necked collar.

"Don't let *her* see that." Jezlynn nodded toward Madeline who sat in the front seat next to Nick. "Ain't ladylike."

Alewine wouldn't have minded being delegated to the back, if Madeline had suffered the same. But the woman had insisted on riding the driver's seat with Nick, saying she needed to help him scout the trail since he'd been gone so long. That bustle-bobbing petticoat had out-and-out lied! How the buzzard beaks could she watch the trail if all she did was gawk at the gambler's face?

"She ain't seeing nothing but your pa at the moment," Aly grumbled, lifting the hair off the back of her neck to cool it. What she wouldn't give for her coonskin right now, but the cap was stored away in the trunk with her buckskins and longhandles. Glancing at Jezlynn, she envied the child's shorn curls and masculine clothing. But there was no use wallowing in pity. No one held a shooter to her back when she promised to wear this lacey noose. Still, there ought to be a limit on how much a lady, or one pretending to be, had to suffer.

She held the collar away from her neck, letting her skin cool. Surely, she could stretch her word a bit until she got somewhere and washed off this traildust. "Reckon your ma would faint if I hike up these here petticoats?"

"Prob'ly be out for days." Jezlynn nodded, giggling as Alewine tempted fate.

Madeline turned and looked over her shoulder, a dark brow arching over one emerald eye. Alewine deliberately raised her hem another inch. Eons passed as glare met glare. Though neither gaze unlocked, challenge emanated from both, drawing an imaginary line in the space that separated them.

I don't like you, Madeline glowered.

I don't like you liking Nick, Alewine scowled back.

Madeline blinked. Aly smiled. Triumph surged through Aly as she watched her opponent concede defeat. Probably a first, from what Aly had seen. The townspeople treated Madeline like she owned rights to

53

the only watering hole in the territory. Jezlynn's mother abruptly shifted toward the team, her neck and spine now ramrod straight.

Wanting to savor her victory, Alewine dug the spurs in a little deeper. "Must be mighty uncomfortable having to act so upright all the time." She wiggled in her seat and pursed her lips like she'd seen some of the crowd do when they were looking on Nick with disdain earlier. "That would make my—"

"Aly."

"Twisted tadpoles! What?" Nick's deep reprimand startled Aly, jarring her from her impish mood. She'd thought he was too busy concentrating on the roadway and enjoying Madeline's adoration to pay attention to *her*. Jezlynn giggled again.

"There's a child present."

"I was gonna say 'backside.' You just didn't let me get it all out."

Jezlynn giggled again. "You was gonna tell a damn lie."

"Watch your language, too, Jezlynn Theresa," Madeline chimed in. "There's company present."

Nick looked as if he might turn around in his seat. Aly jerked down her hem, sat bolt upright and grabbed her collar as if someone were trying to choke her. *She'd roast before Nicodemus saw hide or hair of her underthings . . . yet!*

Madeline reached out to link her arm through Nick's, pressing her head against his shoulder so he couldn't turn. "The heat is bothering me a great deal, Nicky dear." Her voice took on a quivery tone. "May I lean against you? I'm afraid I'll fall out. My strength comes and goes lately." She sighed a bit too deliberately. "I'm sure Aly won't mind, will you, dear?"

"The name's Alewine." *And you're about sick as I*

am married. "Oh, I don't mind. But don't fall out.
That might trouble Jez a fair bit!"

She started to wink at the child but was surprised to
watch the six-year-old's eyes darken.

A quick flick of the reins, urging the team into a
faster gait, warned she'd gone too far. Nick would
wait until they reached privacy then would speak his
peace. Well, let him. She was tired and hungry and
irritated as snake tongue at that vixen in the front seat.
If Nick didn't like it, he could just get somebody else
to play priss for him.

The barouche and the two buggies of invited guests
that followed them headed toward the reddish-brown,
cobbled wall of an ancient pueblo that sat upon the
bank of the Aravaipa. A cool breeze rippled the river's
surface and gave Aly a moment's reprieve.

Despite her anger with him, Aly watched the flex of
Nick's shoulders and arms, admiring his handling of
the horses. His reputation for being one of the best
card slingers in Texas was well-deserved, but the chis-
eled slope of his shoulders, the sun-bronzed tone of
face and forearms, the potent angle of chest to hip,
confirmed he was a man who spent time outdoors
building calluses. A trait she'd grown to admire in the
past year. He'd never hesitated to lend Ben McGuire a
hand in his cornfield or mercantile, nor failed to help
his brother Nash at the livery . . . at least anytime Nick
stayed in town long enough to light somewhere.

Sorry shame he didn't have good taste in women.
But then, he'd had the good sense to leave this one.
Aly snarled as she stared at Madeline's backside then
focused on the panorama just west of Prickly Bend. A
glance at Jezlynn made Alewine almost regret the trail
her thoughts were taking . . . almost.

"How far is it?" Aly spotted the turquoise peaks in

the distance. "Your guests gotta go mountain climbing for supper?"

"Those are the Pinalenos." Nick pointed to the Aravaipa's southern bank. "And over there the Galiuro Mountains. That tallest peak is Holy Joe. And, just beyond Mount Lemmon is Tucson. The Kearney Trail I told you about earlier is around eight—almost nine— miles past Madeline's place. So you can see, Prickly Bend is a great freighting route for anyone with enough grit and the funds to finance it for a year. By that time, you'd have enough customers that it would pay for itself."

Though he talked business, Aly suspected he was reminding her of their agreement. Of her word. Even so, the opportunity to extend her freighting company conjured up lots of possibilities.

Almost *eight* miles past Madeline's place? "Then you just live a mile or two from town?" Alewine remembered that Nick said the Kearney Trail was only ten miles from Prickly Bend. "Where's *your* house, Nick?"

"One-fourth a mile from my home." Madeline looked up adoringly at Nick. "We really enjoyed the closeness when we were younger. Didn't we, Nicodemus?"

"Almost there now." Nick evaded her question as the team's gait increased without any encouragement from him.

"Good. I'd like to get to know the town a bit, if I'm gonna call it home for five months. Glad it's close enough to walk to, if I take a notion."

"Then you intend to stay the full time?" Madeline looked hopefully at Nick. "*Both* of you?"

"Aly and I will stay as long as it takes to convince you Jezlynn should return to Valiant with us."

"I ain't going nowhere I don't wanna go!" Jezlynn

56

folded her arms obstinately across her chest and refused to look at any of her elders.

"We've talked about this before, Jezlynn. You know it's best for you and—"

"It's good for *you*, not me!" Jezlynn half-turned in her seat, letting no one see her eyes.

"You have no idea what's best for you, Jezlynn Theresa. Perhaps going to bed without supper tonight will help you to think twice before running away from home again or causing your friends and mother such concern." Madeline lifted a lace handkerchief and began to dab away the perspiration beading on her brow. "This is all just too, too much, Jezlynn. Why can't you behave?"

"I ain't hungry, anyway!"

"Perhaps that's a bit too harsh," Nick said, defending the child. "It was a long, tiring journey. She's probably as hungry as I—"

"I don't need you to take up for me." Jezlynn glared at him.

"Well, if you think she'll mind any better, then I'll certainly take your suggestion under consideration." Madeline's tone softened slightly. "But I don't . . ."

Their conversation lowered as they discussed the proper way to proceed with Jezlynn.

The manner in which the child's legs instantly drew up, curling her into a tiny ball on the seat, reminded Aly of a prairie dog whose mother had left it behind at Wild Horse Creek. She'd found it all balled up, shivering from lack of more than just warmth . . . just as Jezlynn's words spoke of a hunger for something other than food.

Aly reached out and gently touched the six-year-old's shoulder. Jezlynn jerked away.

Aly's hand hovered. Fetid memories rose from her own childhood and fouled her mind. She willed them away, but could not shed the nauseating sensations left in their wake. Hesitating no more, she offered Jezlynn the one thing she'd somehow hung onto despite the past that had disappointed her, despite the years that had hardened her heart, despite a future that had looked even bleaker at times. *Compassion.*

Yet the girl shunned her attempt.

Gently brushing Jezlynn's shoulder a third time, Aly moved closer. Jezlynn turned to stare. Alewine lifted one arm, offering her the space at her side. Jezlynn hesitated, but Aly's invitation stood firm.

The child blinked, tears welling instantly in the dark lashes that sheltered her eyes. Confusion shimmered in their green depths, replaced by a need so desperate that only one who had suffered the same might understand. Finding that accord, Jezlynn hurled her body against Alewine's. Her small shoulders bobbed as she pressed into Aly's ribs in anguish, yet never uttering a sound.

The silence of the child's misery pierced Alewine's heart as if a perfectly aimed arrow had met its mark. She squeezed her eyes tightly shut, damming back the flood of rejection she had herself suffered those many years ago.

I promise you, little one, Aly let the words flow through her mind and heart, willing them into the tiny body she held. *I'll not only find out why she's trying to make you feel so miserable, but you can count on me to make sure Nick is father enough to heal your sad, little heart.*

"Well, are you just going to stand there and fold them socks, or are you gonna growl at me and get it over with?" Alewine stared at Nick from across the bedroom. They'd been escorted up to this priss parlor ten minutes ago, and he'd done nothing but neatly put away his belongings in the rosewood armoire. His silence was making her as jumpy as a bedbug on a lit mattress.

He faced her, casually shedding his frock coat. "I won't yell, Aly. It wouldn't do any good if you've made up your mind not to help me. You didn't even try to make a good impression on Madeline."

"Who says I ain't gonna help you? I told you I would. And just as soon as I can wiggle into those clean garments over there, I'll play the part just fine." Since the ride with Jez, Aly had made up her mind that the only way to assist Nick and his daughter was to put on the show a bit more for Madeline. "Then maybe the straight-neck will ease up on Half-Pint, if she's occupied with pestering me instead of—"

Her voice suddenly escaped her as Nick took off his embroidered satin waistcoat, then his cravat. His linen shirt and Kerseymere trousers were travel-stained and fit his muscular physique as if they were a coat of paint. When he started to peel off the shirt, Alewine took a step backward and insisted, "Whoa there, Gambler! What do you think you're doing?"

A challenge darkened his eyes into midnight coals. Nick smiled, a beguiling expression that made her flutter where she wasn't sure she had any ruffles.

"I'm undressing, Chick. Getting cleaned up . . . for dinner." He unfastened one button, then another. "You do recall the meal is being held up until we get rid of some of this trail dust? We don't want to keep the guests waiting."

"But I thought you'd, I'd, well, we'd—" As the last button unfastened with Nick's broad shoulders suddenly bared, Alewine stood there with her mouth gaping, her fingers turning the key around her neck. Muscles shiny with perspiration flexed with the mere effort of folding his soiled shirt and laying it on top of the armoire. Some slender thread of propriety told her she ought to turn around and close her mouth, but he looked too good to stop staring.

His smile broadened, deepening each dimple until her own lips curved in response. When it dawned on her that she was staring oogle-eyed at him, Aly did an abrupt about-face. Once, twice, she blinked, finding it difficult to breathe and trying hard to rid herself of his tempting image. She hadn't felt this winded since getting bucked off Ol' Bone-Buster last spring. Attraction to the gambler was flowing through her bloodstream like water from a primed pump.

"Aly?"

The low huskiness of his voice rippled down her spine. "Y-Yeah?"

"Keep that up, and you'll for sure convince Madeline we're lovers."

Chapter Five

All conversation stopped as Nick escorted Aly into the dining room. Every soul sitting at the long table of dinner guests turned to focus on her. She felt like the first nag ever to enter this stable of thoroughbreds. Their silent scrutiny continued, causing her to shift her hips and readjust the bustle of her fringed silk dress. How in the horsehair was a body supposed to sit with this caboose riding dead center?

"Aiiiee, do my eyes deceive me? Madre Santissima, what a wonderful surprise, mi amiga!"

A short, full-figured redhead scooted back her chair and stood, slapping both palms against her high-carved cheeks. Sapphire eyes lit with excitement and approval as the plump woman bounded around the table and flung herself into Aly's arms.

"It *is* you, Alewine Penelope! What in the name of Benito Juarez are you doing in Prickly Bend?"

"I'm here with . . . what are *you*—?"

"I did not have a chance yet to write you and tell you I had moved! How did you know where to find me?"

"I didn't have any idea you—"

"I only accepted Banker Sullivan's offer a month ago," she chattered, not giving Aly time to complete a sentence. "But then, you always know how to surprise me, too, my friend. I am so happy you are here. Come, let me look at you!"

She stepped backward, propping one elbow on her other hand and resting a forefinger against one cheek. Eyebrows that were a shade darker than the woman's auburn tresses arched.

"There is something different about you." Her nostrils flared and a smile spread across her generous, rose-colored mouth. "Something naughty, I think."

I'll strangle you, Alewine decided, wishing she could wrap her fingers around the voluptuous book-keeper's neck. *I'll lace your spicy tongue up with rawhide and sprinkle cayenne pepper on it for good measure.* But that would be considered unladylike in anybody's book, and she'd promised Nick she'd do him proud. Besides, Aly owed Connie too much to ever really be angry with her.

Though Aly had once saved the woman's life, Connie had been far braver by being patient enough to show her how to keep the ledgers at the freighting office. Because of Connie's instruction, Aly owed her friend most of the success of her business.

Crooking her mouth to one side, Aly hoped no one could hear the whispered words to her long-time cohort. "It's the dress, Connie. I ain't wearing my buckskins."

"I can see that, amiga. And so does every caballero here, eh?"

Aly's cheeks tightened with mortification as the truth of the woman's words made her aware of the men's approval. She glanced at Nick and was disappointed that he thought it amusing. He didn't have to take their interest so blamed well. He could act a *little* jealous. After all, he was her pretend husband.

"I haven't had the pleasure of meeting you, senori—er . . . senora." Nick half-bowed to Aly's feisty friend, quickly focusing attention away from his bride. "But you most assuredly must be Consuela Bonita Maria . . . I forget the other names . . . Calhoun. I've heard all about you."

Consuela allowed him to press a kiss lightly against her offered hand. "It is 'senora.' Four times, I am so fortuitous. And I am indeed sorry to say I have not had the pleasure of meeting a man as *guapero*— how do you say in Americano . . . good looking . . . as yourself, senor. But whatever Alewine Penelope told you about me—the truth is much worse, I am certain."

Her laughter shook her entire frame and the rug beneath them.

Someone deliberately cleared their throat. Two of the matrons present at the table leaned over and discussed a private matter with the men sitting next to them. Madeline rose and waved to three empty seats. "Won't you come join us, Mrs. Calhoun? I'm sure everyone here would love to get better acquainted with you, as well as Nick and Mrs. Turner . . . *after* we've served the first course."

Their hostess' countenance never changed from its calm expression. Madeline reseated herself. Aly sensed irritation growing within the woman. Maybe the feeling stemmed from the way Madeline twisted the fork around and around in her gloved fingers.

Ignoring the empty chair next to Nick's former lover, Aly headed for the two farther down the table.

"*Mrs.* Turner?" Connie's smile broadened as her

gaze raked the gambler from head to boot tip. "You mean this fine-looking caballero is the bee that—?"

"He's my husband, Connie. Got married about a month ago," Aly interjected, knowing the half-Spanish, half-Irish fireball might give the women vapors if the sentence were finished.

Aly waited until she saw which chair Connie claimed, then took the other empty one two seats away. She sat, then scooted forward to give the bustle more room. Her shoe slipped on the soft carpet beneath her feet. She teetered into the long-necked matron sitting to her left.

Friction shot up Aly's arm. The matron squealed. Aly grabbed the table's edge to regain her balance, jostling the crystal goblet standing inches away. Her hand darted out to stop the spill, sweeping the fringed silk's three-flounced sleeve across her neighbor's plate and into a basket of rolls that divided the two place settings.

"Sorry, ma'am," Aly muttered, grabbing the goblet in time. She slowly scooted up, letting the bustle ride high, nearly to her waist. Now, she knew how a turtle felt when its shell got cockeyed. "Mighty fine rug. Slicker'n a wad of—I mean slicker'n satin, don't you know."

The long-necked woman's eyebrows angled so high they nearly formed a second widow's peak at the top of her forehead.

Nick smiled indulgently and attempted to draw the attention away from her clumsiness. "Your home is as lovely as I remember it, Madeline."

He glanced to see if there were a chair next to Aly's but found none. He looked askance at Aly. "And dinner smells delightful."

"Nick, will you do me the honor of sitting beside

me?" Madeline motioned him to the chair adjacent to hers as if she were bestowing favor upon the queen's champion.

Alewine fumed as she realized the vixen had purposefully planned the seating arrangements, just as she'd deliberately sent Jezlynn to her room. Madeline's motivation to have them stay the night had nothing to do with Nick and Jez getting to know one another or allowing the Turners to get a good night's rest.

Still, if Nick sat next to Madeline, all eyes would be focused on the former lovers, and maybe everyone would miss whatever future blunders Aly was apt to make. She nodded in approval to Nick.

To her chagrin, Aly noticed the man sitting between her and Madeline was none other than Clay Driscoll, looking very much like a lap dog ready to wag his tail if either she or Madeline favored him with conversation.

How more miserable could this dinner get? Aly took a sip from the cup and found the answer sooner than she expected. Spiced tea, for pistol's sake! She despised tea with a passion.

Everyone voiced their approval of the Gilmore home and Madeline's gracious hospitality, mentioning particularly her special recipe for spiced tea. Madeline blushed with appreciation at the various comments. Aly couldn't bring herself to lie about the taste, but felt it was an opportunity to try some of those social skills Rachel had taught her. Rachel once said, *"If you can't say anything nice, make certain you say something that can be construed as a compliment."*

"This tea is definitely unique," Aly offered, proud of the words she'd chosen. "Like nothing I've ever tasted."

"Why, thank you, Alewine." Madeline dabbed a laced napkin daintily against her lips. "I'll send over a dozen or so bottles of the next batch. But do sip it slowly, dear senora. There are properties within its recipe that are potent to certain ladies' constitutions."

"Just wait until you're invited to your first sewing bee, *mi amiga*," Connie urged. "Senora Gilmore furnishes the tea for the event. The quilt we are working on, it has no pattern. But it is very much fun to stitch. Sí?"

Several of the women looked nervously at their husbands while the bookkeeper paused to take a sip of her tea.

Connie could boast four husbands, but she was a petticoat shy of being a full-skirted female. *Rachel, I need you*. Aly wished her friend from Valiant would appear in the doorway and give her a quick reminder of all the etiquette and good manners she'd been practicing in anticipation of becoming a godmother. But Rachel was hundreds of miles away, and Nick could only sidetrack attention from her for a short time. It was up to Aly to keep her word. If only trying to be feminine wasn't so darned bothersome. Wearing acres of ruffles on her sleeves and strapping a perch on her backside wasn't exactly Aly's idea of fine riggings.

Connie was no Rachel McGuire, but the bookkeeper must have known something about being a lady or she wouldn't have interested those four beaux. Aly guessed she'd just have to make do and weigh everything Connie told her with a careful scale before taking the saucy senora's advice.

Suddenly grateful for Consuela's presence in Prickly Bend, Aly didn't feel quite so much like a pig out of its sty and was thankful she had at least one friend among strangers.

Still . . . how in horse hooves was she gonna get

Connie to teach her to be more of a lady without confiding the truth about her marriage? If Connie caught wind that Nick was good-looking and *available*, the woman wouldn't let the skin under her ring finger tan up before she set her own bonnet for him.

Chapter Six

The meal commenced and the evening wore on. Listening to Madeline laugh at something Nick said, tasting the delicious fare that everyone swore was made from Madeline's own recipes, watching the preening peahen try to jump her claim, wore Aly's temper to the nub. Her appetite left her completely after the first few bites. She squished mashed potatoes through the prongs of her fork, first one way then another until they resembled a checkered mound.

"I don't like the potatoes, either, dear," the long-necked lady's tone was more quack than whisper as she slightly leaned toward Aly, "but try the quail casserole. You'll like it. People wait months to get invited to Madeline's for dinner. She's so ill, you know. Can't have everyone over all the time, but she has a good many. Why just the other day, Mertle Mae McFarland told me—"

Barrel-breasted, Aly decided as she turned from the

sight of the woman's ample bosom that rounded immediately into hips. Tuning out the chatter, Aly took another sip from the silver goblet the servants filled repeatedly. She knew her share of barrel-chested men, but had never hung the handle on a female until now. The thought of men's chests refreshed her memory of the bare one she'd seen less than an hour ago upstairs in the room she and Nick were expected to share tonight.

The sip became a gulp that went down awkwardly. Her throat knotted. Tea burned the roof of her mouth. Her nostrils clenched as she prayed she would not embarrass herself. From the corner of her eye, Aly saw Driscoll's hand snake out and suspected he was about to do the unthinkable!

She waited for the slap on the back, fearing he thought a piece of food had gone down wrong. If he made the expected move, she would spew Madeline's fine tea in a very unladylike manner all over the dinner guests. Instead, Nick reached across the table and offered her his handkerchief.

"Are you all right?" he asked.

She nodded, unable to speak. Pressing the linen kerchief to her mouth and nose, she willed her facial muscles to ease while the tea scalded its way down her rigid throat. Aly flashed him a look of gratitude, blinking back the pinpoints of light that danced before her eyes.

"When I was a new bride, I wanted my Eustace to think I ate like a bird," the large woman said.

A duck maybe, Aly silently countered, pleased yet perturbed that the quacker continued to talk as if nothing had happened. Maybe Aly's lack of grace wasn't that noticeable.

"It was almost a year before Eustace ever saw me eat more than one meal a day." The chatty woman scooped a healthy portion of potatoes onto her fork. "He thought I swooned frequently because I was so excited to see him." She stuffed the potatoes into her mouth, then swallowed. "Actually, it was from lack of eating."

The woman's name fit her well—Ursilla Quackenbush. Aly would have bet her last dollar the lady had long spindly legs beneath that overskirt and waddled when she walked.

"I nearly starved myself to nothing but bones and bonnet before he told me to eat, eat, eat." Ursilla flashed a smile at the equally barrel-chested man who sat farther down the table. "Eustace says a man of the West wants his woman stout and hearty and—"

Silent, Aly added. Keep the wife eating, she doesn't quack as much. Wonder if anyone wanted to wager which of the two women could talk the most—Ursilla or Connie? At least Connie's chatter was sprinkled with a little spice. "Smart man, your Eustace."

"Why, yes, he is, Mrs. Turner. I was just telling him the other day . . . oh, now, dear, that story can wait 'til we know each other better, don't you think? Aren't you going to eat anything?" She moved her large plate over and grabbed the small one holding dessert. "Madeline's prickly pie won first place at the Fourth of July baking contest the last five years straight. You really ought to try some, dear."

"No thanks," Aly countered, attempting to ignore the cinnamon aroma. The pie would have to smell as delicious as it looked. How many more talents did the divine Madeline Gilmore boast? "I'm not very hungry."

Ursilla's tiny mouth pressed together as she chirped, "Oh, my goodness, I'll just bet you haven't quite recovered from the coach ride, and your stomach is a bit bottoms up, isn't it? But you really should eat something, Mrs. Turner. Enough to keep you healthy."

Had the woman taken a single breath? Aly exhaled raggedly as if she were a three-legged horse in a pony express race. "How 'bout some quack—er—crackers? That'll do."

"You aren't already with child, are you, Alewine?" Madeline frowned. "I had hoped Jezlynn would have a bit of time to get to know her father well before sharing him with other siblings."

The buzz of conversation stopped as attention focused on Aly.

Her temper flared. Though Madeline's words implied concern for Jezlynn, Aly didn't like the implication aimed at her and Nick. From the animosity between Nick and several of the townsmen, it seemed clear that Madeline had borne Jezlynn out of wedlock. Aly started to remind the pretender to judge not lest she be judged, but decided that wasn't the right course of action to take. Reminding the guests of Jezlynn's illegitimacy would only give the child more to deal with.

"We've been married a month now, and there isn't—"

"And we're hoping a blessed event won't happen until Jezlynn feels secure with the two of us." Nick deliberately raised his tone until even those at the end of the table could hear.

The warmth of Nick's gaze ignited a possibility within Aly that had lain dormant for so long, she'd forgotten it even existed. Motherhood. The one fantasy she believed would never be realized. The one fear she might never conquer. The only dream she could not gain alone. It took all the will Aly could muster to look away from the dark gaze that made her believe *every* dream had a chance . . . if she were only courageous enough to take it. But their marriage was in name only.

"Besides, I run a freighting office in Valiant, and I

want to continue working for a while. You know . . .
put some money in the bank for when times are
tough." She focused her attention on the men in the
group, knowing from past experience that to gain busi-
nessmen's respect there must be eye-to-eye contact.
"I'm thinking of extending my freight line to Prickly
Bend and the Kearney Trail."

"You run a freight line?" Madeline's brows knit in
curiosity. "What does that mean exactly? Do you keep
the ledgers . . . schedule the deliveries?"

Aly's chin lifted proudly. "All of that. Consuela
here taught me the hard part—keeping the books. But
mostly, I make deliveries. And on time. You can set
your clock by me."

Several of the ladies at the table shifted uncomfort-
ably as their hostess closed her eyes, distress clear in
her pallor.

"Then who intends to watch over Jezlynn when her
father is working?"

"When she ain't in school, she can hitch a ride with
me. From what I've seen, she's got a travel bug up her
bonnet. Might like skinning them jennies and jacks
down the road."

"Indeed. Skinning?" Madeline took a long, deliberate drink from her teacup, then asked, "And what pray
tell is that?"

"Mule skinning. Skinning to those in the business."
Aly flashed everyone an enthusiastic smile. "Why,
there ain't anything"—she remembered the company
she was in—"*isn't* nothin' better than smelling God's
good earth churning up beneath the hooves of a mule
team six jennies deep, knowin' that I'm delivering
necessities to somebody who's grateful I take them
just what they need right when they need it. That's a
mighty good feeling."

Disapproval filled Madeline's expression, but a

short, balding man cleared his throat, drawing all attention away from her and to the other end of the table. He bit his lip, raking his lower teeth over the bottom of his handlebar moustache. "A freighter, you say? I'm Silas Sullivan, the banker in Prickly Bend. If you need any financial assistance, please come see me at the Three Rivers. I'll see what I can do to extend you a loan, if necessary. Your friend, Mrs. Calhoun, will tell you I'm a fair man."

His offer set off a volley of remarks pertaining to the lack of commerce in the township. Apparently, the offer of a year's worth of free mortgage had not aroused the interest they'd hoped.

When someone brought up the subject of allowing a brothel, Ursilla and her husband were on opposite sides of the issue. Surprisingly, she felt a red-light district would not be of too great harm. After all, any town that was of any quality had its soiled doves. And men would come from all over the Gadsden to spend their money in various ways—hotels, saloons, restaurants, and gambling halls would sprout up once there were patrons enough to sustain them. Eustace wanted the same type of repercussions, but not by bringing in the "wrong" element.

"Mr. Turner makes his living as a gambler," Ursilla interjected. "Some feel he's one of those wrong elements. But every man here has gambled at some time in his life, or they wouldn't be living in Prickly Bend. You're gambling by trying to make a town thrive here in the cactus and sand where others less hearty than you have given up and gone back east. If the doves bring in commerce, let them. Sometimes actions justify themselves in the end."

"Though I don't think brothels are the answer to your problems and wouldn't want them brought in myself," Nick admitted, "I do agree that taking action

73

to rectify a bad situation is the only way to achieve the result you want."

Aly sensed he was talking to her more than he was the others. He seemed to be asking her to bear with him, not to let Madeline ruffle her feathers, to give him a chance to prove what he'd told her about wanting to raise Jezlynn. To know he was against bringing in one of the very businesses where his gambling game thrived showed Nick meant to change for Jezlynn's sake.

As Aly listened to the others discuss their opinion of the matter, she gently slid a biscuit and chicken leg from her plate to the folds of the linen kerchief Nick had given her. She stuck it inside the pocket of her silk dress.

When the discussion heated up, she felt compelled to support Ursilla's view. "We have a saloon in Valiant called the Lazy Lady. Some folks say ill repute goes on under the roof. Me, I think what's your business is your own, and nobody has a right to mind yours for you. So if you feel like ill-reputing, have at it. But just to set the record straight, so you know, a lotta good gets done there, too. Ophelia, that's the saloon keeper, donates twenty-five percent of her profit to the town orphanage on a weekday, more come Saturdays. Are any of us willing to be that generous?"

Not an eye would look at her directly, answering her as surely as if each guest had spoken.

Eustace's shoulders squared, his expression stern. "Our town has made a point of keeping scandal from our doors. Avoiding costly mistakes. For more than seven years now, I might add. Unfortunately, trouble has a way of returning unannounced when you least expect it. Dens of so-called 'delight' would surely do the same."

"If you're talking about me, Eustace"—Nick met

the man's gaze squarely, but Eustace quickly looked away—"I left Prickly Bend so there wouldn't be any trouble. Believe me, I wouldn't have returned if it hadn't been necessary."

Madeline stood. "Please, friends . . . neighbors. I invited Nick back, and I hope that you will forgive him as I did those many years ago. We were young and foolish." She looked directly at Nick. "And terribly in love. Nick's new home apparently has something to teach us . . . if we're willing to listen."

Aly watched silence fill the dining hall as surely as if her hostess had raised a finger to her lips and hushed them all. Every ear seemed tuned to obey her command.

"Perhaps Prickly Bend does need to follow in Valiant's footsteps." Approval lit Madeline's eyes. "Form a profit fund. If each business or family gives even five percent of what they earn, enough could be raised to build another business or at least enough to acquire a loan from the Three Rivers Bank. Isn't that correct, Mr. Sullivan?"

The banker nodded, jarring the long strand of hair he brushed from one side of his head to the other to bridge the ever-widening gap at the crown. "Depends, but it might just be possible."

Surprised that Madeline defended Valiant, Aly wondered if her encouragement was true interest or an effort to please Nick.

"I don't have five percent to give," one of the townsmen complained.

"My Harry isn't making enough as it is."

"We want progressive ideas. Ideas that will increase our incomes, not set us back," someone else admonished.

"Who asked your opinion anyway, Turner? You don't plan to make this your home. Why should we trust the likes of you?" the same man asked.

75

"I might. If I can get an old friend from Tucson to go in partners with me."

"Valiant still has its problems," Clay Driscoll admitted, eliciting even more glares in Nick's direction.

"What about Neil Sorgensen's idea? We could harvest the saguaros for cactus jelly." Ursilla glanced at Madeline for approval. "Or Phillip Dolan's notion about raising horses for the cavalry?"

"Thorne McCandless and his daughter, Gila, already have those two businesses well underway," Banker Sullivan reminded. "And why deal with us when Tucson's closer to Fort Lowell and Yuma? We need something uniquely our own."

"Did you consider Jaco Patterson's idea?" Consuela asked. "He's wildly handsome, rich and—"

"Two chambers shy of a full load. He hasn't had a sensible thought in his head since eighty-one." Disapproval straightened the banker's mouth into a grim line.

"*Que suerte!* I like an unpredictable vaquero." Admiration radiated from Consuela's gaze.

"What do you mean, *what luck*?" Ursilla challenged. "A man like that is no one to toy with or stake your future on. He doesn't take kindly to those of us with a gentler nature."

Well, that did it, Aly decided. Consuela would waste no time in proving Ursilla wrong. The bookkeeper felt it was her God-given calling to entice such reluctants toward the finer points of wedded bliss. Trouble was, she ended up marrying them herself. Consuela Patterson. She had to admit the handle had a nice ring to it, if Aly said so herself.

"What about a ferry boat across the San Pedro?"

Eustace's upper lip curled at Nick's suggestion. "That's about as useless as selling brooms for a sandbox."

"What about bringing in more mining business?" Several grumbles followed Nick's newest suggestion. "Copper seems in great quantity here."

"Takes too much capital to start," the banker informed.

"What about enticing the railroad to survey the area?" Nick ran down a list of possible industries that might find the region appealing. "Or, offer more than a year's free mortgage."

Every suggestion Nick gave was ignored, making it clear he would have a difficult time re-establishing his place in the community, much less in this conversation.

Aly had about all she could endure. She bolted to her feet, not caring if Ursilla saw the boots she refused to take off from beneath the fancy dress she wore. "If you mule-headed jackasses would loosen some of that starch out of your longhandles and quit thinkin' your way is the only way, you just might be able to save this mustang of an outpost. But from what I see, and no doubt what I hear, you ain't doing nothing but sticking burrs under one another's saddles."

"*Olé!*" Consuela shouted, flinging her hair back as if it were freshly rinsed and lightly tossing her kerchief in the air.

The action had its desired effect. Everyone realized that the argument had escalated into a full-blown fight.

"Please, everyone. *Please*." Madeline's voice was breathless as she held both palms up in front of her. "We can't possibly solve all of Prickly Bend's troubles tonight. I'm sure Nick and his new bride, as well as Mr. Driscoll, must be extremely tired from their long journey."

A trembling hand went to her brow and wiped away a crease that had formed on the lovely porcelainlike skin. Her green gaze focused on Aly. "Alewine, if I may impose upon your kindness, will you finish my

77

hostessing duties for the evening? Frankly, I've over-taxed myself and desperately need to take a walk. Nick, I would appreciate having you stroll alongside me, in case I become dizzy. Do you mind?"

Nick stood abruptly and offered his arm. Aly thought his action too quick, too eager, but she realized she had no real right to protest.

To make matters worse, her hostess truly looked ill. Her skin had paled. Tension pursed her lips, forming white circles around them. If this were anyone else but Madeline, she wouldn't hesitate to fill in, no matter how ill-prepared she was to face these society sharpshooters.

"Aly?"

Nick's questioning tone gentled her. He wasn't demanding or expecting, merely awaiting her decision. Respect got her every time. Her downfall. The one thing her best friend never failed to give her.

She didn't like the thought of Nick and Madeline alone, but she knew his patience with the townsfolk and their conversation had reached its limit. He needed an escape from their narrow-mindedness—one she could easily give him. She owed him the same respect.

"Y'all go on. I'll entertain the folks."

"Y'all come back and see her anytime she's feeling better and has less company." Aly waved as the guests climbed into the wagon. Or so she thought. Clay Driscoll's long legs hurdled over the back of the buckboard, and he took the porch steps two at a time. "Did you forget something?"

Driscoll took off his hat and halted in front of Aly, only inches from her face. "Just wanted to let you know that I'll be stopping by often to see you, Aly-girl. You and Nick, of course. I think we Valiantites ought to stay together." He winked and gave her a slow, sexy smile. "From the looks of things, you might be needing someone to spend time with, and we never got much chance before."

"I'm married, Driscoll." Aly held up her left hand. "You saw the ceremony."

"I saw it, but there was something mighty peculiar about what went on. And why did that fellow from Clarendon do the marrying, instead of Brother Caleb?"

Aly sighed. "I told you, Driscoll. Caleb was out of the county, and Nick wanted to get on down the road." Gratitude filled her as she saw Connie lower herself from the wagon and approach.

"You might just want to strike up a special friendship with me, Aly-girl." His gaze raked her from head to hem, then his head nodded in the direction Nick and Madeline had taken. "From the looks of things, it's going to get mighty lonesome now that Turner's come home."

Alewine took a step closer until she was eye-to-eye, nose-to-nose with him. "You might be one to mince words, but if you got any notion in your head that I'm a hike-my-petticoat-kinda woman, you better—"

"Trouble, *mi amiga*?"

Grateful Connie arrived when she did, Aly decided there had to be a more civil way to deter the man. She chose her words carefully. "Saddle up now and ride back to Texas. 'Cause, this here ring"—she touched the gold band Nick had placed on her finger— "says I love, honor, and don't betray Nicodemus Turner."

A hundred more colorful suggestions came to mind, but Aly refrained from resorting to them. Rachel would have been proud. Connie's presence was definitely a godsend.

Driscoll backed away slowly, holding up his palms

as if a gun were at his back. "Just offering friendship, Aly. Just a little friendship."

"Keep it that way."

"Can't blame a man for trying to stake what looks like a shaky claim."

"Do it at your own risk, Driscoll. You know what happens to claim jumpers."

"Yeah, sometimes they get lucky." He half-bowed, then joined the others.

"What's that all about, *querida*?" Consuela looked up sharply at her friend. "What did he mean . . . peculiar?"

Should she take a chance and confide in the book-keeper? Connie had always been a wonderful friend, but the feisty fireball was not good at keeping secrets. Particularly secrets that screamed for advice Connie was only too willing to offer. Besides, if she took the time to explain now, Aly would miss what was happening between Nick and Madeline.

"Such a serious expression, my friend. I think you will not tell me this night. But tomorrow, the sun will shine again. Your worries will not seem so dark and gloomy. Maybe then you'll tell me about this Driscoll gringo and the handsome caballero, eh?"

"There's nothing to tell, Con."

"We'll scrub your house good side-by-side. Then you'll talk. The elbows make the mouth rattle." She hugged Aly good-bye. "I've seen it many times. Trust me, amiga."

If only I could tell you, Aly thought, wanting more than anything to tell her the marriage to Nick was a sham. The key felt heavier around Aly's neck. She'd never be able to convince the much-married woman she and Nick were lovers. Connie was an expert on such things.

Aly watched the buggies roll out of sight, then wondered how much time had passed since Nick and Madeline had left everyone's company. She hadn't heard them return, and twilight already stretched across the horizon in ever-darkening hues. Hunger rumbled in her stomach, reminding her that she would have to wait until breakfast to satisfy its cravings.

She started to step off the large porch that encircled the house, but stopped in midstep. Jezlynn would be hungry, too. While Nick and Madeline were outside it would be the perfect time to sneak her something to eat. But it was also the perfect time to spy on the former lovers. The perfect time to see if their walk was as innocent as it seemed, or a planned rendezvous.

Not that she cared one way or the other, but she needed to know where she stood.

Chapter Seven

"Quit being stubborn as a tick on a tendon, will ya? I've got something to give ya. Open up." Aly waited, but Jezlynn didn't comply. Rattling the knob, the freighter realized the door had been unlocked all along.

"Don't want nothing from nobody," came the muffled reply.

Don't want nobody to know you're hurting, Aly countered silently. She had lived with that deliberate isolation enough times herself to recognize it now. For that reason, Aly rapped on the door again and waited for permission to enter. "Guess this chicken and biscuit will go to waste then. You got a dog who'd want to gnaw on the bone?"

Aly could hear the patter of feet going away from the door. A hiss of shifting wood sounded as if the child had raised a window.

"Dogs makes Mama sneeze. Door's unlocked."

Jez's voice sounded farther away than before. What was the imp planning? "Thank you kindly," Alewine remarked as she crossed the threshold. Catching sight of Nick's daughter, she demanded, "Why'd you climb out there?"

The child sat on a massive ponderosa branch that sheltered her bedroom window. She pointed up at the moon. "I like it better out here in the dark."

Not that Aly blamed her. Pink frills on the bedcover, pink lace curtains tied back, and pink rosebud designs on the wall were enough to point out any self-proclaimed tomboy's feminine failings. Aly shuddered, remembering a similar room she'd been ordered to sleep in.

"Mind if I join you?" Aly strode across the distance that separated them. Just as she tried to hike her leg up high enough to hook her heel on the window ledge, she realized she was still shackled by the confounded tea gown and petticoats Nick had demanded she wear to supper.

"You aren't scared, are you, Mrs. Turner? It ain't nothing but an old branch." Jezlynn looked down, then back at Aly. "Can't be no more than fifteen or twenty feet if you fall. At least, that's what Mama says."

Aly had jumped that far from the roof of the livery onto Pug's haywagon on a dare. Still, she wasn't wearing one of these gutclutchers at the time neither. "Sassy little perch-sitter, aren't you?"

Aly untied her petticoats, then thought better of it. If Madeline happened to walk past, Nick would surely disapprove if he looked up and found Aly straddling a branch, much less without petticoats. With all the grace she could muster, she turned and planted her bottom on the window ledge, then grabbed a higher branch and raised herself until she was standing on the ledge.

"You're gonna fall." The child's eyes sparked with half concern, half challenge.

"Not this gal," Aly assured her. Good thing she wore bloomers. Otherwise, anyone passing under the tree would get an eyeful. "I'll just swing my legs as if I was butt-jumping one of my old jackass—er . . . mules."

With a rustle of petticoats, she threw both legs to one side and mounted the branch like a lady riding sidesaddle. The gown tugged at her waist, threatening to split the garment and making the sitting position uncomfortable. Aly shifted awkwardly yet was able to relieve the bind. "See there? Ain't nothing to it."

"That's what you Texans call butt-jumping?" Jezlynn giggled.

Embarrassment burned Aly's cheeks like hot coals branding them. Rachel McGuire would have her mouth washed out with lye if she caught wind of that slip of the tongue. "Well, uh, *some* Texans call it that. Polite ones say it's mounting a horse from behind. Mostly done at a dead run."

"So you're not a polite Texan?"

The imp sure knew how to put a gal in her place. As Aly mulled over a fitting answer, the child shrugged her shoulders.

"Not that I wanta know any of you Texans anyway."

The child fell silent. Aly suspected she was stewing about Nick. After all, he'd made Texas his home. Maybe she could get Jezlynn to open up, and talking about her papa would do her some good. But try as Aly might, Jezlynn closed up tighter than a cavalry cinch at full gallop.

It felt awkward just sitting there, so Aly focused her attention on the pinkish glow coming from the frosted glass lamps inside the room. The room was so sickeningly sweet looking, she could almost feel her hair curling at the roots to cascade in precious little dangles. Suddenly, her mind lit with a possibility. Nothing made a body talk more than mentioning a burr in her saddle. She motioned to the gas lamps. "Pink your favorite color?"

"It's Mama's."

That explains it. Alewine's heart clenched for a moment when she heard the resignation in the child's voice. "Used to have one like it myself when I was a girl." Aly whistled low. "Great gobs of succotash, that was the ugliest fancy room I ever saw."

"Worse than mine?" Doubt crossed Jezlynn's features. Still, she giggled, studying Alewine from head to hem. "You used to be a girl?"

Though Alewine disliked pretending to be Nick's wife, it aggravated her that even a child couldn't imagine her in such a feminine role. "I figure you got the rougher end of the stick with all that pink. At least my room had a few daisies in it here and there. And I happen to have been a girl all my life. In fact I'm probably more girl now than I've ever been, all gussied up like this. Why don't we go in and talk about how we can fix up the room Nick'll get for you back in Val—"

"Ain't gonna do no talking. I'm sitting right here and no amount of yelling's going to change my mind." Jezlynn threaded her arms across her chest. "I'll just keep scooting all the way to the end of the branch if you try and make me go in." The child moved over for effect, deliberately not using her hands to help with the maneuver.

"I don't know you good enough to yell at you yet." Aly wasn't taking any of those daredevil chances in this dress. Besides, she talked too often with her hands. It would be better to use them and the overhead branch to guide her hips across the limb she sat on.

A ripping sound warned that she'd have some

explaining to do to Nick. Maybe it was time to head on back and try to get the dress patched up before he noticed she'd damaged it. He wouldn't like knowing she'd spent her first night at Prickly Bend in a tree. Maybe Jezlynn would come back in if Aly left.

Holding on to the tree with one hand, Aly dug into the pocket of her gown to retrieve the kerchief. She thrust it out toward the little girl. "I'm going back in now. But I brought you this in case you're hungry."

Jezlynn accepted the kerchief, opened it up and looked at the contraband meal, then let it fall to the ground.

"Why'd you do that?" Aly stared hard at the child. She could understand her need for privacy, but that was just plain meanness.

"I don't know you well enough to take a bribe."

"Got me there." Aly disliked the child's method but sure admired her spunk. Jez reminded Aly of herself. Too much, in fact. "How does someone your age know about bribes?"

Jezlynn's lips lifted into a sneer. "Everybody knows if you're gonna be a bank robber, you gotta know how to bribe someone. Bribes are so you can make people think you're good, when you're really bad."

"Plan on being a bank robber, do you?" Aly remembered when she'd wanted nothing more than to be a trail boss riding herd on a bunch of longhorns heading to market. She'd had to settle on freighting and eating prairie dust behind a team of mules.

"The best bank robber in the whole territory." Jezlynn's emerald eyes lit with the moonlight rising high above the Arizona countryside. "And I've been doing lots of practicing."

"Being good so they'll think you're not bad?" Alewine spread her skirt slightly so the spider that had crawled down the trunk could have safe passage over her lap. *Get along little dogie*, she willed it to move faster, *before I have to smash you clean into the hereafter.* "I thought you were being punished tonight because you disobeyed your mother."

"I was being mean. Mean, ornery, low-down, good-for-nothing—"

"Whoa there, range-rot. I get the drift. You want everybody to think you're one bad hombre, don't you?"

Jezlynn nodded. "The meaner I am now, the more they'll be scared when I rob the bank."

Alewine kept her tone serious as she voiced the comical thought that almost made her chuckle. "You mean you plan to rob the bank here in town that has no money?"

"Gotta start somewhere." Jezlynn tossed her head so her midnight-colored hair would be out of her eyes. "Besides, if I get caught, they can't keep me if I didn't steal no money. Seems a smart place to start learning."

The sound of voices warned that someone approached. Feminine laughter echoed like a volley through a canyon, making Aly squirm to see what was so funny. The sight of Madeline clinging to Nick's arm, her face beaming with joy, hit Aly in the pit of her stomach as if someone had fired a shotgun at her. "Why, that low-down, no-good, card-dealing, dirty flirter. Just wait until I get down from here. I'll—Aiiieee!"

Aly's bottom slipped from the branch she and Jezlynn had been sitting on. Her fingers clutched desperately at the overhead branch and held. She dangled there, the weight of her petticoats and bloomers threatening to pull her down.

"She's gonna fall!" Jezlynn shouted to the walkers below. "Somebody help her!"

* * *

Nick couldn't believe what he saw. Aly dangling from a tree limb so high she'd break her neck if he didn't do something quickly, and his daughter perched even farther out on a limb. What in the hell was Aly thinking? "Hold on, Aly. I'm coming. Jezlynn, just stay put. Don't try to help."

Racing up under the tree, he craned his neck to focus on her exact location. Nick adjusted his distance, then clapped his hands together and motioned her down. "I'm under you now. Let go and I'll catch you . . . like that time we jumped out of the loft."

"Nick." Madeline kept her distance. "She'll break her neck or yours."

"She's right," Aly said through gritted teeth. "You ain't no pile of straw and that loft wasn't this high. It'll hurt if I land on you."

"It'll hurt more if you don't. So let go." Nick braced himself, preparing for the impact.

"Hell of a way to spend a honeymoon." Alewine howled all the way down.

"Will you quit yelling at me? I wasn't trying to be a playmate to the imp. I was doing my best to get her to eat something." Aly paced the room like a caged bobcat.

Nick reached out and gripped Aly's forearm as if she were a recalcitrant child. "Look at me."

Aly stopped pacing and glared at him.

"Not like that. Look like you're really going to listen . . . That's better."

At the sight of Nick's bare chest, Aly took a deep breath and blew out some of the frustration that had been building while he escorted Madeline to her room and checked on Jezlynn. "All right, I'm listening, but you've got to do the same."

Disapproval bracketed his mouth. "If you continue to do things like climbing and falling out of trees,

Madeline's too smart a lady not to suspect this is a sham. Be more careful what you let her see you do." His voice softened slightly as he gently knuckled her chin up so their gazes would meet.

"You've spent more time with Jezlynn than I have. Tell me she'll be better off with her aunt than me and I'll confess everything to Madeline in the morning."

After defending him to the townsmen, Aly was annoyed that Nick scolded her like a child. That and the fact that he was only reminding her what was at stake—Jezlynn's future—was even more frustrating. "She'd be better off with us . . . you," Aly admitted reluctantly, staring into the most mesmerizing eyes she'd ever seen.

"Then let's get some sleep. It's been a long day for all of us."

"All right by me." Aly looked around and remembered that they were expected to share the same bed. Hope leaped into her thoughts, but she quickly dashed them. Nick would insist on being a gentleman.

Nick must have noticed her concern. "I'll take the chair. You take the bed."

Can read him like a day-old trail. "We'll switch in a few hours."

"There's no need." Nick yawned, stretching his arms and tensing every cord of his muscled body.

"I-I always take my time at watch when I'm on the trail." She sure enough planned to take it tonight and have her fill of it, too. Nick Turner was sure something to look at.

"You're not on the trail here, Aly. You just get some rest, so I can. I'll turn my back if you're wanting to undress."

Changing clothes was the thing she most wanted to do, but with Nick in the room, that was pushing temptation too far. She knew when to say whoa or give

89

quarter. As much as she hated the thought of one more moment in this gutclutcher, it looked like she'd be locked in its cage the rest of the night. "I'm sleeping in it. Might as well get more use out of it."

"Suit yourself," Nick sighed, already folding his long frame into the chair and crossing his muscular arms over his chest.

Aly grabbed a pillow and threw it at him. "Sweet dreams, Gambler."

"Same to you, Chick."

Dreams wouldn't come. Aly's thoughts raced so hard, she felt she'd been ridden hard and put up wet. How long had she wanted to share a life with someone to watch a sunset with her? Someone to snuggle up to? Someone to share the glory of her days and magic of her nights? Now that she lay here in bed, she had no idea what to do with herself or those longtime wishes. All she knew for certain was that such dreaming was impossible.

Aly listened to his breath slow in sleep, smelled that wonderful scent that seemed all his own. The fact that he slept barechested shouldn't have bothered her. She'd seen him that way a dozen times when he'd helped Ben McGuire in the fields.

But tonight was different. Tonight they were alone in a room as man and wife. That heif—*Be nice, Aly*, she told herself, almost able to hear Rachel's soft admonishment. That *lady* downstairs expected there to be some man-wife things going on up here. If Aly admitted the truth to herself, she sort of wished they would live up to the woman's expectations.

But while she and Nick were playing Madeline false, the Lord, in His occasional sense of humor, had seen fit to pull one over on Alewine P. Jones.

Chapter Eight

Thunder rattled the windows. Other noises filtered through Nick's subconscious. A voice? Perhaps two? The dream vanished, leaving him with a deep sense of disappointment. He wanted to finish the dream, capture the elusive moment that escaped him when awake—a moment when he pursued his growing affection toward Aly to determine if she might be willing to become more than his friend.

In his dream, they had been wrestling in the soft hay piled in Ben's loft. When she'd pinned him, he'd started laughing. His nose had honked like a goose, embarrassing him and initiating a fit of giggles that had made Aly's freckles bunch in clusters around her nose. Her golden eyes lost themselves in the sandy lashes that sheltered them, tears of laughter squeezing through.

All of a sudden, she had thrown her arms around Nick and hugged him, thanking him for always making her feel so damned good. Aly's words warmed him to the soul and, before he realized what he'd done, Nick's arms encircled her. He pressed the tenderest of kisses upon her lips. The feel of Aly in his arms was something that dreams were made of, branding him with a quest to experience the real flesh-and-blood woman. The kiss became a flame of yearning, searing away the restraints that kept him from making her his own.

But someone knocked on the barn door insistently. Then the boom of gunfire broke them apart. The dream vanished.

The gunfire was no threat from an unseen assailant as first believed, merely the boom of thunder ravaging the heavens outside Madeline's home.

Nick squeezed his eyes shut, trying to regain the dream, but it eluded him. A deep sigh rose from the pit of his stomach and exhaled into the shadows of the room. Guess morning would take a little longer in coming than he hoped. It wasn't easy sleeping in a reading chair while Aly rested only a few feet away.

The nights since they'd left Valiant had been nothing but pure torture for him. Watching her had become a habit to while away the hours when sleep escaped him. She looked all soft and, what was the word . . . ? *Tame*. Like she didn't have to battle anyone and could let down her guard.

She was surprisingly pretty without that usual fierce expression that dared anyone to test her. The odd combination of white-blond hair and eyes the hue of ripening wheat gave her a more exotic appearance than most. The fact that she wouldn't be caught dead using a parasol had tanned years of sunshine into her skin, giving her a honeyed glow of health. The rigors of commanding an eight-mule team overland had carved her figure into one any sculptor would hold in reverence. Aly was probably one of the most beautiful women he'd ever seen, once he'd started noticing her as a woman instead of his friend. But she'd knock his jaw into his throat if he ever told her that.

The first inkling of the depth of his feelings had been at Rachel's tea party, the first time he'd ever seen Aly in a dress. He'd been so surprised by how feminine the freighter looked, he couldn't get her out of his mind. Since then, he'd encouraged her on several occasions to take up more womanish pursuits, but the minx always refused.

Aly had never told him the reason she felt the need to prove how tough a character she could be. And he had respected her enough not to ask. But one thing was for certain . . . whatever the reason, it had to do with a boarding school and must have compelled her to help him win custody of Jezlynn. And, if his suspicions were true, the same reason she'd refused to pursue a family of her own.

Nick couldn't remember a time when Aly ever allowed herself to be the gentle soul he suspected she'd buried years ago. A soul that silently wept when she witnessed her friend Rachel sewing clothes for the coming baby. That true soul shone clearly on her sleeping face.

Maintaining his promise to keep their marriage in name only was harder than Nick ever imagined. Yet, there was one promise nothing on this earth would ever prevent him from fulfilling. A promise made out of more than friendship to the lady freighter. It was a vow he'd made to himself that Alewine Jones would have at least one gentle season in her life, one time of love and laughter.

Nick's eyes flashed open, taking in the degrees of darkness layering the room. They automatically focused on the bed, certain to see Aly's form stretched out comfortably. Lulled by his peaceful thoughts, his ears tuned themselves to hear the sound of her shallow breathing.

Bolting upright, Nick disbelieved the sight before him.

Aly had suddenly let out a noise of surprise and begun bouncing in the middle of the ticking, causing the headboard to strike the wall repeatedly.

"Ahhhmmmmm, you're jumping on the bed!" A tiny voice scolded from beneath the four-poster.

"What the hell do you think you're doing?" Nick demanded, rushing over to grab Aly's arm as she crashed down in another bounce. "Stop that!" he hissed.

Propelled by momentum, Aly sailed upward instead. "I just got a good bounce going. Gotta get a rhythm, they say. And quit cussing in front of your daughter."

"Hello? Is everything all right in there?" Madeline's voice came quietly from the opposite side of the door.

"Alewine is jum—" came the small voice again.

Nick let go of Aly and dropped to his knees. He lifted the bottom edge of the covers and stared at the tattletale about to make his night worse. "Shhh," he pleaded, holding a finger against his lips.

The black curls swayed as she shook her head and grinned. "How much?"

"How much what?" Nick glanced back at Aly. "Will you please quit bouncing? You're going to knock a hole in my child's head, if you don't."

"Turkey pi"—Aly's gaze shot to Jezlynn before quickly amending the curse— "pi-leeeased to do so."

"I said how much you gonna give me?" Impatience filled Jezlynn's tone.

"For what?" Nick fought the urge to drag her out.

"For not telling Mama about Alewine jumping on

the bed. She doesn't like anyone jumping on the bed. *I know.*".

Nick considered telling Madeline himself, but not until he found out the exact reason Aly felt compelled to do such acrobatics. For now, he would indulge the little swindler and give Aly a chance to explain herself. "Name your price."

"A dollar, and I don't have to go with Mama back to her room."

"Deal." The fact that the child preferred to stay here with him when he was a virtual stranger made Nick wonder why Jezlynn disliked being near her own mother.

The child spat in her hand and held it out to Nick.

With a grimace, he accepted it. Having a daughter would take some getting used to. "Provided you wash your hands before I give you the dollar."

Jezlynn giggled.

"Jezlynn, are you in there?" Madeline called in an exasperated voice. A light shone beneath the door, indicating she held a lamp.

In unison, the three conspirators held a finger to their lips. Silence ensued.

"I guess not," Madeline finally said.

Lightning streaked across the sky outside the window, illuminating the room briefly. Jez's eyes rounded, her expression turning to sheer terror. She was obviously afraid of the thunder and lightning. It was probably her reason for hiding.

An overwhelming need to protect her engulfed Nick, making him react instinctively. He pulled Jezlynn from under the bed and into the wall of his chest. Before he knew what he was doing, he began to pat her small back and say, "There, there now. Papa's . . . I'm here."

"Now, ain't that just the sweetest thing you've ever done, Nicky Turner." Alewine grinned at him.

"I don't need you." Jezlynn flung herself away from Nick. "I don't need anybody." She crawled back under, then refused to come out again, despite Nick's insistence or her mother's concern.

"Got a mind of her own, doesn't she?" Aly smiled. "And the grit to trick you out of a dollar, Gambler. Yep, she's sure as snuff your kin."

Feeling awkward, he glared at Aly. "Get me out of this, will you? Madeline might barge in here any minute to search every cranny for Jez. Whatever explanation we come up with, we can't let Madeline know she's here. Your bed-jumping got us into this. Now get us out of it."

"That's what I was trying to do in the first place." Aly frowned as she tugged on his arm and pulled him away from the bed. She shook her head and held a finger up to her lips again, her gaze slanting to where Jezlynn hid under the bed. "Understand?" she whispered.

He was tired, not blind. She didn't want Jezlynn to hear. "Not completely," he whispered back.

"If you're awake, please open the door." Irritation made Madeline's tone shrill.

"When I get through, Miss-Nose-In-Our-Business will sniff at someone else's door." Devilment lit Aly's eyes. "So pucker up, gambler, and make it feel convincing."

He'd seen that ornery expression before. She was about to pull a prank that would challenge all his wits. Wits that weren't in their best condition at the moment due to a lack of sleep.

Aly took one more glance in Jezlynn's direction. Nick followed her gaze and saw that his daughter had not budged from her haven.

"Good . . . little eyes are looking the other way. Here goes, gambler!"

Aly suddenly threw her arms around him and planted a hard kiss upon his lips. He flinched as she ground her mouth against his. Nick unlinked her arms from around his neck and abruptly shoved her away. "Aly, what are you doing?" He tested his front teeth, making sure they were still rooted.

"Please open the door. We need to talk." Madeline broke in, warning that she would not be put off any longer.

"Trying to look like I've really been kissed," Aly whispered back at Nick, suddenly seeming angry. "That's why I was jumping on the bed, so Madeline would think we were . . . you know . . . doing married kind of things. Why . . . didn't I do it right? I seen my share of prairie dogs kissing."

Nick chuckled. "That's how they say hello, Chick. They *smell* each other's teeth. Haven't you ever seen humans kiss?" He paused and addressed the door. "Yes, Madeline. Coming."

Aly's golden skin blushed—an uncommon sight since she rarely let anything fluster her. "Well, sure I have. You can't be around Ben and Rachel for a single day without watching those two kissing. I swear, they're about the kissingest bunch of—"

Jezlynn giggled.

Madeline's patience wore thin. "It really is unkind of you to make me stand out here in the hall."

"Be right there." Nick regretted the time he'd lost that he could have been teaching Aly the finer art of proper kissing. "Put your arms around my neck again, Chick."

When Aly complied, Nick pulled her close. Even through the clothing that separated their bodies, he could feel her warmth. "You do it like this," he murmured, slowly moving his lips from her forehead down the tip of her nose to pause only an inch away from her mouth. "That lets you taste the skin and gives your heart time to catch up with your pulse."

"How did you know?" Golden eyes searched his, widening with astonishment.

"Because mine is doing the same." Nick's mouth covered Aly's, his teeth gently tugging at her bottom lip. She opened in response.

Suddenly, all that had happened in the past month fused into this moment together. He had only wanted to show her how tender a kiss could be. How a man and woman could savor the taste of each other. How the joy of sharing surpassed being alone. But Aly would have none of his gentleness. Her fingers threaded through his hair, her fists closing in the mass to tug him closer. Her kiss became a searing flame, setting his blood afire with passion.

Nick's arms tightened around her, crushing her breasts against his chest. This time, he kissed her with all that he was . . . so she would not forget the taste of him. He kissed her with all that he hoped to be . . . so she would know his dreams of late included her. Then he kissed her with every boldness in his soul, so she would know he offered her a place where she could belong . . . if she wanted to.

Aly tensed beneath his touch and slowly pulled away, as if forcing herself back took great effort. Her eyes looked dazed, her lips slightly swollen from his kiss. She shuffled to the door, opened it and allowed him full view of Madeline.

His ex-lover stood there, dressed in a gown so sheer the light defined her every curve. But it was Aly's form that held Nick captive, Aly's voice that drew his attention.

"Sorry things got a little rambunctious in here, Madeline. Got carried away, I g-guess. Nick's trying for a full house."

Madeline's lips formed a perfect oval. She craned her neck to see around Alewine, but Aly took a step in the same direction, preventing the woman from looking past.

"We're alone, Madeline." Nick reassured her as he winked at Aly. "Just the three of us. Everything's fine. You don't look like you feel very well. Why don't you go on back to bed; we'll get dressed and look for Jez. Are you sure she's not in her bed?"

"Very sure. She put pillows under the cover to make me think she was there."

"Then I'll go to the outhouse and see if she had to make a visit in the rain." Knowing his daughter was safe inside, he added concern to his voice for Madeline's sake. "You don't need to be getting chilled."

"If you find her there, tell her that I will talk to her in the morning about letting someone know she's gone out."

When the woman turned and left, Alewine shut the door and leaned against it. "Smart thinking, Gambler." A frown creased her brow. "But everything's far from fine. You and me have to talk, too."

Chapter Nine

"Yes, we do," Nick concurred, moving closer.

The broad span of his bare shoulders beckoned to Aly like a coat offered to ease a December cold spell. She wanted to throw herself into his embrace and let him wrap his warmth around her. A shiver of attraction blazed through her, so hot it melted any notion of winter.

"One more kiss, then we'll talk," he whispered, reaching out to fulfill her wishful thought. "Just in case Madeline comes back and needs more convincing."

A tiny giggle erupted from under the bed. Suddenly, Aly remembered Jezlynn and pressed her hands against the velvet granite of Nick's chest. "I'll bet a week's staples that little ears are twitching, even if her eyes aren't peeping."

When Nick's hold on Aly instantly slackened, disappointment for herself and respect for the gambler fought for dominance within her. But respect quickly overshadowed Aly's discouragement in not getting to explore the new path of feelings where Nick's kiss had led her. If only her heart would quit pounding like the hooves of a ten-mule team at full gallop.

Yes, ma'am, Mrs. Madeline Gilmore, Aly thought. *Our Nick is definitely father material . . . whether or not he knows it yet, and whether or not you've a mind for him to.* Madeline's reasons for asking him to return home stemmed from something more than determining whether he was fit father material. Aly'd seen that right off. The woman wanted the gambler here for more personal reasons than assuring a daughter's proper raising.

Aly decided she had best haul her attraction to Nick up short for a while. She didn't know Madeline well enough to guess how their hostess would react if she discovered Jezlynn's presence in their room. But Aly could smell a prairie fire long before it grew into a full burn. Best get the blaze under control before somebody got blistered.

"Jez don't know you're on trial here," Aly reminded. "And Madeline seems to be the sole judge and jury. Better not give her any reason to call us unfit. She wouldn't like us carrying on in front of little britches there." Aly looked at Nick uncertainly and said loud enough for the child to hear, "Even if it was for show, best find out why Jez wants nothing to do with her mother."

Nick's thumbs rubbed gentle figure eights on Aly's arms as if he seemed reluctant to let her go completely. Finally, one hand returned to his side while the other raised to brush back the disheveled hair at his temple.

"You're right. Losing Jezlynn is a gamble I can't take. Let's see what's bothering her."

As Nick bent to persuade his daughter to join them, Aly turned away and pretended the shirt he'd tossed over the back of his chair needed attention. She grabbed the garment and tried to do what she'd watched Rachel accomplish a hundred times over. Her friend could fold the material to look store-ready, but all Aly managed was to wrinkle the sleeves.

Aly's frustration exited as a sigh. Her lack of talent with handling the garment clarified why she would never make Nick a true wife. His decision not to give any rein to what was stirring up between them only served to shift her longing for him into a load of pure misery. Though she'd been the one to stop the kiss, he might as well have said, "You're right. Kissing you isn't worth losing my daughter over."

Aly blinked back stinging tears, telling herself she was acting loco and better straighten her backbone a notch. Feeling sorry for herself was a post she'd never hitched to. Besides, she'd think a lot less of Nick if he hadn't considered the child's welfare first.

It's that blamed key, Aly decided. *I just want to open the present. But I gave my word.* In frustration, she tented material away from her bosom. *And this dress. These stays are so tight they're squeezing the air from my lungs. Making it hard for blood to pump to my brains. I don't care what Miss Mind-Your-Manners Madeline says, I'm dressing in my buckskins tomorrow. Let her think it's only so I can clean house easier. Me and Consuela will know the real reason.*

"Come on out, Jez," Nick encouraged. "We just want to talk to you a minute."

Aly glanced at the gambler who now lay prone on the floor, his head under the bed, his elbows winging on either side of him. The view of his bare back and muscular arms balancing his weight stirred up a fancy or two. Looking for a distraction from her thoughts, Aly asked, "Need some help, card man?"

He scooted back and maneuvered until he sat with his elbows on his knees. "Be my guest."

Aly smiled and crawled under the bed.

Nick laughed, despite his exasperation. "If you can't defeat them, you have to join—"

"Got that right, Gambler." Aly had to admit she'd grown plenty since the last time she had hidden under a bed. "A badger won't crawl outta his hole unless somebody moves in on his territory." She deliberately bumped Jezlynn with her hip. "Scoot over, half-pint. I'm jumping your claim."

Jezlynn scooted completely out, just as Aly suspected she would.

"There you go." Nick stretched out one of his legs, patting his thigh. "Why don't you sit here and tell me why you don't want your mother to know where you're at?"

Aly stuck her head out from under the bed, attempting to join them. Jezlynn eyed her, the chair Nick had been sleeping in and, finally, his offered lap. The child elected to sit on the floor next to him, blocking Aly's further retreat.

The little burr did that on purpose! Aly wouldn't give the six-year-old the satisfaction of knowing she'd won this round. Aly shifted beneath the bed to find another escape, bumping body parts that had already seen too much restraint lately.

"She'd just make me sleep with her." Jezlynn folded her arms across her chest, her lips pouting. "She always does if she doesn't find me in my bed."

Jez didn't like cuddling next to her mom? Aly wondered what had happened between the two to cause such a breach.

"You okay, Chick?" Nick peeked around the footboard where she attempted to break out.

"I got myself into this," she huffed and puffed, placing her hands on the back of the footboard and scooting her shoulders clear. "And like you said"—another scoot—"I can get myself out."

The gambler shrugged. "Okay, but don't snag your dress. You wouldn't want to get a—"

"I'll snag *you* if you don't move out of my way so I can get out from under here. This dress is about as *snagged* as it's gonna get. As you can see, Gambler, I've got things under control here. Now, get on over there and help your daughter."

Nick did as he was told. "I never thought sleeping with your mother was so bad, Jez."

"Great," Aly muttered, bumping her knee.

Nick must have thought Aly was commenting on his reassurances to Jez, for he quickly amended, "I . . . uh . . . mean, don't you like sleeping cuddled next to your mother?"

"Not on rainy nights."

The gambler reached out and ruffled Jezlynn's hair. "You aren't afraid of a little thunder, are you?"

The tiny head jerked upward as emerald eyes glared back at him in defiance. "I ain't . . . I'm not . . . afraid of no thunder."

Finishing her slide from beneath the bed, Aly shooed Nick over so she could take a seat beside them. "It's good to be a little afraid of thunder, Jez. That means you respect it and you won't do anything foolish to get in its way."

"Really?" Jezlynn stared up at Aly.

Knowing she had the child's attention, Aly nodded. "If you don't respect the dangerous side of something or somebody, then you ain't smart enough to fear what it can do to you. Fear's a good thing to feel sometimes. It keeps you smart. Makes you aware of what's going on around you. And I'd say you're about one of the smartest six-year-olds I've ever—"

"I'm almost seven," Jez interrupted.

"You're about the smartest almost-seven-year-old I've ever met." Aly kept her expression as serious as the child's.

"Mama don't think so. She says being scared of thunder is nonsense. Mama isn't afraid of anything. Not even dying." The little girl hung her head, then continued in a low tone, "Except one thing."

Nick lifted her chin. "What's that?"

Misery etched Jezlynn's face. "She said she was afraid of loving me. Told me so."

The child's dark lashes blinked as her eyes shimmered with newborn tears. "I'm nobody to be scared of, am I?" Her tiny shoulders shrugged. "At least not yet."

Nick reacted before Aly could. He picked Jez up and set the child on his lap, enfolding her in his arms. She resisted at first, then finally decided to just sit there, letting her hands dangle at her sides and erecting an invisible wall to his compassion.

"Your mother loves you, Jezlynn," he assured her.

Jez shook her head but didn't speak.

"Sure she does." Aly nodded at the child. "Ain't that why she was so glad to see you climb outta the stage?"

Jez leaned into Nick's chest, her tiny body looking much like a sail losing its wind. "She just wanted people to notice her looking happy to see me. She likes to be noticed. But she wasn't really happy 'cause of me."

Nick and she weren't the only ones who needed to talk, Aly decided, setting her will to the task. Before the day's activities began, she was going to have a long, long talk with Mrs. Madeline Gilmore and set things straight . . . no matter how much sicker it made the woman or whether Nick Turner liked it or not.

Chapter Ten

For someone who was supposed to be terribly ill, Madeline looked remarkably spry and fit in her riding skirt. Aly sauntered closer, watching the beauty stroke the nose of a stallion. The beast's shiny coat rivaled the luster of Madeline's rich ebony hair.

"I thought you'd sleep longer this morning," Madeline said before turning around. Then, with grace born of long practice, she faced Aly and lightly tapped the quirt she held in her gloved hand. "After all of last night's activity, chasing down Jezlynn that is."

Intimidated by the woman's polish, Aly's stroll to the corral took on a little less stretch of the legs. She tried to put a wiggle in her backside like she'd seen Rachel do on several occasions. The fringe at the bottom of her buckskin shirt seesawed left and right, punctuating each exaggerated jerk of the hip. By the time Aly reached the corral fence, she decided walking like a lady was something she'd have to spend more time on. *You win this round.* She glanced at her hostess. "You been riding this morning?"

Madeline stroked the horse again. "I like riding at dawn. The horizon stretches into forever and gives me an impression that nothing ever ends."

Surprised they shared something in common, Aly halted next to her and hooked a boot heel on the lowest post. "I'm up before dawn myself but usually hitching up teams and tallying freight. You can count on a Texas sunrise stretching into the hereyonder."

Eying Madeline for a split second made her all the more aware of how the woman looked good in any light, definitely a clear difference between them. Aly spit a wad of frustration into the grass and wiped her mouth with her forearm. Revulsion filled Madeline's expression.

Nick is gonna kill me. Realizing her blunder, Aly pretended to have something in her mouth. She spit and sputtered, trying to explain herself out of this one. "Pardon me. Dadgum fly-bys. Can't open your mouth without someone wanting to set up housekeeping in it."

Madeline reached inside her skirt pocket, produced a white lace handkerchief and offered it to Aly. "Dab your mouth with this."

Accepting the hanky, Aly heeded her instructions. The delicate material smelled and tasted slightly of perfume—primroses, if she guessed correctly. An elaborate *M* had been embroidered in one corner.

"Obliged," Aly mumbled, her mouth constricting as she fought off the perfumed taste. She started to return the handkerchief to Madeline then thought better of it. "I'll see it gets washed and return it later."

Madeline shook her head. "Keep it, if you need it. I have several more." She leaned back against the fence and folded her arms below her breasts, defining the reason her figure attracted attention.

Aly folded her arms to see how well *she* stacked up. Surprised and pleased, she decided that she gave a fair showing.

"Now tell me, why did you come out here to talk to me?" Authority exuded from Madeline's tone. "You obviously wanted to catch me alone."

Aly stuck the handkerchief up her left sleeve for safekeeping. "You're right, I did. I've got some questions about how things are gonna be concerning your daughter."

Emerald eyes leveled on Aly. "Don't you think that's Nicodemus' responsibility . . . to do the asking?"

"He will, when he gets around to it. Right now, it's my duty to know as much as I can about that little girl, if I'm gonna be any kind of mother to her."

"So you and Nick are really married? This is not some scheme he's cooked up to get custody of Jezlynn?"

She was smart. Aly would give her that. "Got the marriage license if you need proof, but Jez's future with Nick is the question I'm concerned with." Aly studied the woman. "I can't help her unless I know her past."

"Fair enough." Madeline turned from Aly's intense stare and focused on stroking the horse. "It must be obvious to you that Nick and I were once very much in love. When he decided to leave town after the shooting seven years ago, I didn't know I was with child. By the time I knew, I had already promised my hand in marriage to Judge Gilmore. There was no need for Nick to know."

Shooting? Nick had left town because of a shooting? She wouldn't take Madeline's bait by asking. Nick could cast his own line when they were alone.

"So you passed Jezlynn off as the judge's daughter?" Aly's dislike for the woman deepened. The judge should have been told the truth, and Nick had a right to know, too, long before now.

Madeline laughed, a strange hollow sound that seemed to straighten the woman's back. "I thought it was true, until a few hours before my husband died. He confessed he'd never been able to have children. He had mumps when he was younger. He knew all along about Jezlynn's true lineage and had never said a word."

"Was he good to Jez?" Buried feelings from Aly's own childhood spurred her question. She knew the hurt of being considered less because she was not blood-related.

"He loved her like his own."

"You're a lucky woman twice, Madeline Gilmore." Aly glanced back to the house and the window of the room she shared with Nick. "The judge sounds like somebody I would've liked to have known. And, Nick, well . . . he's willing to love Jez whether or not she's really his."

"That's good. That's very good." A genuine smile graced Madeline's lips. "Because I've decided something—something that should happen as soon the rest of the household awakens. It will make the transition easier for all involved."

"Transition?" A fancy word for change. Aly wondered if Madeline meant to test her education. "What kind of change?"

The woman looked impressed. "I shall allow Jezlynn to live with her father, now instead of later. I need to see how well they get along, whether the two of them suit each other. The remaining five months should be sufficient enough time for them to get accustomed to each other."

Though Madeline's decision made sense, Aly couldn't quite let it go unchallenged. "Why doesn't your daughter want to be near you, Mrs. Gilmore?"

A hand splayed across Madeline's bosom. "W-whatever do you mean?"

Aly thumbed toward the house. "Jezlynn said something that bothers me. Something no six-year-old should be fretting about."

"She's precocious, always telling extravagant stories and pretending she wants to be a bank robber. Jezlynn plays *escape* so often I can't leave her alone for any length of time. That's why I keep extra servants . . . to help me watch her. But I sent them home after the dinner party to give them a night off. She's simply a daredevil and a wanderer like her father." Madeline rubbed the top of the braided quirt against her brow, as if to erase the frown that creased it. "Of course, she doesn't like me telling her that I will not tolerate such antics. She doesn't care to be around me because I expect more of her than tomboyish tricks."

"We're talking about a six-year-old child here." Disapproval echoed in Aly's reply. "Did you ever think maybe she did all those *tricks* to get your attention?"

"You've only known my daughter a few days. Don't presume to tell me how to raise her." All semblance of courtesy had evaporated from Madeline's voice.

Aly's temper bolted, but she reined it in for the moment. "I'm telling you that your daughter thinks you're afraid of loving her. So afraid that you won't let her close. Said you even told her so."

"I did," the woman stated flatly.

Madeline spun halfway around. Aly didn't trust the words of someone who wouldn't look her in the eyes.

"I told her, because I *am* afraid of loving her. I had to tell her so she'd understand. So she would find someone she could trust more." Madeline's voice lowered. "So she can let me go when the time comes."

You're either a very good actress, or I've misjudged

you. Suddenly, Aly thought she understood. Madeline was scared of dying . . . of endings. Of leaving behind a brokenhearted little girl. What she didn't realize was that Jez's heart was already in pieces. "Maybe you ought to reconsider. Instead of pushing her away, why not grab on to every second of life that's left in you and love Jez with all you are? Maybe, just maybe, those memories would be enough to keep her smiling through the rest of her days."

Aly's thoughts went to another place and time. She hesitated, then gingerly reached out to grasp Madeline's shoulder, offering comfort. "Some folks need a whole feast of love, Madeline, but others . . . well, others just need a scrap or two to survive."

The last thing Nick had expected to see this morning was the two women together. He cautiously joined the women at the corral, noticing Aly's buckskins and Madeline's split skirt. Had they gone riding together, or were they about to go? "Glad to see the two of you are getting better acquainted. Are you saddling up?"

Madeline moved away at the same moment Aly's hand returned to her side. "I've already been." She eyed Aly's buckskins from fringed seams to neckline, as if noticing her guest's odd attire for the first time. "It looks like your wife intends to ride. Plan to go with her?" Madeline glanced at the house. "I suppose Jez-lynn is still sleeping?"

"Just checked on her. And, yes, if my bride wants a morning ride before we start our day, I'd love to join her. You don't mind lending us a couple of horses until I purchase some, do you?"

"Not at all. You can borrow the wagon as well."

"Just until I dust off the one that should still be in my barn."

"Use it as long as you need." Madeline frowned.

"Little scamp shouldn't be allowed to oversleep, she certainly won't let anyone else do so when she's awake. That's why I took to riding in the morning."

Nick shared a conspiratorial glance with Aly. "She must have been exhausted from the stage ride."

"Among other things." Madeline motioned to the black stallion she'd been petting. "The black will be more to your liking, Alewine. He's a superb mount. I'm sure you must be quite the horsewoman if you can handle a mule team."

"Quite." Aly smiled, but the gesture didn't reach her eyes.

The air between the women was charged with something like the perfume of a prickly pear blossom that lured a victim closer to its hidden needles.

Nick decided he had to put a stop to this contention now, before Aly broke her fool neck trying to prove the point. Madeline spent part of her life in England, learning from world-reknowned trainers. Day-to-day experience had taught Aly her remarkable skills. But she had been riding a stage for a month and might be a little rusty. Better to get their minds back on Jezlynn and away from rivalry. "It's good Jezlynn was able to get back to sleep after her trip outside. The thunder and lightning kept me awake most of the night."

"That's most unlike her. When I heard the storm worsening, that's why I checked to see if she was still in her bed. She is terrified of the thunder. I realized none of the servants could help me search for her since I'd given them the night off. I appreciate your trek in the rain to see her safely inside." Madeline sighed heavily. "She's just too much to handle lately. She won't mind, and she seems not to care how much it upsets me."

Aly's brows veed, one eye narrowing to display her rising temper. "Maybe if you'd—"

"I'll say it so you won't have to, Chick." Nick linked his arm to Aly's, hoping by pulling her close she would follow his lead. "What she means to say, Madeline, is how would you feel if we take Jezlynn to live with us now instead of later? I'll bet she'd have fun helping us get the house ready. And I'd like her to live in it for a while before we go back to Valiant. After all, one day it'll belong to her."

He hoped the gentle squeeze on his arm meant Aly approved.

"Good. So, we're in agreement." Madeline's smile rivaled the morning's brightness. "Alewine and I had just discussed that possibility."

The gentle squeeze became a pinch. Nick tightened his forearm against Aly's assault and glared at her. "Is that all right with you, Dear?"

Aly's eyes glared her disapproval before she ever opened her mouth to speak. "I ain't . . . didn't have my say on the matter. I agree it'll be good for you and Jez to live together a while before we head home, but I'm not sure today's the best day to hitch her wagon to the team. Don't we need a couple of days to settle in first? We won't be doing much more than cleaning and toting and checking for repairs. Can't be much fun for a youngun."

The lady freighter loved children. Nick knew she got along with them better than she did with most grown-ups. She'd always been the first to volunteer at any church social to be "in charge" of the children's activities. Aly was stewing on something, and Nick had to find out what. "My wife has a point. Tell you what Maddy . . . give us some time to discuss this, and we'll let you know our feelings on the subject when we get back from our ride. Fair enough?"

"Meanwhile, I'll see that Jezlynn is up and dressed. It won't take long to pack her now that the servants have arrived." Madeline headed for the house. "I know you'll see the sense of taking her with you now. In fact, I'm so sure you will, I'll order her things packed this very minute."

Aly exhaled an exasperated breath and mumbled low, "Can't wait to get rid of her, can you?"

Nick patted her arm, seemingly to calm her.

"Well, she can't." Disgust filled Aly's tone. "I let her rope me in for a minute, but I sure won't do it again. I'll be watching for the next loop."

Nick glared at Aly and was grateful when she quit muttering. Whatever fueled her grumbles had chafed the hell out of her better humor. Just what had the two women discussed this morning? There was only one way to find out. "Let Jezlynn sleep a little longer. We won't be back for at least an hour."

"I'll see that she's fed." Madeline gently slapped the quirt against her left thigh. "She'll be starving since she had no supper last night."

"I'm going." Aly yanked her hand from Nick's and headed toward the corral gate. "If you're planning on riding with me, you better hightail it now!"

Madeline shouldn't have reminded Alewine about the child being sent to bed without supper. Nick realized Aly was doing all she could to control her temper, and he appreciated her effort. But he knew if he didn't get Chick away from Madeline this very minute, feathers were sure to fly.

Feathers or something more personal.

Chapter Eleven

Aly reined to a halt, laughing with triumph. The black was, without a doubt, the finest piece of horseflesh she'd ever ridden and was just the salve needed to soothe her itch to be in the saddle again. Riding for weeks in the stagecoach and pretending to be a wife sure cut back the range she normally would have roamed—a condition she'd change if she ever truly married. No man would ever fence her in.

"Good fella. Let's rest a minute." Aly dropped the reins so the black could crop grass. She stroked the animal's sleek neck as it lowered. Bursting with the need to tease Nick about having won the race, Aly swung around to watch him catch up. Her heart leapt so high she was certain it had lodged in her throat.

Nick's dark hair and the horse's mane whipped like black banners of fire. The gambler looked as if he had been carved from the horse itself, one in form, one in unrivaled coordination, one in the flex and rhythm of power.

Desire blazed through Aly, setting her bloodstream afire with a fierce longing. *Whoa there, gal.* She exhaled deeply, then realized she'd been doing that a lot lately—breathing heavy and sighing. *It ain't like you've never seen a man sit a horse before.*

If she hadn't been wearing her buckskins, she would have blamed the lung trouble on the confining dresses she'd worn lately. But that would have been a lie. The sight of Nick Turner made her feel all hot and breathless inside.

Maybe wearing all those frills and flounces had rubbed some kind of gal notions into her skin. But it wasn't her skin stirring the pot of possibilities; her head seemed full of thoughts about Nick these days. Nick pledging his oath "till death do us part." Nick with his bare chest, and the kiss last night that had sent her soul crow-hopping like a bronc in need of busting. Nick and his skill at making her feel she was some-thing more than what she seemed.

The gambler made her dream . . . even when she was wide awake.

Aly wanted to believe that Nick might find her appealing enough to love as more than a friend. But her mind kept fencing off that prospect. He liked women lovely and delicate. She was about as delicate as a porcupine sitting on a bolt of silk.

Aly had lost a lot of things in her life—family, respect, the dream of mattering most to somebody. Still, she always managed to survive life's ride and mount again when she fell. But all that stubbornness and grit counted for nothing unless it was Nick's pony she mastered. If he ever spurned her, her biggest dream would be trampled. Best thing to do was not set herself up for that kind of fall.

Close your trap, Aly told herself, deliberately shutting her gaping mouth and willing the attraction to cool in her veins. She forced herself to yell, "What's the matter, Turner? Stop to pick the burrs off, did you?"

Nick halted alongside Aly. A broad grin made him look even more handsome as he untied the bandanna from around his neck and mopped his forehead. "A month in dresses hasn't slowed you down any."

Though pleased by his flattery, Aly pretended he meant it as a jest. "I'll take that as a compliment, but we both know Madeline's praise about my horsemanship was because she wanted me to act a fool and get bucked off."

Nick laughed and stuffed the bandanna under the saddlehorn. "You may be right. Quiet and dignified, she could have handled. I don't think she ever expected me to bring home a woman like you."

Home? The word twisted inside Aly, sending her humor into a deep slide. He considered Prickly Bend home. Did that mean Valiant had simply been someplace to bide his time? Would he remain here after Madeline's death? Feeling miserable and insecure, she grumbled, "You saying I'm loud and common?"

Nick stared at her, his eyes softening as he reached out to touch her arm. "Where'd that come from? You know you're my closest friend. Common is the last thing I'd call you."

Aly's gaze met his. There was a time when being his best friend would have been enough. But life had spurred her in a new direction. "I guess I'm all out of sorts this morning and looking for a fight. I'm mad at Madeline about the way she treats her daughter. I'm mad at you because you had to choose somebody so danged beautiful, there's no way anyone's gonna believe you favored me over her, and . . ."

Aly sighed again, exasperated. Her eyes started to lower, but she willed the insecurity away. Instead, her shoulders squared. Aly glared at him as if defying him to criticize how she felt. "I'm mad at myself 'cause I *care* that those strangers don't think I fit with you."

"Aly, Aly, Aly," Nick crooned, reaching to cup her chin gently. "Maybe between the two of us, we can help Maddy be more patient with Jez. And you shouldn't be worried about comparing yourself to anyone. Maddy's beautiful, but you have the kind of quality that makes people want to look twice at you. More important than that, Chick, you've got a spirit that charms anyone who knows you." He leaned down and pressed the gentlest kiss on her lips. "But I'm glad you want others to think we fit."

A sweet sadness filled Aly. She should be pleased with his words, *pleased that he was pleased*. But she didn't fit him. She doubted she ever could. He was all polish and wit. She was all burrs and backbone. Aly brushed his hand away. "Well, wanting and doing are two different things. I don't exactly sit this wife saddle with the best of them, if you've noticed."

"Is that why you don't want Jez to move in with us now?" Nick half-turned and rested one forearm over the saddle horn.

Aly knew he'd deliberately done so in an effort to keep her attention. All he managed to do, however, was drive her temperature up several notches. The shirt he wore veed open and gave her a partial view of his chest.

She tried to focus her eyes elsewhere, but her attention kept wandering back to the dark wisps of hair triangling downward. "You know as well as I do, I don't know hide nor hair how to be a wife, much less a mother. I can hold my own on most accounts, but tending the needs of a six-year-old who acts like she's going on twenty?"

Aly noticed the rhythm of his breath made his shirt expand and contract, defining the broadness of his chest and the curve of his muscular arms. "You . . . um . . . forget . . ." Distracted, she forced herself to concentrate on what she was saying. "I was just like her."

Jezlynn, she reminded herself. *We're talking about Jezlynn and me not being worth my salt as a mother.* "I know how much attention that requires. Besides, what'll I do if she gets hurt and I don't have a notion how to help? That's just the everyday could-happens. Did you ever wonder what we're supposed to say when she asks why we don't kiss and do things like other husbands and wives? I ain't fool enough to think those kind of weeds ain't gonna crop up now and then."

Aly motioned to his clothes. "And what about my normal wife duties? Cooking and cleaning? You've eaten my cooking. Lucifer himself would pitch me outta hell 'cause I'd burn the brimstone too crisp." She yanked on the fringe seam of her trouser leg. "Ever wonder why I buy clothes a couple of sizes too big?" Alewine didn't give him time to answer. "I've shrunk everything I've ever washed."

Nick smiled at her candor.

"Let's see if you're still grinning after a day or two of my cooking and cleaning. Hell, there's spiders who keep house better than I do. Don't you think I need a little practice before Jez moves in? If for nothing else, to protect y'all from a bad case of sour belly."

"You'll do just fine, Chick. I've got faith in you."

The softness of his tone and his belief in her thrilled Aly. Did he truly think she could pass herself off as a lady? "You do?"

"Sure." A smile quirked his lips. "I also have the faith that you're going to keep Jez so busy, she won't have time to notice your blunders."

Aly started to laugh, then wondered what the heck was so funny. It was all right for her to criticize herself, but he didn't have to agree she'd stumble! "Wanta bet I'm a quick learner, Gambler?"

"Shall I name the prize?" The challenge was apparent.

He had that look about him again—the one that warned she'd followed him down a deliberate trail and stuck her foot in the trap. The last time she'd slipped up, she had to marry the man. No telling what he'd ask of her now. "No, *I'll* name it this time. If I fix you a meal you don't have to toss out as slop before the week's up, I get twenty-four hours of doing nothing but being Alewine Jones. I don't have to pretend to be your wife, Jez's soon-to-be mama, not even a *lady* for Madeline's sake."

"And if I win?" Nick gathered his reins.

Two choices came to mind. The most logical was the safest—Aly would stake Nick's pot at the nearest poker game and give him twenty-four hours of no responsibilities. A day without a daughter, an ex-lover, or a pretend wife.

The second possibility called to her like a voice echoing from a canyon, *Take a chance, Aly, Take a chance. Where's your gumption? Why wonder when you can know?* Before she could change her mind, Aly followed her heart's fancy and her mind's bullheadedness. "If you win, Gambler, then I'll do anything you want . . . one last time."

A full moon challenged the sunset, staining the western horizon a fiery orange and the adobe homestead the hue of a ripened peach. Nick brought the team to a halt in front of his childhood home and set the brake. When such a moon soared higher in the sky, it would cast the sandy countryside with a pinkish-white glow that allowed visibility for miles. He could have stayed longer in town, but he suspected Aly would wonder what delayed him. If he arrived late for her first cooked dinner, he'd never hear the last of it.

A look at the goods in the wagonbed pleased him. He'd made sure they had the necessities first—staples, smoked meat, fresh linen and blankets, oats for the horses. Then he'd decided Aly and Jez needed some kind of gift for general purposes. Aly for trying so hard to prove herself, and Jez for not putting up a fuss about going with them. Choosing for Aly had been easy, but Jez . . . what did he know of a six-year-old's wants?

Deciding to leave Jez's package in the wagon until later, he headed inside. Curiosity filled him with an eagerness to learn how Aly and Jez had fared their first day alone. He scraped the soles of his boots across the threshold and was pleased to find a rug in front of the door. Caches of rainwater still patched the ground. As hard as they'd been cleaning all day, he didn't want to track in anything.

A glance at the parlor revealed the room had been given a fair amount of scrubbing. Turquoise-colored tapestries lent a quiet beauty to the adobe walls, while the flagstone floor gleamed like polished mahogany. He supposed the women had made the gathering place for visitors a priority.

The fragrance of desert verbena and pinon permeated the air, pleasantly displacing the mustiness of a house that had been boarded up too long. The cowhide furniture was rearranged, the windows dusted and curtains freshy washed. Though the day had been a scorcher, the adobe cooled the room to a pleasant temperature. Aly must have been very busy.

Dia Hunter

A lamp atop the fireplace mantel cast an amber glow across the gun pantry by the door and the rows of bookshelves that lined one side of the parlor.

Father's critical eye would have caught every imperfection, Nick realized, *but he would have been pleased with their effort, nonetheless.*

The first thought of his father in years forced Nick's attention to the gunrest. He reached out to admire the cool ponderosa planks hewn by Travis Turner's own hands. But the happy memory of watching his father fell the tree mixed with the nightmare of why the storage cabinet remained locked until this very day. Nick's hand began to shake uncontrollably, and he forced it to return to his side.

"Did you finish your chores? It took you longer than you said it would."

Nick turned and found Alewine standing in the doorway, looking like she'd been caught in a twister. Her hair was spiked at odd angles. Dirt smudged one cheek, her bodice, and the lower half of her trousers. She'd obviously been crawling around on her knees. "I didn't intend to be so late," he apologized, "but it looks like you have things well in hand around here."

"Far from it." Aly sat in the nearest chair and stretched out her legs, rubbing her neck as if it had a cramp. "At least this room's livable. Connie and I worked on it most of the day until she had to leave. If the rest of it takes that much scrubbing, I might finish by the time we're ready to head back to Valiant." Her lips curved to one side. "Guess that's stretching it bit, but I'll sure enough need to hunt up a hot spring to ease these ol' bones."

"A night's sleep will do us all some good." Nick turned away from the cabinet. "It's been a long day. A long month, as a matter of fact. And none of us got much rest last night." Would he be able to sleep in this

122

house again? How could he sit here in this room, chatting about everyday details when tragedy had occurred less than five feet away?

Nick willed the tension to leave his body but failed miserably. Perhaps if he visited with his family for a while, the exhaustion would finally kick in and send him into the oblivion of sleep. *Family.* How long had it been since he could say he had a family? "Where's Jez? Did you two get along well today?"

"Upstairs." Alewine motioned above her. "Connie suggested that we clean Jez's room after this one. She said that would give Half-Pint a proper place to bunk down for the night and somewhere to play so she won't be in our way. I told her that wasn't the way things were going to be around here. Seeing Jez has a place to sleep is one thing, but if Half-Pint wants to be in the thick of things, then she can work right alongside us. Connie means well, but danged if I'm gonna take advice about raising kids from a woman who doesn't know any more about them than I do."

"Did she?"

"Did she who? What?"

"Did Jezlynn help you?"

"You must've stayed out in the sun too long." Aly shook her head, her eyes glinting like newly cooled gold. "She did everything she could to make my job harder. Moved my soap water. Hid my duster. Bumped me when I was cleaning those hundred million glass danglebobs on that fancy chandelier over your supper table. I thought I was going to bring me and all hundred million crashing down on top of her."

Aly rolled her shoulders and yawned. "If I wasn't so darned tired from all this bending and reaching, I'd probably take her out to the corral and show her how to hogtie a mule come branding season. Don't josh yourself, Gambler. Mothers, natural and otherwise, are the bravest souls to walk this earth."

Nick saluted her. "To mothers everywhere."

Aly saluted back, her fingers just missing her forehead. "And to fathers who need to come home a little sooner to help with their little darlings."

Hearing the irritation behind the jest, Nick apologized again. "When you see what I brought you, Chick, maybe it'll justify my delay. It just took longer to clean up than I thought it would. I wanted to surprise you."

"Surprise?" Aly looked somewhat invigorated by that. "What kind of surprise?"

Nick was glad he'd taken the extra time now. This was just the thing Aly needed to make her feel at home. Enduring a month of stage riding and accepting Madeline's hospitality ought to offer some reward. He rose and went to the window, holding back the curtains so she could look outside. "This one."

Aly grasped the arms of the chair and boosted herself to a standing position. It took a moment for her to steady her legs. She really must be tired, Nick noted. The woman could control an eight-mule team easily and had more stamina than most of her counterparts. He'd never seen her this exhausted.

"I didn't know scrubbing could be so tiresome," she admitted when he refused to quit studying her. "Guess I'm working muscles I don't normally use when I sit a wagon."

As tired as she was, Aly kept going. Nick worried about the weariness in her eyes and the slow gait that moved her to the window. Doubly glad of his gift for her tonight, he promised himself Aly would be rewarded further when they returned to Valiant with Jez.

"A wagon! Oh, Nick, you cleaned your wagon."

Aly closed the curtains and threw her arms around him, hugging him fiercely. "For me?"

When he nodded, she unthreaded her arms and wiggled her fingers in front of her as if they itched. "Can we take it for a ride now? I want to get the feel of it . . . hold the reins in my hands. Gosh, I've missed skinning them jennies."

Excitement replaced the weariness in her eyes, her expression exuberant. Wishing she'd remained in his arms a few minutes longer, Nick tried to match her enthusiasm. Sleeping had been impossible after the wild kiss he'd shared with Aly. The rest of the night had been spent fighting his need to touch her and to see how she would react to him as a man rather than as a friend. Riding with her in the coming moonlight would be no easy task. Tired as he was, he didn't trust himself not to take a liberty or two.

Despite the moon bathing the countryside in light, it wouldn't be wise for them to wander too far until Aly and Jez were more familiar with their surroundings.

Jezlynn. He could take Aly for a short ride, but his daughter would have to go with them. They couldn't leave her in the house alone. She would be a natural barrier to his attraction to Aly. "I would imagine you and Jez are as tired as I am by the day's activities. Let's grab her and take a short ride so you can get the feel of the wagon and I can show you around the place."

An unrecognizable look darted across Aly's face, then she nodded. "Guess you're right, Gambler. A longer ride can wait till morning. I am considerably tired."

"Let's see what my darling daughter is up to." Nick noticed a slight haze filtering through the doorway that led to the back of the house. The lamp's amber glow took on a grayish tinge. His nostrils flared as he breathed in the smell of smoke, an acrid taste singing his throat. "If I'm not mistaken, something's burning."

Frustration bunched Aly's freckles into a single blotch as she groaned and raced toward the smoke.

"Let me guess . . ." Nick followed close behind, stifling a chuckle, not daring to laugh. "Supper will be delayed."

Chapter Twelve

Three days had gone by and still Aly hadn't managed a meal worth eating. How could heating a skillet, kneading a wad of dough, or boiling a pot of coffee be so troublesome? She suspected Nick agreed to take Jezlynn into town every day for more reason than to have what he called "father-daughter time alone." More than likely, the two of them filled their bellies at the hotel restaurant so they wouldn't starve to death when they came home. Not that she blamed them. She ached for a well-cooked meal herself.

Aly stared at the pan of biscuits she'd just finished baking and wondered why the blamed things were flatter than flapjacks. She chose one and bit into it. Hard as tack with the taste of old leather. Frustration boiled inside her. She threw the biscuit across the kitchen.

"Ahh, mi amiga. You have trouble again today, I see." The full-figured woman bustled into the room and laid a large valise on the table. Connie bent to pick up the biscuit and examined it. "More soda and . . ." She glanced at the bowl Aly had used to mix up the dough. "Remember, good cooks never clean their bowl for the sourdough starter. Still, these are better than yesterday's."

Aly wanted to scream and throw away every ounce of flour left in the cupboard. "I can't do this, Connie. The Almighty must have left out an ingredient in His own recipe when He whipped me into shape, 'cause I sure ain't got it in me to cook. Hope to hellfire I ain't practicing burning things for a purpose, and He's trying to tell me something."

Consuela patted Aly's hand. "Patience, amiga. Patience. Good cooking comes from knowing how to satisfy." One eye winked at Aly. "That, too, is learned with time. Which reminds me . . . are you and Nicodemus still sleeping in the parlor?"

Their sleeping arrangements for the last three days had proven equally frustrating. Aly had been so intent on making sure Jezlynn's bed was ready she'd forgotten the remaining bed in the house had been chopped into a million pieces. When she'd asked Nick what happened to it, he'd merely said to order a new one from Tucson.

"The ticking hasn't arrived yet," Aly informed the bookkeeper, twisting her wedding ring around and around.

A sly grin added playfulness to Connie's expression. "I think I would like such a predicament myself. A handsome husband"—Connie spun around with a sweeping gesture, setting the auburn curls near her brow into motion—"a new home. Why not christen *every* room? What's one more day or two? Save the bedroom for last, I say."

The suggestiveness in Connie's tone left no doubt

what she meant by *christen*. "Is that all you think of, Consuela Bonita Maria Calhoun?"

"Is there anything else, amiga? Love is the spice of life. Ah, but you are new to its flavor. Wait until you've added four and five more names to the pot." Connie giggled and strolled over to the table where she'd left her valise. "I see I have shocked you. A present is needed so you will forgive my boldness." A cinnamon aroma wafted through the room as Consuela lifted a basket covered with a kerchief. "Let's see . . . what smells so delicious?"

At the sight of Connie's offering, Aly's mouth watered with hunger. "You brought cinnamon rolls!"

"Si. I thought your handsome Nicodemus and his daughter would enjoy the treat. It's difficult to cook for one, so I brought the extra in the hope they would not go to waste."

"Stop your yarn. We both know you just don't want them to starve to death around here." Aly laughed more at herself than at Connie. "God bless their souls, they keep trying to eat my meals, and I keep finding greasy spots in their pockets where they've stuck the grub so I wouldn't see them spitting it out. We all appreciate the rolls, Connie. It's mighty kind of you."

"It is my privilege to help you, amiga, in any way I can."

Connie's implication was clear. She wanted to give Aly advice on more than cleaning the house and settling into the routine that was expected of her as Nick's wife. The bookkeeper wanted Aly to discuss the spicy details of what she believed were Aly and Nick's lovemaking. Aly wouldn't have done so, even if anything was actually taking place. She thought that kind of thing ought to be kept private between lovers.

Lovers. The thought of being close to Nick sent butterflies winging in Aly's stomach. She'd never tasted passion before, but figured it must be something worth anticipating if Connie liked to sample it so often. Heck, Nick always rubbed her tired shoulders when Aly had lifted one too many crates and never failed to scratch her back where she couldn't reach the itch. He'd touched her a hundred times without stirring up everything inside her. But that was before she stood at the altar and said, "I do." Before she'd shared a room with him. Before he'd kissed her mindless.

She had to concentrate on other things or Connie would sense her mood and pester her to talk. Aly knew better than to get into a deep discussion with the book-keeper, because Connie had a way of making Aly say more than she intended. But she had somehow managed to keep the existence of Ophelia's present a secret. "Tell you what, you can help by taking down four glasses. I promised Jezlynn we'd have milk for breakfast this morning, so I'm going to head out to the springhouse and grab a jug. Poor kid must think soaking the biscuits will soften them up."

Laughter followed her out the back door.

Aly returned to the kitchen and realized that the rolls and glasses no longer sat on the table. Hearing the sound of voices made her decide that everyone had congregated in the parlor.

She carried the milk down the hall, past Nick's study and the extra room Nick had converted to a sewing room for his mother after his older brother left home. When she entered the parlor, Aly was surprised at the scene before her—Nick and Connie's faces were animated with laughter. Jezlynn's cheeks moved up and down as she vigorously chewed. Madeline Gilmore's emerald eyes stared adoringly at Nick as he took another biscuit from the platter she offered. And

Clay Driscoll was inspecting their bookshelves like they hid some great secret.

Thunder! News about how bad a cook she was traveled fast around here. First Connie brought edibles. Now Madeline. She should have been less surprised to see Driscoll. He always hitched a ride on a free food wagon. It was one of the things she disliked most about him—he rarely fended for himself.

Aly glared at Consuela, thinking the bookkeeper had started the mercy mission. But Aly could forgive Connie, because her friend's craving of food came second only to her wanting of men. Connie had brought rolls so she'd have plenty to eat while she helped clean. Madeline's gift of food had a parsimonious purpose behind it. Despite that knowledge, the biscuits' aroma required every ounce of Aly's resistance to ignore.

"Care for a little milk with that?" Aly lifted the jug to let them see its frosty surface. "The springhouse is about as good as they come. Thought I'd have to fetch some gloves to handle this jug."

"I'd love some, thank you." Nick set the biscuit on one of the saucers meant to hold a cinnamon roll. They still lay on their platter, as yet untouched. "Here, let me pour, and you sit down." His attention went to their new guest. "Aly's been working her fingers to the quick since she arrived."

Nick glanced at Aly, and she realized he wished she'd been more femininely dressed. Aly had reveled in wearing the buckskins the past few days, but the cleaning was almost done and she had no excuse to wear them after that point.

Driscoll's blond head turned, acknowledging Aly's presence. "You're looking . . . comfortable, Alewine. Decided to forego the normal trousseau?"

"Madeline was neighborly and brought by some of

131

her famous sourdough biscuits and fryback," Nick announced, drawing attention away from Aly. "They've won the Fourth—"

"Of July cookoff for several years." Aly nodded as she interrupted him. When Nick frowned at her, she frowned back. "Mrs. Quakenbird—er—*bush* told me that first night at Madeline's."

"The dear. Ursilla always brags on me, though heaven knows why she feels the need." Madeline chose to ignore Aly's slight and, instead, changed the subject. "Mr. Driscoll"—she shared a glance with the Valiant businessman—"*Clay* joined me this morning so that I could show him where your home is located. He arrived about the time I had Clement bring the wagon around. When I mentioned I would be checking to see how Jezlynn has enjoyed her stay so far, Clay was kind enough to accompany me."

Driscoll's smile could have outshined the sun. "My pleasure, indeed."

Madeline's cheeks stained a becoming pink, making Aly want to throw up. Trouble was, it would be a dry heave because there had been nothing edible since she'd taken over the cooking.

"How is my daughter faring?" Madeline's attention focused on Aly.

"Why don't you ask *her*?" Aly demanded, exasperated at the woman for talking as if the child were not in the room. "She still talks, you know."

"But she has her mouth full." Madeline's tone warned Aly to be civil—she would not tolerate the insolence.

"Give her a minute. The kid hasn't eaten anything decent in a few days." It was difficult for Aly to admit the failing, but Jezlynn had the right to finish her bite.

Madeline's brow arched disapprovingly.

"Aly's done a great job with the house, don't you

think, Madeline?" Nick ran his boot sole across the polished flagstone to point out Aly's achievements.

Though Alewine appreciated his effort to take the attention away from food and her inability to master the meals, she couldn't take all the credit. "Couldn't have done it without Connie's and Jez's help. There ain't enough of me to go around."

Surprise filled Madeline's face as she actually focused on her daughter. "Jezlynn helped?"

The girl continued to ignore her mother's indirectness.

Seeing a chance to make the child feel important, Aly nodded. "Yes, she keeps her own room. I told her I wasn't going in there a single time unless I saw the ceiling splitting from all the weight of her personables. It's to be her private sanctuary—with three rules. She has to sleep there, keep it clean, and decorate it the way she wants."

The child finally looked up at her mother. "And nothing's pink."

"Well, we'll see that your curtains and covers are brought over later this afternoon." Madeline rose from the chair as if to leave.

"My schedule is free today," Driscoll declared. "If you like, I could ride over with you again."

"Thanks for the offer," Aly interrupted her guests in her most formal voice. She didn't want Driscoll feeling he could come calling any time he wanted. "But that's unnecessary. Nick and I feel Jezlynn needs to choose a different color, to help her adjust to the new environment. Don't we, Nick?"

"If you and Jez agree, I'm with you." Nick waited until the child quit chewing. "Is that what you want, Jezlynn . . . a different color for your room?"

Jezlynn nodded. "Pink is for babies. Mama still thinks I'm a baby."

"Then I guess we'll have to find a young-lady color of some sort." Nick frowned at Jezlynn, as if he silently scolded her for criticizing Madeline's choice of furnishings.

"Green," Jezlynn quickly interjected. "I want green."

The color of her eyes, Aly thought. At least it would blend with some of the tapestries, but there was nothing they could do about the pink cast to the adobe walls. "Green it is, then."

Nick reached for Madeline's cloak that hung on the chiffonier near the door. Opportunity presented itself, and Aly stood. "I hate to see you go so soon, Madeline, but I certainly understand that you shouldn't tire yourself."

She hurried to the door and swung it open wide. "Clay, you tell all the folks in Valiant that me and Nick and Jez are doing just fine. It's always a . . . surprise . . . to see you."

Being a gentleman, Nick frowned at her for rushing their guests off so quickly. "Of course, you're welcome to stay a while and eat breakfast with us. We're having wonderful biscuits and cinnamon rolls for dessert."

"You're a dear, Nick." Madeline allowed him to place the cape around her shoulders. "But I only stopped by to bring Jezlynn some homecooking and see how she's doing. I see that she's coming along well with the transition. Now, as Alewine said, I really had best get home before I tire myself. Will you walk us to the wagon? I'd like to have a word with you before I leave. Consuela . . . Alewine." Madeline turned as she bade them good-bye. "I hope the day goes well for each of you. The house looks quite lovely . . . better than I ever dreamed it would, frankly.

You have a treasure of a friend in Mrs. Calhoun. I hope you appreciate her, Alewine."

Aly bit back the words that raced to mind for the sake of not arguing in front of the child. She knew Madeline meant to imply Aly couldn't even clean house on her own and had to have Consuela's help. The woman had meant to barge in, find a mess, her daughter unhappy, and the three of them starving. At least, only one of those charges had any justification. Aly couldn't let Madeline leave feeling she had the upper hand. "I appreciate her most, Mrs. Gilmore, because she's friend enough to help me. Some folks are so lazy, they just sit back and criticize instead of lending a hand."

Jezlynn rose from her chair and left the room immediately after her mother departed.

"Do you believe that woman?" Alewine's temper flared as she stared out the parlor window. "She said good-bye to everyone but Jezlynn. She cares about as much as a preacher cares for someone who steals from the collection plate. She no more came here to check on her daughter's welfare than I married Nick for—." Aly caught her near-blunder. "Than I married Nick for his mule-skinning skills."

"Come away from the window, amiga." Connie tugged on Aly's arm. "She would love to catch you watching. It's what she wants."

Aly swung around, knowing Connie was right. "What more does she want from us, Con? Does she expect to romance him for as long as she still has to live?"

"You worry needlessly, Alewine." Connie took a bite of one of the biscuits, chewing slowly, then licking crumbs that stuck to her fingertips. "She is a wonderful cook, but he does not love her. In fact, I do not think the man ever loved her truly."

"There seems to be a lot of that going around this morning. From what I've seen of Madeline, I doubt she's ever loved that precious little thing in there who's crying her eyes out. Listen."

All conversation stopped. Compassion saddened Connie's eyes. "Let us go to her."

"No, leave her alone for a minute." Tears stung Aly's eyes and words she'd never spoken to anyone before offered a wisdom long marooned in her soul. "That's what she wants at the moment."

How well she knew the misery that gripped Jezlynn now. Loners tended to isolate themselves further so everyone would think it was by choice. The truth was, letting anyone see how badly they hurt was more painful than the rejection itself. Years never purged the pang of being the unwanted child. "She has to deal with it in her own way. Just like I have to overcome my feelings about Madeline and Nick."

"What feelings?" The bookkeeper grabbed the bait Aly offered.

Aly needed advice, and Connie was obviously eager to give it. If she was forced to seek further guidance, she could always contact Ophelia in Valiant. The saloon keeper shot straight from both hips, and Aly had learned a long time ago that the truth was the best direction anyone could give. But she knew her friend well. The saloon keeper would hop a stage and spend a month riding out here and a month back just to give her advice. Ophelia had a business to run.

"Reckon I should pack my bags and leave town?" Aly motioned toward Madeline. "Let her have her last days with Nick? If I did, Jez would have a home with both her parents, for a while."

Connie shook her head. "You should stay, amiga,

for many reasons. The child will need you to comfort her. Nick will hope that you can help him adjust to fatherhood. But most of all, you must stay because you care for him and fear those feelings might change if he shares the remainder of Madeline's life as her lover."

Yes, she would definitely send Ophelia a telegram and see if the saloon keeper agreed with Consuela's judgment.

"I ain't going back with her," a tiny voice announced from around the edge of the door that divided the parlor from the rest of the house. "*Ever.* I'll run away if you make me."

Alewine found Jezlynn sitting with her back against the wall, her head bowed between her arms that crossed over her upraised knees. Aly slid down the wall and mimicked the six-year-old's position. She waited, without speaking, grateful that Connie honored their wish for privacy by remaining out in the parlor.

"You know, Jezzy . . ." Alewine finally spoke. "We usually run away from the very thing we want most."

Chapter Thirteen

Aly waved good-bye to Connie, thanking her for the morning's help. The afternoon sun burned brightly overhead, sending heat waves shimmering along the road back to town. "Tell your boss I appreciate him letting you change your schedule for a few days so you could help. I think I can make it on my own now."

It was an out-and-out lie, but Connie didn't need to spend her entire week scrubbing. She'd done enough.

And so have I. Aly's eyes focused on the adobe barn just beyond the stand of Joshua trees. She'd heard hammering there for much of the afternoon and envied Jezlynn when Nick had asked his daughter to help him repair the stalls. Aly supposed Half-Pint agreed more out of need to get away from housecleaning than a desire to spend time with her father.

They all deserved a break from the chores. A glass of sarsaparilla sure sounded good. They could stop at the hotel restaurant first, then she could survey the town and find a building for the new freighting office she planned. Ought to be plenty of buildings to choose from since the townsfolk were trying to drum up business.

"I'll tell my mama on you!"

The threat echoing from the barn increased Aly's gait. Someone had stirred up Jezlynn's temper. Nick? "What's going on—"

"You won't have to tell her, I'll do it for you. I meant what I said."

Alewine raced through the corral gate and into the barn. She found father glaring at daughter as he scraped his boot on the prong end of a pitchfork. Jezlynn sat sulking on a bale of hay with her arms folded across her chest. Both glanced at Alewine and returned to their former positions, their silence layering the barn with tension.

"What's going on here?" Alewine strolled closer.

"Don't come any clos—"

The minute she stepped in it, Aly knew exactly what had happened and exactly what she'd stepped in. "Horse dung?"

"That's about the size of it." Disgust etched Nick's face into stone as he offered the pitchfork to Aly to scrape off the manure. "Jezlynn Theresa Turner, you apologize to Alewine this minute."

"I'm sorry," the six-year-old mumbled.

"She didn't hear you." Nick's voice boomed, warning he would tolerate no more nonsense from the child.

Jezlynn looked up at Aly. "I'm real sorry, Aly. I didn't mean for *you* to step in it. Honest."

"That's better." Nick said. "I'm afraid we have surprises all over the place. She was supposed to be pitching some hay for the animals, but it seems she was laying traps. It's hard enough to dodge the ones the horses leave."

Tears welled up in the child's green eyes. "I didn't know Aly would step in it. I was playing a trick on *you*!"

Alewine's heart went out to her. How many times had she played a prank herself and discovered she'd hurt someone unintentionally? She wondered if Nick would recognize Jez's true remorse and calm his temper.

"Having fun is one thing, squirt, but when it causes someone problems, it's no longer a prank. It's cruel." Nick's eyes softened. His tone became less sharp. "You may not have meant to hurt Aly, but think what might have happened if Aly had broken a leg slipping on that? She would have been laid up for days. Besides, horses tend to make messes on top of the hay, not underneath it."

The child rose and grabbed a shovel, almost as big as herself, and began digging through the hay. "I'll clean 'em all up, I promise. But them dumb ol' horses can do their own."

"I'll muck up after the horses." Nick had a hard time hiding a grin. "You just shovel out the ones you hid."

Aly watched father and daughter work side-by-side, pleased that they'd gotten past the squabble. While the child shoveled, Aly joined Nick at the first stall. "Just what did you intend to tell Madeline?"

"That if Jezlynn didn't quit setting traps for me to step in, I'm going to make her wash every four-legged creature her size and charge admission to the show."

"Hey, now that's a dandy idea." Aly slapped him on the back good-naturedly. "A critter-wash just might be the thing this town needs."

"You best go back in the house, Chick. The heat has scorched your brain."

"I'm serious. I'd bet there'll be dozens of parents

who'd like their children kept busy for the day. The kids could charge for each washing. The older ones can rub down the horses or oxen. Some can scrub the goats and such. Half-Pint could be in charge of dogs, rabbits, and the likes. Think of it, Nick. A critter-wash would teach the children some enterprise and maybe help raise money for the bank. Trouble is . . ." She eyed Jezlynn. "Reckon we could find a youngun who'd want to be in charge of telling everybody what to do? Something that important has to have a leader."

"How old's a leader gotta be?" Jezlynn fell for Aly's ploy.

"At least six, I'd say." Nick caught on and held his palm up to the height of his daughter. "And at least this big."

"Could I be the leader?"

"Well, I don't know." Nick rubbed his chin as if in deep contemplation. "You'd have to be extremely good. Leaders are people everyone wants to look up to."

Jezlynn's chin fell. "Everybody would have to look down at me. Guess I can't be no leader."

Don't you dare laugh, Gambler. Aly shot Nick a warning glance while she tried to stifle her own chuckle. "Sure you can, Half-Pint. That's just an old saying. If someone looks up to you, that means they admire you and think you're special."

"I think you're special." Nick bent down to meet his daughter eye-to-eye. "It takes a special kind of orneriness to pull one over on me."

"I won't be ornery when I'm washing the critters." Jezlynn's gaze darted back and forth between her elders. "I promise."

"Well, that settles it, then." Alewine wiped her hands as if dusting off any reason to deny the child's wish. "Guess we have a leader here, Nick. I'd say the next thing in order is to hitch up the wagon and head for town. I need some sarsaparilla, and we've got to stir us up a team of followers."

"And I've got just the thing to celebrate our decision. Ladies . . ." Nick bowed and motioned them to proceed ahead of him out the barn. "First one into the house gets to choose one present at the mercantile, and I'm doing the buying."

The child was out the door and through the gate before Nick could finish the sentence. Just as he'd intended.

Nick was surprised at how quickly the news spread. They'd been in town for a couple of hours, and already people were asking when Aly planned to open for business. Aly had settled on the building adjacent to the livery for her new freighting service. She handed him a broom—one of the items she'd sent Jezlynn to buy at the mercantile. He thought his daughter too small to entrust her with the task, but she'd returned with everything on the list Aly had given her.

"Turnabout is fair play," Aly announced and tied an apron around his clothes. "I got spruced up for you." She eyed her blue calico dress with disgust. "So, it's time you spruced something up for me. Dust the cobwebs in the corners, if you will. My guess is we're about to have company and a lot of it. I gave Jezlynn permission to pass the word."

Aly's prediction proved true sooner than he expected. Jezlynn must have told every child in sight about the critter-wash, because families now gathered outside the freight office. Nick hoped Aly's new commerce and Jez's critter-wash were all that aroused the crowd's curiosity. He knew from experience that big gatherings could turn mean if there were other purposes behind the interest. He hadn't been gone long enough from Prickly Bend to believe all had forgotten why he'd left town.

Several questions echoed through the crowd. The minister held up his hand, and the gathering immediately quieted. The man of God smiled at the little girl standing on the porch behind the hitching rail. She revelled in her sovereignty.

"We've caught your enthusiasm, Jezlynn," the minister complimented. "Some of the parents want to know how they can help."

"Well . . ." Jezlynn looked at Aly, then Nick for advice. "Well . . ." she repeated.

Think fast, Nick encouraged his daughter silently. To his delight, she proved to be quick-witted and resourceful.

"Tomorrow everybody can bring some food and tables like you always do after church. We could have a whole bunch of pies and cakes and cookies. Then maybe we could charge everybody money for eating."

"That's a wonderful idea, Jez." Nick was proud his daughter had inherited her mother's ability to organize a community. But his pride developed a tarnish when the six-year-old stated her real motive.

Jezlynn faced the children. "If our parents are eating, they won't be griping at us or telling us how to wash."

Snickers erupted in the crowd, and one man shouted, "I sure enough won't jaw at my Johnny if you add some grown-up food to the lunch table."

Nick had Clay Driscoll to thank for that particular life lesson taught to Jez. At least she'd been smart enough to see through Driscoll's offer to feed her during the stage ride.

Noticing Driscoll make his way through the crowd, Nick lay the broom against the doorjamb. He deliberately moved alongside Aly and wrapped one arm around her shoulders, pulling the woman close so all would see that she belonged to him.

Then, Aly did the most extraordinary thing. She wrapped her arm around his waist and leaned her head against his cheek. Nick hadn't realized how perfectly she fit him or how good it felt to have her molded against his side. She was up to something. Had to be. If she'd been in Valiant, she would rather be dragged down the street at the end of a rope than do anything that tagged her as female. But now every soft curve reminded him of just how much woman he held.

"Time to play bride, Chick?" Nick gave her a gentle squeeze. Temptation coursed through him and he dared to be bold. Nick swept Aly up into his arms to carry her across the threshold of the new freighting office.

"Kiss me, Gambler," Aly whispered, her golden eyes gleaming.

"You don't have to ask me twice." Nick kissed Aly soundly, savoring the taste of her—part temptress, part innocent. His heart drummed erratic beats as desire surged through him, demanding him to hold her even closer.

A slight moan, so whisper-soft he wasn't sure if it came from him or her, made Nick end the kiss. If he didn't stop this now, he wouldn't be able to meet their visitors for several minutes. "You've officially been carried over the threshold and given a welcome kiss, Mrs. Turner."

Raw need in Aly's eyes fed the blaze her lips had ignited within him. The lovely blush staining her cheeks exposed the passion he had stirred. Could it be possible that Aly wanted more out of life than rawhide and rope burns? Was it possible that she *could* find happiness as the real Mrs. Nicodemus Turner?

"I think we convinced him," Aly whispered.

Her words were like a bucket of cold water thrown over Nick. He lowered her to the planked flooring and turned to find Clay Driscoll standing out on the porch. Nick's heart felt as if someone had placed it in a vise and a strongman had been chosen to squeeze it. "No doubt," Nick muttered brusquely, then gave voice to the hurt. "We convinced *me* there for a moment."

Alewine softly pressed her hand against his chest. "I'm sorry, Nick. It was the only way to make a believer of him."

"Use me anytime, Chick." Nick pretended to pat her hand, but the action was meant to lightly push her hand away. He didn't want her knowing how vulnerable he felt at the moment. "After all, that's what friends are for, eh?"

"Nick, I—" Regret lurked in Aly's tone.

"I can't remember a time when you looked so pretty, Alewine. You ought to dress in that color more often," Driscoll complimented and moved ahead of the crowd.

"You got business with my wife?" Nick ignored what had just transpired between him and Aly and played the role she needed him to play to get rid of Driscoll.

Driscoll's blue eyes rounded in innocence. "No more than to tell her that her bed's here. From the looks of things, I'd say she'd be happy about its arrival."

Men chuckled and women tittered. One little boy asked, "What does he mean by that, Mommie?"

"That means that Mr. Driscoll sticks his nose in where he has no business, son." Aly glared at the Valiant businessman and dared him to deny the charge.

"Just being neighborly, Aly." Driscoll held his palms up and backed away. "Just being neighborly."

Dia Hunter

Conversation buzzed through the crowd, and Nick could tell that while some agreed with Aly's anger at Driscoll, others thought her too haughty. Nick raised one hand to silence everyone and turn the crowd's attention to something other than Alewine. "Speaking of being neighborly, folks, my daughter Jezlynn and my better half"—he waited for the last conversations to die before continuing—"have an idea how to raise some money for the town. Some of you already know a little of what they have planned, but they would like to talk to the community as a whole. That way, you can pass the word along to your relatives and neighbors who haven't come in to town today. We hope everybody can attend church tomorrow and the critter-wash afterward."

"You say it's your wife and daughter's idea?" A rough-looking rancher shouted.

Nick's jaw set, his feet planting themselves into the planked flooring, bracing himself for what he knew would come next. "Yes, Simon. I had no part in it."

Simon tipped the brim of his hat in respect to Aly. "Then you can count me in, ma'am."

"Me, too," said another man.

"I'll help," added yet another.

Nick started to head back in and sweep again, but an adamant tug on his arm prevented him from completely turning. The next thing he knew Aly had linked her arm with his and stood beside him, her chin tilted at a defiant angle.

"I suggest you all wear your best Christian charity to church tomorrow and lace it with a little forgiveness. This here critter-wash is supposed to be a *community* event. Nick and Jezlynn will be attending church tomorrow and scrubbing critters with me afterward." Aly glanced up at Nick and winked. "Lord knows, this family won't mind paying our share for some decent grub."

146

Chapter Fourteen

"Thanks, Aly." Nick helped her settle the new mattress against the headboard. He stretched his arms and back.

Bless his hide, he'd cleaned the office from roof to floor, arranged for plenty of wash buckets and the livery troughs to be used during the critter-wash, then came home and helped her put the bed together. He looked tired to the bone. She ought to help him brush down the horses after supper. They all needed to get in bed early.

Bed. Aly had been sleeping in Jezlynn's bed beside her while Nick used the davenport in the parlor. Though they'd used the excuse about not having a bed to fend off Jezlynn's questions about their sleeping arrangements, the child would expect them to sleep together tonight. The image of lying next to Nick with his arm around her stirred up an uncommon heat within her.

Aly realized she hadn't answered him, because she'd been so distracted. "You're welcome. I'm used to toting a lot heavier—" Her words ended abruptly as Nick's hand captured hers. When had he managed to move around the bed and so quietly?

"I meant thank you for *everything*, Chick. For pretending to be my wife, understanding my daughter, standing up for me in front of the crowd. I couldn't have asked more."

She shrugged her shoulders. "Nothing you wouldn't have done for me."

"You don't even know why they hate me." Nick raised Aly's hand to his lips and pressed a gentle kiss against her fingertips.

Her eyes met his and locked. *It doesn't matter why. You're my friend, my pretend husband. The man I want to* . . . She tried to withdraw her hand, but it had a will of its own and remained there. His warm breath skittered along the surface of her fingers and up her forearm, kindling heat in a hundred different places inside her. "Don't need to know till you tell me."

Nick pulled Aly close and hugged her. "That's what I like most about you, Chick. You accept a man for what you know of him, not hearsay."

She wanted to linger in his arms but suspected the risk in doing so. She was exhausted by the day's events and guarding Nick from the town's vexation with him. Most importantly, she tired of trying to determine what was real and what was pretense between them. Was that true caring in his eyes or merely gratitude that she'd rallied behind him?

Too tired to think properly, Alewine stepped back from his piercing gaze and complimentary words. She wanted to be completely of clear mind and sound body when, and if, she ever invited Nick Turner to her bedroll.

148

"What do you say me and Jez get supper going and you brush down the team?" Aly glanced at the room and found it all finally in order. "While everything's cooking, I'll come out and help you."

Nick smoothed back a wisp of her hair and settled it behind her ear. "I took the liberty of buying some roast turkey. After all the work we did at the office, I thought you might appreciate a night off from cooking. I hung it in the smokehouse until you're ready to serve it. We can take care of the horses first, then I'll help you do the slicing."

His thoughtfulness reminded Aly of how good a man Nick was. What had he done to the people of Prickly Bend to make everyone dislike him so much? "What about Jez? She'll get hungry before then."

"I asked her a minute ago if she wanted something to eat, but she said she's too busy drawing up plans for the wash to want to eat. I even told her . . . now don't hit me . . . that you wouldn't be cooking the meal." Nick laughed as Aly swatted his shoulder. "But she said she'd eaten plenty in town. I think she's saving her appetite for tomorrow's banquet."

"Can you blame her?" Aly's laughter joined his. "Everyone will be chomping like cows with tasty cuds. Even me. Ain't nothing worse than a new cook."

The saffron rays of dawn shone through the window, awakening Nick to the new morning. Sunday . . . his favorite day of the week. People were more charitable today, more themselves than what they pretended to be all week. On God's day of rest, everyone seemed to relax and live the day how they wanted to live every day. He couldn't wait to take Aly and Jezlynn into town—to watch his wife and daughter's success in being accepted by his hometown.

The womanly curves nestled against his left side felt

so warm and cuddly, he almost didn't want to leave the bed. When Aly discovered that she'd thrown her leg over his and snuggled into him during the night, she'd be up in a flash!

He admired the blue calico dress she slept in and how well it fit her. His bride had *slept* in more dresses since she'd been here than she'd worn in all the time he'd known her. Aly never thought twice about stripping down to her red longhandles when they'd gone fishing and taken a swim. Did pretending to be his wife make her feel that much like a fish out of water?

Toying with the lace at the bottom of her puffed sleeve, Nick noticed her bronzed skin had begun to fade. "I need to let you drive the wagon more," he said aloud without realizing it. "After all, it's your gift."

The whitish-blond head nestled against his shoulder as she mumbled, "You don't *let* me do anything, Gambler. I just do it."

A grin split Nick's lips. She could hold her own even when half-asleep. "Wake up, Chick. You're a few hours away from eating honest-to-goodness home cooking. The women will try to outbake each other, and the men, they'll have plucked enough chickens and turkeys to feed us till Thanksgiving."

"Mmmmm." Aly shifted slightly.

Did the mention of food or the comfort of resting against his shoulder arouse that throaty little moan in her voice? Nick liked the feminine noise and gambled on instigating another. He gently pressed her closer. "Warm, Chick?"

"Sure am," she grumbled. "Now go back to sleep, will ya?"

Nick lay there, amused at her feisty reply and pleased with himself and the fact that it hadn't been food she'd been thinking of. He played with a tendril of her hair that lay against her breast, admiring how the silken strand curled around his finger of its own accord. The rise and fall of her bosom defined the gentle woman hidden beneath the hellraiser role at which she played. He marveled that it had taken him so long to recognize how much her beauty moved him.

Her sleeping wiles affected him more than those belonging to ten wide-awake women. All because she didn't try to seduce him with her beauty. Aly demanded that he accept her for what she was, not what she thought he wanted her to be. Somewhere along the way, Alewine Jones had captivated him with her strength of character and charmed him with her integrity after they'd become friends. Admiring her outer beauty was like being dealt the final card in a royal flush—the other cards increased the stakes, the final one made it . . . and Aly . . . a sure bet.

His fingers draped the curl so that it outlined the rounded swell of her breast like an artist's defining stroke. *Beautiful*. Everything inside him wanted to touch her, to hold the soft mound in his hand and measure its weight, to memorize the feel of her. But friendship and respect held him back. He wanted her to welcome his touch.

"Better wake up, Chick." He pressed a kiss against the top of her head instead of where he wanted to and willed desire to quit coursing through his body. "You might want to change into something a little less wrinkled."

Aly's eyes opened, staring up at him. She smiled, glancing down to look at her fingers threading through the wisps of hair curling along Nick's bare chest. Her mouth formed an oval, and she abruptly sat. "How long have I . . . ? Did we . . . ?"

Her eyes rounded like twenty-dollar gold pieces.

"Don't look so horrified." Nick chuckled. "Nothing happened. And you slept like that most of the night."

She wiped her hands on her skirted thighs. "Must've been really tired. Sorry about that."

Nick lifted her chin and planted a kiss on the tip of her nose. "I'm not, wife. Not one bit. Now scoot." He grabbed his shirt and playfully popped her on the behind. "Fetch my daughter and some grub."

"Keep your hands to yourself, Gambler." Her glare, as she rubbed her hip, turned to a twinkle the instant her eyes challenged him to chase her out the door. "Sometimes."

"I'm after you, Chick." He followed her hoots of laughter downstairs. "And I plan to catch you, one way or the other."

The critter-wash was quite a success. Nick hadn't expected such a turnout from the community. He had wrongly assumed at least half the crowd would stay home once they discovered he had any role in the event. Aly and Jez should be proud of themselves. All along Main Street, washtubs had been placed several yards apart to allow teams of the smaller children to clean the animal of their choice. Over at the livery, bigger boys used the troughs for soap basins and lathered up the horses.

"Done!" Jezlynn pushed the goat her team had been washing, but the beast wouldn't budge. "Move, you old billy, or I'm gonna kick you good. We'll get behind."

Nick laughed. Sometime between yesterday and today, his daughter had come up with the bright idea for the teams to challenge each other in how many animals they could wash. She had a special prize in mind for the winning team—one that would, hopefully, bring them lots of money from the spectators. She'd borrowed a skunk from Johnny, one of her school friends. It seemed Johnny's pa had found the tiny skunk left to die by its mother. The poor thing apparently had been unfortunate enough to have been born without a "perfume trigger." Culley, as Johnny called him, had been born a cull. But Jezlynn said no one would know that until after they started washing.

He needed the darn goat to move, too, or his team would lose, and he'd be out a pocketful of money. Never one to miss an opportunity, Nick had thought some side bets among the men were in order.

"Something got your goat?" Clay Driscoll called from the sidewalk that ran along the saloon front. The owner had set up kegs and promised that all today's profit would go to the children's proceeds. Clay and many of the men elected this as the best way to participate in the fund-raising.

Everyone laughed.

"Got a rope, anybody?" Aly pushed through the crowd, glancing from one hostler to another.

She looked the picture of womanly perfection. Though Aly had insisted that she wear the buckskins for a critter-wash, Connie had persuaded her that she needed to be dressed more demurely for the occasion. After all, the children were supposed to do the washing, not the adults. Nick had thought the bookkeeper's logic sound.

Connie had adorned Aly's hair with a gold ribbon that matched her eyes and allowed the white curls to dangle over one shoulder. Aly chose the new white dress he'd bought to match the one purchased for Jezlynn. His bride looked like the prettiest angel Nick had ever seen. Still, he'd bet his whole next winnings that she wore boots or moccasins underneath.

"Now, Aly." Clay tipped his hat to her. "I didn't mean nothing by it. Just having some fun."

"The rope ain't for you, Driscoll." She pulled up one sleeve that kept riding down her shoulder. When it wouldn't submit, she pulled down the other one to match it. "Though I've seen plenty of times I'd like to have hogtied ya."

Madeline stared down at Nick.

"Have she and Mr. Driscoll known each other long?"

Nick nodded, suspecting where Madeline's question led. He pulled his hat down over his eyes so she wouldn't see the amusement in them. *Madeline was jealous of Aly! Now, that was a switch.* "Long enough to know she has no use for him."

"Oh."

Disappointment echoed in Madeline's tone, but she quickly praised, "He's been nothing but a gentleman with me."

"As well he should, Maddy." Nick didn't rally to her insinuations, preferring to ignore her impression of Driscoll. He wanted to see what Aly had in mind.

Someone tossed her a rope, and Aly caught it one-handed. Nick watched her do some fancy finger work with the rawhide and begin to build a loop above her head. His ankles unlinked from the top of the railing where he'd rested them. Nick leaned back in a chair, enjoying the shade of the mercantile's overhead veranda. Several others stood around him, taking advantage of the offered shade from the bright Arizona afternoon.

With each circling movement of her wrist, Aly's breasts and bare shoulders moved, defining her cleavage and curves to every man at the gathering.

"Mmm, mmm, mmm, would you look at that!" A cowboy spat a wad of tobacco into the spittoon standing next to the mercantile door. "Wouldn't I like to have me some of that—"

Nick shot out of his chair and plastered the man against the wall.

"—wildcat." The cowboy swallowed the rest of his tobacco.

Madeline pressed a restraining hand over Nick's fist, making him hesitate. "Nick, he has no idea who she is." Her eyes slanted, indicating the crowd watched. "Don't make a scene. I-I don't think I could endure it."

"Then sit down, Madeline." He turned his attention back to the cowboy. "That's my wife you're talking about, and I'll have none of it." Nick refused to lower his arms and listen to Madeline's voice of reason. To hell if he made a scene. Aly was no strumpet. "Apologize, if you don't want to swallow a few teeth along with that wad of tobacco."

The cowboy lifted both palms. "Sorry, mister. Meant no offense. I was just saying that gal is about the prettiest thing I'd seen in a long time and . . ."

"I heard what you said." Nick tightened his fist at the man's throat.

"And God bless you for being the lucky man who lassoed her first. My apologies to you, sir." The cowboy nodded at Aly. "And to the missus."

Rawhide whipped through the air and looped around Nick's arms, roping them tightly to his sides.

"Let him be, husband," Aly hollered, shortening the end of the rope as she urged him backward. She took a gun from the pocket of her skirt and aimed it at the cowboy. "Don't go taking any notions, hombre. Just 'cause I pulled my husband off you, don't mean you can throw a punch at him. Read me?"

"Loud and clear, Mrs. Turner. Loud and clear."

When Nick reached her, she grabbed his hat and set it on top of her head, thumbing up the brim to acknowledge the cowboy. "Apology accepted, mister." She nudged Nick around to face her. "You'll make him think we ain't friendly 'round here."

"Let me go, Aly." Staving off a fist fight was one

thing, but Nick figured she had some other trick up her sleeve.

"Uh-uh. Got you right where I want you, Gambler." Aly put the derringer away and tugged on the rope, just to remind Nick she held the cards at the moment. "I've been cooped up cleaning and cooking for days. Got me an itch to do something fun, and I mean to scratch it today. Connie . . . you got those extra barrels ready?"

The bookkeeper bustled over to the wagon Nick had given Aly and let down the gate. Dozens of buckets lined the bed. Wet circles ringed the buckets, warning they were not empty. "It took some doing but, yes, amiga, they are ready."

"Okay, kids, it's time." Aly loosened the lasso and shouted. "Gonna do a little baptizing this Sunday, folks! Last *two*-legged critter still dry gets dunked in the river!"

Nick threw the rope off him about the time a tidal wave of water came at him from all directions. Soaked from the top of his head to the bottom of his boots, he stared through the curtain of dark hair plastering his face. "Baptize somebody else, will you? I've had enough!"

Someone threw a bucket of water on Aly. Instead of complaining, she howled like a coyote and filled the street with hooting laughter. Chick seldom listened when she was having so much fun. The angel had sprouted horns.

All wet and sassy and full of spit and vinegar, her eyes gleamed with righteous intent. "Bet your boots, I will, Gambler. Now, where's Driscoll?" She stomped down the street to seek him out.

Everyone followed, including Madeline.

"Come on out, yellow-hair," Aly taunted Driscoll as she stared into storefront windows. "I'll teach you to follow me anywhere."

Nowhere on the street or sidewalks was safe. Children soaked parents, parents splashed children. Anyone who could throw a loop, or empty a bucket, did.

Ursilla Quakenbush urgently untied the ribbon beneath her chin to loosen her prized hat. Clutching it behind her, the woman edged down the sidewalk sideways, dodging frontal attacks. Nick nearly split his britches when she stepped into the alleyway between the mercantile and the telegram office and stumbled on her hem. She landed bottom-down, the hat lost beneath her. A bucket of water drowned her cry of anguish. There stood her husband, a sheepish grin on his face. She stared at him, he stared back. Suddenly, Mrs. Quakenbush yanked Mr. Quakenbush down in the mud alongside her. They both started laughing and hugging each other.

Three little boys, who could barely tote the buckets they carried, threw water at a woman who must have been their mother. One of the woman's hands balled against her hip, the other pointed. All three boys obeyed. They ran over to the trough and dunked their own heads.

The animals hitched to various posts kept turning their heads to see the commotion going on behind, beside, and in front of them.

Madeline Gilmore was the only dry soul in sight and was looking indignant.

"Aly . . ." Nick attempted to catch up with his bride. "We'll never hear the end of this from Madeline. She's—"

Aly stopped long enough to glance at her adversary. "That ain't mad you're seeing, Gambler. She's got one of those I'm-left-out kind of looks. Tell Jez to hand her a bucket."

Jezlynn had other things in mind. Before the words could leave Nick's mouth, his daughter and her team

157

drenched Madeline completely. Her bustle went askew, and the feather in her bonnet drooped. When she sputtered, Nick wanted to laugh but didn't dare. Several men rushed to her rescue with offered kerchiefs. Madeline seemed to glory in all the attention. Maybe Aly was right . . . Madeline just didn't want to be left out.

All of a sudden, Driscoll appeared in the doorway of the livery with a skunk in his hands. "Stand back, Aly. Stand *waaay* back. If you so much as throw a rope on me or one bucket of water, I'll let this thing loose."

Jezlynn ran up and kicked the man in the shin. "Let my skunk go, mister!"

Upset by the noise and the gathering crowd, the skunk hiked its tail just as Nick hollered at Aly, "Don't worry, Chick. That's Culley—Jezlynn's surprise for the winning team. It doesn't have its trig—"

The foulest smell this side of purgatory drenched everybody within the length of two buildings. Madeline gasped and took a step backward.

Jezlynn's gaze darted from one grown-up to another and another. "Johnny wouldn't let me borrow his dumb ol' skunk. I had to find me another one." Her skin paled considerably. "Surprise."

Chapter Fifteen

When Driscoll dropped the skunk, it ran into the livery. All hell broke loose inside. Horses screamed in insult. Hooves kicked against stalls so hard, the sound of splintering wood echoed over the gathering. The old building's timbers shuddered.

"It'll bring down the roof if someone doesn't get it out of there!" Nick shouted and reached for Aly's lasso. Everyone else seemed too surprised to move.

"*I'll* get a rope around him." Aly kept the rope and began building a loop.

"I can help." Jezlynn rushed toward the door, her little legs weaving through those that blocked her way. "I caught him the first—"

"No." Nick ran after her. "Pardon me. Excuse me. My apologies, ma'am." Finally catching Jezlynn, he gently pushed her out of the pathway to the livery. Though exhausted, he laughed. How did Aly ever manage to keep up with her? "I think you've helped quite enough today, Half-Pint." He patted her behind playfully. "Now, go see Connie and let her figure out how much money you've earned for the bank today."

To his surprise, her wish to help the bank overcame her desire to catch the skunk. She headed for the book-keeper. Laughter rippled over the crowd, making light of the serious situation. The horses would hurt them-selves, and maybe even people, to get away from the skunk's offensive odor.

Inside the livery, Nick could see the skunk's trail by the ferocity of kicks as it dodged between hooves.

"Quit laughing, Gambler." Aly twirled the rope over her head, looking for a clear target. "The way we smell, they'll think there's *three* polecats and kick us all to high heaven."

Nick spotted the skunk heading for the door that connected the livery with another building. "There he goes, Chick! He's heading for your office."

I just cleaned that, Nick thought miserably. His imagination took an offensive whiff of what might happen.

"Whoa there, stinkweed!" Aly let the loop fly. The lasso sailed onto its victim and stopped the skunk in its tracks.

"Everybody stay back." She held up a warning hand not to come any closer. "I'm gonna try to lead it to the edge of town. Not sure how old the stinker is. If he's a youngun, it'll take him five or six hours to spray again. If he's an old codger, we could get it as soon as his perfume stirs up, for sure within the next hour. No need for all of us to take another shower." She eyed her brand-new dress and grimaced. "Besides, I don't think I can stink much worse than this."

Nick couldn't let her go alone and tagged along beside her, making sure he kept as far away from the skunk as the rope allowed. But it didn't take easy to the rein. It stopped at every food-laden table that lined the sidewalk, sniffing out breakfast, dinner, and supper, it seemed.

Aly gently tightened the rope when the skunk became too distracted and walked slightly ahead, forcing it to move. Each time the skunk raised its tail, nothing happened. By the time she managed to convince the polecat he was better off roaming the desert, they discovered that it must have been a fairly young skunk. The little bandit hadn't been able to pull the trigger a second time.

When Nick and Aly returned to the center of town, they found a good portion of the crowd still waiting on them. Some were already taking soap to the outer walls of the livery. A line of shoppers had formed at the mercantile that apparently had been opened to fill the demand for tomatoes. Nick had heard that tomatoes and their juices helped scrub away skunk stench, but he doubted there were enough tomatoes in stock to clean this many! If Aly had her freight business going, she could make a fortune hauling the next few days.

"Did you get sprayed again?" someone in the crowd asked.

Aly shook her head. "Guess he couldn't reload quick enough. But that ain't a whole lot of luck." Her nose wrinkled. "Heck if stink don't get stinkier the more you wear it."

All noses wrinkled in unison. Realizing what they'd done, several people laughed.

"This is no longer a laughing matter," Madeline proclaimed, opening her parasol in a lame effort to block the odor issuing from the people around her. She eyed Connie Calhoun who stood with the collection box resting against her hip. "I can't imagine anyone still wanting to participate. I think it's time to call a halt to the proceedings."

"Shoot, Maddy-girl. I'd bet there's a hundred men in this town would give a month's pay to wash that odor off ya!" Aly's grin stretched from ear to ear, her hands resting on her hips and her legs planted apart.

Women gasped and some of the men lowered their heads so no one could see their faces. Nick couldn't help himself. His deep, rich laughter volleyed over the crowd. Madeline spun on her heels and marched up the sidewalk, her soaked bustle bouncing crookedly, her parasol at an angle as rigid as her back. Several townsfolk followed.

"Much as I hate to admit it, Chick . . ." Nick's laughter faded into a grin. He pinched his shirt away from his skin. "It's going to be a long ride home. We might as well grab Jez and get started." He glanced over the crowd and didn't see her. "Anybody seen the captain of our wash brigade?"

Folks turned to see who stood next to them, then faced Nick again. No one spoke up. Nick shared a glance with Aly. "Have you seen her?"

Aly shook her head. "Not since you stopped her from going into the livery."

"I did." A young boy stepped up, rubbing his eye. "I seen her headed toward the river and told her I was going with her, but she socked me in the eye." He glared at an older boy who laughed. "Said she doesn't like dumb ol' boys tagging along. That includes you, Pete."

The two boys broke into a fight. The man nearest them separated the two, letting both sets of parents claim their slugger. "Madeline's right, folks, it's time to disperse. We've had our fun for the day, and we've all got our share of real washing to do now."

The man turned just enough that Nick spotted a deputy's badge pinned to his vest.

"Mrs. Calhoun will tally the earnings and deposit

the money in the bank for us. Preacher Simmons will announce the total Sunday." As the crowd broke apart, the deputy added, "Thank you all kindly for coming, and have a safe trip home."

Nick noticed Aly heading toward the river. "Alewine, wait."

"You catch up," she hollered back over her shoulder. "I'm finding Jez."

Her gait ate up the distance. He ran as fast as his legs could carry him. Reaching out to grab her arm, he forced her to stop. "Listen, Aly, I'll find Jez. I probably hurt her feelings or something. I shouldn't have laughed when I pushed her out of the way. But it all was so funny, and I didn't want her going into the barn where she could be hurt."

Aly eyed him and looked as if she were contemplating his logic. Finally, her head bobbed. "All right, Gambler, but if you ain't back here in fifteen minutes, I'll come looking for the both of you."

"We'll be back," Nick assured her and ran ahead. He hoped Jezlynn hadn't wandered too far. Sometimes he forgot she was such a young child. She always acted a lot older and was headstrong like Aly. Even if her intentions were to wash off the smell, she could go too far out into the current and be swept away.

Suddenly, fear iced his veins. He didn't know how strong a swimmer she was or if she could swim at all. In fact, there was little he knew about his daughter. Nick realized that he hadn't had much time to learn about her. He'd been too busy trying to convince Madeline to give him custody of Jez. Nick pledged to spend more time with his daughter in the coming days. "Jezlynnnnnnn . . . where are you? I need to talk to you."

No answer. He ran up the bank of the Aravaipa but didn't spot her among the cattails and prairie grass.

Reasons she shouldn't answer him came to mind—she barely knew him, he would be taking her away from Madeline, he had not let her help with the skunk, which meant he'd not allowed her to correct her own mistake. . . . Nick retraced his trail and began searching the bank downstream. "Come on, Jez. If you hear me, speak up. Aly says if we aren't back in fifteen minutes, she'll come looking for us. We shouldn't worry her, don't you think?"

"Over here," a small voice yelled back.

Nick studied the outcropping of trees that sheltered the small inlet he'd swam in as a boy. He should have guessed that's where she'd feel safest to wash. Quickly closing the distance, he didn't take time to talk. They needed to head back to town. Relieved to find her only ankle deep in the water, he swooped her up into his arms.

"Hey, let me go!" Jezlynn wiggled.

"I'd like to, Half-Pint. You smell worse than sulphur, but we don't need to worry Alewine any more than necessary." Jezlynn continued to wriggle making it difficult for him to hold her. Nick's grip tightened. When she yelped, he realized he must have hurt her and eased up. He'd have to watch his strength around her. "Sorry, I didn't realize how hard I was holding you. Please quit squirming, and we'll get home a lot faster."

She finally obeyed. "I don't want to go home with you. I don't like you."

"Why not?" Nick kept walking. He thought they'd been getting along fine, for the most part. Was she *that* angry with him for pushing her away from the livery?

"Because you think I'm little, and that I can't do nothing. It was *my* skunk. I coulda caught 'im. I did the first time, you know."

How she'd managed that was something he'd ask

later. The most important thing to know now was how he could explain to a little . . . a girl . . . why sometimes it's best to let others help when you've made a terrible mistake.

He thought of his own past and how he could have spared his mother a lot of grief if he'd been wise enough to listen. "Yes, you could've caught him again. And, yes, it was your mistake. But you had friends and family who were willing to help you correct the error, Jezlynn. That's important. You helped us by letting us help you."

Jezlynn looked puzzled as she deciphered what he'd said. "Huh?"

Nick smiled. "I'm your father, Jezlynn. Like it or not, that's the way things are. I don't know you as well as I should, but to be fair . . . I didn't know you existed until a few weeks ago. Now that I am your pa, I want to know all about you. What you like, what you dislike, what you want to be when you grow up—besides a bank robber." Nick nodded when her eyes rounded in surprise. "Yes, Aly told me about your dreams of bank robbing. That's usually a short-time profession for most. I think you should have something other than prison in mind for the rest of your life."

"Prison?"

He could tell she hadn't contemplated being caught. "Prison or worse . . . hanging. Sometimes they just string up thieves."

"Even if there's a whole gang?" Her hand rubbed her neck.

"Sure." An idea popped into Nick's mind as he realized how he could persuade his daughter to seriously reconsider. "Particularly the leader."

She fell silent for a moment. He could see her mind working, gauging, adding to, casting off. When she started to speak, Nick was sure she had shed her dreams of bank robbing.

Jezlynn shrugged. "I guess that means I just gotta be careful and not get caught."

Yessir, he had to spend more time with her in the days to come. And when the time was right, he'd tell her all about his last days in Prickly Bend seven years ago. He'd tell her so she would understand how a good person could lose all he had simply by making one wrong choice.

Chapter Sixteen

Aly would never dare say so, but the tomatoes she'd used to bathe the child made Jezlynn's skin glow pink. Jez might hate the color, but it didn't make her look any less lovable. Scanning the horse trough filled with pink suds and the now empty Mason jars that had stored the tomatoes, Aly decided she and Nick would have to use other means to get rid of the smell.

She nodded toward the towel she'd draped across the kettle. It sat next to the trough they'd moved to the back of the house. "You'll have to grab the towel yourself, Jez, and wrap it around you. I can't get too close, or I'll just stink you up again." Aly issued a challenge. "Guess you can get out by yourself, can't you?"

Jezlynn cleared the rim easily and grabbed the towel. Aly wondered if she dared stand close enough to braid the child's hair. Surely it couldn't be any more difficult than braiding a rope. She grabbed the brush and reached out to run it through Jezlynn's hair. "Want me to brush it for you, skunk wrangler?"

"How come you're always calling me names?" Jezlynn swatted away Aly's attempt. "What's a skunk wrangler, anyway?"

"I call people I like different names because sometimes it shows how I feel about them. Take 'skunk wrangler,' for instance. I'd say it's someone who can pick up a fully loaded skunk and not get sprayed. So I'm proud of you when I call you that. How did you manage to catch him the first time without getting perfumed?"

Aly listened intently to Jezlynn's tale of capturing the skunk. She nearly jumped out of her skin when a hand gently caressed her left hip. Aly swung around and ran smack dab into the middle of Nick's chin.

"Whoa, Chick. It's just me. I've got more water warming, so I thought I'd see how things were coming along out here."

"Don't go sneaking up on me like that." Aly didn't want him to know how much he'd startled her nor how his presence made her skittish. Sleeping curled up to him all night and helping him chase skunks today had been the best time she'd ever spent with him—give or take the smell.

"There's a lady in a towel here." Aly cleared her throat. "It ain't polite to approach unannounced."

"You're right. My apologies, Jezlynn." Nick bowed at the waist and backed away. He put his hands over his eyes. "May I join you ladies? I have an important question to ask my wife."

Jezlynn's eyes rolled upward as she sighed. "I got a towel on, for goodness' sakes. You seen my head and my feet before."

Nick chuckled.

Aly liked Jez's spunk and tapped her on the shoulder with a gentle fist. "Don't go so easy on him."

Devilment sparked Jezlynn's eyes. "You can come closer, but only if you'll show me how to play poker. And you can't get mad at me if I make a mistake. I want plenty of chances."

"Deal." Nick let his hands drop to his sides.

Aly looked from father to daughter and wondered what she had missed. Their pact dealt with more than teaching and learning poker. Something else was being agreed upon. "Now what question is so all-fired important it couldn't wait till the lady is done bathing?"

Nick pointed to the wagon. The tarpaulin she'd tied over the items had been pulled back to show several boxes and jugs. "I'm a little puzzled by the purchases you made at the mercantile. Shouldn't you have bought more tomatoes?"

A smile split Aly's face. She had hoped Nick would have enough tomatoes stored to survive three skunk washings, but logic told her to prepare for an empty cupboard. "Tomatoes would have been a good thing, but the shopkeeper was sold plumb out by the time he got to me. So . . . I bought some whiskey and baking soda, another remedy I've used before."

"Never heard of that one." Nick laughed, challenge lighting his eyes. "It'll be the most interesting bath I've ever taken."

Images of rubbing a paste of whiskey and soda into Nick's back and other parts sparked a longing within Aly. A longing she was too tired to restrain. She tried to focus on the task at hand. "Jez, I'd appreciate it if you'd head on in and get ready for bed. I set out some milk and oatmeal cookies Connie sent for you, if you get hungry before we get through with our bath . . . er . . . baths."

Her tongue stumbled along the path her mind took. She imagined sharing a bath with Nick. Every part of her suddenly felt like hot, sweet mush. Grateful for the twilight that had just begun to blanket the countryside, Aly turned away from Nick so he couldn't see how fired up she felt. What was it about the gambler that made her go all soft inside?

It was the day, their antics, his laughter. The fact that she truly cared for him and he for her no matter if this marriage had began as a scam. All those things and, if she admitted the truth, the way he held her lately, made her feel like a woman. *His* woman.

Remembering the child was still in their presence, Aly fought back her attraction to Nick. Some substitute mother she was! "Maybe the cookies will keep you till supper."

Jezlynn shook her head, her eyes bright with anticipation. "I don't want no supper. I'll just eat Connie's cookies. Besides, I'm getting sleepy."

"When you're finished with the cookies, say your prayers. I'll come up and tuck you in, okay?"

"Okay." The child yawned as she headed toward the house, her towel wrapped securely around her. A second later, Aly was surprised to find a disapproving expression on Nick's face. "What?"

"She should eat something more substantial than cookies."

Duly chastized, Aly couldn't help but defend herself. "She ate plenty at the gathering before the critter-wash, and I wouldn't exactly call anything I cook substantial, would you?"

Nick eyed her from damp strand of hair to soiled skirt hem and laughed. "Not so far. What's it been, Chick . . . a week or so?"

"Quit smirking. You won your wager, Gambler. I owe you a day all on your own." Aly should have been irritated at losing the bet, but she couldn't muster any anger at the moment. He stared at her in a way she'd never seen—like she was the deed to a gold mine and he was in the mood for prospecting.

"Don't guess I'd mind much if you take tomorrow for your own," she offered. "Ain't sure the whiskey and baking soda will get all the smell out, but I figure most folks will be able to tolerate you if you . . ." She'd been so concerned with Madeline's flirting with Nick, she'd little more than noticed the soiled doves in town, but she'd bet money they'd noticed him. "Stand downwind, and don't get too close to anybody."

"Show me what to do with the remedy, Chick. I'm ready to get started."

Nick's eagerness seemed for more than washing. Even she was woman enough to recognize that the timbre of his voice had lowered. His gaze pored over her body like sweet icing over warm cake. The tips of her breasts hardened beneath the white muslin bodice, still damp from the day's deluge. A bath sounded good to cool things off for the moment.

"Get a kettle and pour most of the whiskey into it," Aly instructed. "Don't add the soda till I say. Dump the tomato water and rinse the trough out. I'll go in and check on Jez. I think I may have scrubbed too much of the feistiness out of her."

"Do I build a fire under the kettle?" Nick began to strip off his shirt.

You're building one in me. Aly shook her head. "Not unless you intend to *scald* the stink off of us." She laughed to get rid of her nervousness.

"I'm going to save a couple of pints." Nick took a swig from one jug and set it near the trough. "It'll relax us for the scrubbing we're going to give each other."

The heated intention behind his words sank in and

made Aly lightheaded just thinking about the possibility. Had he read her thoughts?

She'd plotted her own course ever since she'd left her home back East, trusting her instinct to determine the right direction. But she'd waited a long time to cross a path that would lead her toward a new horizon—the path toward home, children, and a true husband. If curling up next to Nick and taking care of Jezlynn was even a pinch of what made family so tasty, she wanted a bigger bite.

Her lonesome road had finally reached its fork. Now was the time to choose which way to travel—the familiar path of friendship or the unknown passage to love. Whichever she chose, she knew there would be no turning back. Perhaps she'd get to use the key one day soon.

"Don't get too far ahead of me, Gambler," Aly advised as she hurried toward the house. "I want you sober enough to know exactly what you're scrubbing."

The sight of Nick's muscular arms stretched on each side of the trough's rim made Aly's knees weak. The clothes discarded on the ground assured her that he was naked beneath the suds. His eyes were closed, a wisp of a smile curving his mouth.

Aly swallowed hard and set down the lantern she'd lit to give them light in the growing darkness. When Aly realized she didn't dare touch the covers to tuck Jez in, Jezlynn had settled for the telling of one of Aly's freighting stories instead. The storytelling had taken longer than expected.

All the tasks she'd given Nick earlier were done and the trough refilled with fresh water. She wiped her sweaty palms on the legs of the pantaloons she'd donned so she wouldn't be completely bare. Treading with a little caution seemed in order, in case his intentions were not the same as hers.

Taking a deep breath, she announced her presence. "Is there room for me, Gambler? You're looking mighty comfortable."

Nick's eyes drifted open. The sensuous smile that followed nearly melted her where she stood.

"You're looking mighty *clothed*." Nick sat up and grabbed the jug of whiskey. "Come, Chick. Sit and relax. You've always got a place next to me, if you want."

Aly felt a coward. She had planned to rush outside, shuck her clothes and jump in, but at the last minute an unfamiliar shyness overtook her. What had she been thinking? The fancy bloomers and chemise Connie had suggested she buy did little to place a barrier between her and the way she felt when Nick was so close. "I—I couldn't find my longhandles, so I thought I'd give these bloomers a try."

"What about the skin under them, Chick? I'll need to scrub it, too."

Desire flamed in her bloodstream, searing her throat to the point she could barely speak. "If you think it's necessary."

"It's my responsibility now, Chick." Nick scooted over to make room for her, stretching his legs out the length of the trough. "As your husband, I'm supposed to take care of all your needs."

The man knew how to seduce a woman, that was for dang sure. She had to keep some sense about her. *Concentrate on the smell*, she reminded herself. *That'll keep your mind off other things*. "Let me empty a box or two of soda into the kettle. "No"— she held out one palm as he attempted to stand—"don't get up. I'll do it."

173

She couldn't have handled him standing stark naked in front of her at the moment. She just wasn't ready for that.

Nick laughed and took another swig of whiskey. "I'm a patient man, Chick. Now tell me how we're going to use this concoction you're stirring up." He closed one eye and looked at her askance. "You mix a medicinal remedy better than you cook, don't you?"

Aly ignored his jibe. She walked over, and took the knife out of his left boot and slit open the boxes of soda, then returned the knife to its hiding place. "As you can see, there's no cooking involved. It'll make a paste we have to smear all over our bodies—like a poultice."

"I'll smell like I've been on a week long drunk with a skunk."

Aly giggled and nodded. "For about twenty-four hours, you will. Just long enough to see you through your day off." She stirred the concoction until it began to take on the texture of thick mush.

His eyes leveled on hers. "You're offering me tomorrow on purpose."

"Me?" Aly grinned. "When have I ever done anything to keep you from enjoying yourself at the gaming tables?"

"I don't think it's the gaming tables you're worried about tomorrow, Aly-girl."

Aly's hands halted at her task, and she raised up to stare at him. "D'you think I'm pretty?"

"You're more than pretty. You are, without a doubt, the most beautiful woman I've ever known."

"Don't guess you've known too many women, have you?" Excitement leaped within Aly. Nick thought she was beautiful. She supposed she should repay the compliment. "But, I always thought you have the makings of a fine-looking man yourself."

Nick roared with laughter and winked. "Is that the best you can do, hellcat? I expected a little something more daring from you."

"Daring? I'll give you daring. Scoot over." Aly plopped down into the water and held her pasty hands up, facing him from the opposite end of the trough. Her nose wrinkled. The smell hadn't been part of her daydreams. "Now what?"

She didn't trust the look in his eyes. It reminded Aly too much of how the night could wake her and leave a yearning for something just beyond her restless sleep.

"Discarding your clothes seems to be the first order of business." He bent his knees, scooting closer.

Her knees tented, locking in place. "What are you doing?"

"Just moving closer, Chick." Nick grinned. "To untie the ribbon."

Aly straightened her legs. Her breath caught in her throat when he scooted between them and as his feet came to rest only inches from touching her *there*.

"We wouldn't want to get whiskey and soda on your clothes, would we?" he asked, unlacing the ribbon that held her chemise in place.

Unable to speak, to breathe, Aly shook her head. When the last piece of lace came unbound, he gently removed the garment.

"Nick, I—"

"Shhh, Chick. You have no need to be shy with me. I've seen you in every way but this."

"I'm not shy, Nick. I want you as much as I think you want me." Cool air rushed over her bare skin, immediately replaced by the heat that warmed Nick's eyes. "I'm just not sure I've learned enough about being a woman to—"

"You know more than enough. And what you don't

know, you'll figure out as we go." He lifted the chain from around her neck and held the key up to study it.

"Careful." She grabbed at it.

Nick held it just out of reach. "I've seen you wear this since the day we left Valiant. I just don't remember you having it before then."

"It's a wedding present from Ophelia." She snatched it from him and put it back around her neck.

"A wedding present?" Nick toyed with the key as it rested between her breasts. "A key? To what? Oh, I know now." His eyes lit with certainty. "That locked box in the first drawer of the armoire."

"You didn't look inside, did you?"

"I could have," he teased.

"But you didn't, did you?"

Nick's expression sobered. "I wouldn't do that. Your privacy is your privacy." He delved into the water and brought out a bar of soap. "Are you saying you haven't opened it, either? You don't know what's in it?"

Aly couldn't share the exact terms Ophelia demanded. Neither could she lie. "She told me when she wanted it opened. The time ain't right yet, is all."

"Let's forget the key and Ophelia and everything else that tends to keep us from enjoying each other." Nick handed her the soap. "Shall I wash you first, or would you prefer to wash me?"

A sensual haze surrounded Aly until a breeze wafted across the yard and reminded her of the need to rid themselves of the unpleasant odor. But she couldn't allow him to touch her now. She would collapse from the sheer want of him and drown herself in a trough of soapy water. Scrubbing him would give her time to regain some sanity. "You get washed first."

"Here, scrub my hair, Chick."

To her surprise, Nick twisted around and lay his head back against her breasts.

"Hmmmm, that feels wonderful."

She stared at his upside-down smile. "I haven't done anything yet."

"I know." His lips broadened devilishly. "But it still feels wonderful."

Pleasure radiated through Aly at the compliment. She'd always considered herself a strap of rough leather with sun-bleached hair.

Aly soaped his dark locks then rinsed them with water. "And by the way, I'm giving you tomorrow because I heard there's a regular Monday poker game over at the saloon. Connie said the banker and blacksmith are two of the players. Maybe there will be room for you."

"I'll look forward to it."

She scooped some of the soda mixture from the kettle and worked it into his scalp.

"Are you sure that really works?" He sat up.

"Settle down." A pasty hand urged one of his shoulders to return where it had rested against her. She liked the feel of him there, his head against her skin, his mind listening to the sound of her heart. "Yes, it works. The whiskey opens your pores, and the soda brings the smell to the surface."

Aly began to wash his shoulders with small circular strokes, then moved to include what she could reach of his chest and abdomen.

Though she was the one scrubbing, the motions lulled her into a state of relaxation. A curious thirst collected in the lower part of Aly's throat, and she realized she was hungering for his kiss. "I-I think I need a sip of whiskey, Gambler. Can you reach it for me?"

"I'll need to turn."

177

Nick moved so quickly, she didn't have time to protest. His hand reached over the side and grabbed the jug. Instead of returning to his former position, he handed her the jug and twisted around to face her.

Dark eyes locked with hers. "Sit on my lap, Aly. Wash me wherever you like."

Was it the whiskey or flames of desire warming his gaze to the color of midnight? The amber liquid seared Aly's throat as she drank fully of the night and Nick.

When she stretched to return the jug over the side of the trough, his hands covered hers and relieved her of the task. Suddenly, he pulled Aly close, forging his molten lips to hers. She threw her arms around his neck and kissed him feverishly, wantonly, without hesitancy or thought of any consequence.

Nick needed no further encouragement. Aly wanted him as much as he wanted her. Her shyness was gone now. As he removed her pantaloons, she pressed her lips to his brow, his eyes, each cheek. The hot tip of her tongue traced a long lazy circle of ecstasy from his neck to his shoulder. A low moan escaped from somewhere deep within him. He crushed her to him. Aly was an innocent but borne of a passion as fiery as her temper.

His breath came slow and uneven as her fingers caressed his shoulders then twined into the dark curls of hair that spanned his chest. When she tugged playfully, he muttered a pleasured oath.

She leaned back, allowing her fingers to toy with one of his nipples. It hardened in response. When her head bowed to lavish the peak with her tongue, she innocently moved her thighs closer, touching his burgeoning desire. What glory!

Her hands encircled his neck, pulling him backward. "You'll drown!" he teased, his palms forming a pillow to cushion the back of her head. He lay over her full-length now, reveling in the way their bodies fit so perfectly.

Aly's fingers cupped his buttocks, kneading the rounded flesh as her breasts pressed against him. He shivered when she raised slightly, her mouth claiming his once more to sear him with a white-hot flame of eagerness.

The kiss branded his soul with the sweet taste of love offered without bounds. A hunger like none he'd ever known engulfed him. He wanted more of her. He wanted to give her all of himself.

She writhed against him, muttering incoherent words of want and need. Nick knew her craving, for it was as immeasurable as his own. "Are you sure, Aly?"

Passion heated her eyes to molten gold. "I want it to be real between us, Nick. No more pretending."

"It may hurt." He poised at the brink of her welcoming womanhood.

"I've never been afraid when I'm with you."

Her body stiffened as he filled her, confirming his suspicion that Aly had never known a man in this way. "It will only hurt once."

She didn't cry out. Her gaze locked with his as her chin lifted stubbornly. Then, she began to move.

"Easy," Nick urged, his voice echoing with the strain of holding back his passion. "There's no need to hurry."

"I can't. I want to be closer. Hold me closer, Nick."

The quest was upon them and neither could turn from the fervor that carried them. He could do nothing but answer her persistent plea. Nick moved with her, cherishing her. His mind whirled as the water eddied around them.

Lost in the rapturous movement of their bodies, Nick climbed the pinnacle he'd been searching for all his life—the place where he and the woman he loved would become one breath, one heartbeat, one soul.

Aly, the hellcat. Aly, the innocent temptress. Aly, his wife. In that moment, she became every woman to him, and he would yearn for no other.

The need to make her his for all eternity rose within him, spiraling Nick upward, higher and higher, until, at last, his soul found its zenith.

Now he knew exactly where he belonged.

Chapter Seventeen

Sunlight shone through the bedroom window, warming Aly's face and stirring her awake. She yawned and started to stretch her arm, then halted. Nick's head pressed against her breast, his hand laying claim to the flat plane of her belly. His right leg intertwined with her left one, holding her snugly against him.

She felt as if she'd been riding a twister all night, touching down to earth occasionally to shatter all her misguided notions about being female enough for Nick. She was sore but in all the right places and for all the best reasons. Aly had never ached so good.

A smile so big it could have rivaled the width of a canyon spread across her face. Heated memories of last night's lovemaking sent a tremble through her. Rather than consider it weakness, she welcomed the fact that her body delighted in yielding to his. For the first time in her life, Aly was glad to be a woman—Nick's woman.

"You cold, Chick?" His nose nuzzled her bare breast, then he scooted slightly higher, taking the nipple into his mouth.

"Not for long, I reckon." Aly's fingers delved into his hair to draw him closer. "I'm for some carrying on." She tousled his hair. "How 'bout you?"

He pressed his hard body against her. Desire as untamed as a dust devil spun through Aly. Her fingers traced a trail down the slope of his shoulders, to the muscles defining his arms, urging him upward to feed the craving for his kiss.

"I'd love to, Chick."

When his lips covered hers, Aly's tongue raced to taste the power of his passion that had transformed her dreams into reality last night.

Nick shifted, demanding a more intimate touch. Aly opened to him gladly, wanting the sensations surging through her never to end. Her hips arched against him, demanding that he forget the chatter.

Dark eyes lit with amusement. "Patience has never been one of your better qualities, Aly."

She flipped him over onto his back, giggling as her hair cascaded across his startled expression. For once, the strength she'd gained from hauling freight proved itself useful in female endeavors. "You're right, husband, I am impatient. Especially now that you've shown me what I've been missing with all this pretending."

"Wildcat," Nick whispered, his hands gently grabbing the key and its chain to draw her closer for a kiss. When she straddled him, he crooned, "What have I just let loose on the world?"

He filled her so completely, Aly's answer exited in a tone full of raw need. "On you, Nick. Only you . . . not the world." Her lips lowered to his and halted only a breath away. "All that I am, I am for *you*."

She began to move, riding the winds of fate, staking her claim on forever.

Aly couldn't stop staring at Nick as his horse faded into the horizon. Something inside her twisted, making her run out into the yard to get one more glimpse before he disappeared over the rise. All of a sudden, the horse reined half-quarter. Nick lifted his hat and waved a broad good-bye, yelling something she couldn't hear from that distance.

Tears from the deep well of emotions she felt for the gambler flooded Aly's eyes. "Get a hold of yourself." Aly spoke the reprimand aloud as if it would make the words easier to obey. "Don't want him to think you've become some kind of mush melon with all this squalling, do you?"

She waved back and yelled, "I think I love you, gambler!" Then in a slightly lower tone, she continued, "I know you can't possibly hear it from where you are, and I know I should have told you already, but I couldn't. Dang it all, I'm scared to say it when I don't know for sure how much you feel for me."

Aly's arms crossed over her, her palms trying to rub away the loneliness that now engulfed her. She was impatient like he said, but she had it in her to tell him now or be sick from wanting to.

The door to the house opened behind her. Aly had forgotten their guest! How much had Connie heard? Watching Nick's image disappear over the rise gave her enough time to regain some semblance of control and face the woman behind her. Aly quickly wiped the tears and hoped the morning sun would be too bright for Connie to notice.

Connie stood at the door, an apron tied about her waist. "Have you seen Jezlynn?"

Aly nodded. "She was headed for the outhouse a while ago. Why?"

"The cinnamon rolls and milk are still where I set them on the table. Uneaten."

"She's pouting this morning." Aly sniffled, then pretended to cough, as if she'd gotten something in her throat. "She wanted to go to town with Nick. I told her we had to leave him be today. But she said he promised to show her how to play poker, and a deal's a deal. I wouldn't be surprised if she's laying a trap for me in the outhouse. I'm on her get-even list."

"It is not her I worry so much about, amiga. I wonder if you know your own mind and heart so well?"

Aly should have known she couldn't hide anything from Connie . . . especially when she stood out here shouting her thoughts to the world. "What's a piece of rawhide like me know of loving a fella?" Aly shrugged. "I ain't exactly had much to measure that stick against."

"How does he make you feel, amiga?" Connie's eyes and voice warmed with the sultriness of a woman who'd known the pleasures of a man's true love. She shut the door and headed out into the yard. Halting alongside Aly, the bookkeeper shaded her eyes with one hand and stared in the direction Nick had taken. "Can you put it into words?"

Aly had often wondered if her initial interest in Nick's company could have been something other than love. After all, the gambler was the only man she'd never been able to sling out of her wagon when she'd had the need to do so. That showed he had grit, and she respected someone with grit. "Up until last night, I was convinced that love was just a mountain peak at the end of a road two people decided to travel together."

She smiled, recalling her early days with the gam-

184

bler. "We shared a lot of the same road, Nick and me. We went fishing, played poker, and even tried to out-howl a pack of coyotes one night. We've gotten drunk together and told each other things we wouldn't dare tell anyone else.

"Guess somewhere along the way I started hoping we could find more to like about us than wanting to outsmart each other. Ain't that what everybody calls love, or something close to it?" Aly's fingers splayed against her belly. "Surely it ain't this wild yearning he stirs inside me or this need to hold him so close I can't tell where he ends and I begin. I can't seem to breathe right without him."

"I, myself, always fall in love in the heat of the moment." Connie laughed, a sensuality to her voice. "Are you certain he is the one, amiga? Is he all that you need?"

Spending all her days and, particularly, the nights with Nick offered a welcome future. Aly knew most of his failings and admired the man more than she did any others. One reservation kept her from answering a definite yes—Nick had not said he loved her last night.

Doubts began to flood Aly. Before she could stop herself, she blurted out everything to Connie. About the bet and how she suspected that Nick had somehow arranged for Ophelia to give him the winning cards. About the true reason they had "married" and the bets made against the marriage lasting. She even admitted wondering whether Nick had placed some side wagers of his own over the matter.

Ophelia! Aly rubbed the key she wore around her neck.

If you ever have to yell at him how much you love him, it's time to open the box.

"Ain't you expected at the bank soon?" Aly tried to hurry her friend to work. She wanted to be alone to

185

open that box. "I appreciate you bringing the rolls to Jez. Banker Sullivan will be at the poker game, won't he? It's Monday."

"I told him I would be stopping here first," Connie said. "There's very little to do at the bank these days. I am caught up on the books. Everyone knows he spends this morning at the saloon." She folded her arms across her breasts. "Now, why did you not tell me about you and Nick when you first arrived? Could you not trust me with the truth?"

Aly felt as if she were a lone shooter facing a posse a hundred guns strong. "I was afraid when you found out we weren't really hitched, you'd take a shine to him and make him husband number cinco."

Connie threw back her head and laughed. "If ever there was proof you love him, you have just spoken it. You want no other woman to have him. That is what we call jealousy, my friend. Green-eyed . . . *golden*-eyed jealousy."

She was right! Aly's heart leaped so hard, she thought it would break through bone and muscle. She'd yelled that she loved him. She'd meant it, too. Only now she understood all that she was trying to say to him. "I gotta tell him, Connie." Her hands caressed the key between her thumb and finger. "Face-to-face. It's beating strong in me, and I feel like I'm gonna burst."

"Then go to him, amiga." Connie laughed again. "He has not ridden that far ahead of you."

Aly eyed the direction of the outhouse. "But what about Jez?"

Connie shooed Aly into the house. "I'll ask which she prefers—for me to stay with her or for her to go with me to the bank. Now, you must decide what you shall wear. When you tell a man you love him, you wear something you'll want him to remember the rest of your days."

Aly hurried to their bedroom and shucked the calico dress she'd put on to see him off to town. She opened the armoire and riffled through the dresses until she found her buckskins. If she meant to catch him before he reached town, she needed less restraining clothes. The buckskin pants slid up her legs easily. The shirt took only a few seconds more.

Though there was plenty of room because of her tendency to buy clothes slightly bigger than necessary, Aly discovered they no longer felt right. "I can't wear these," she grumbled and stripped down to her chemise and pantaloons again. "They don't fit anymore!"

Living like a man no longer appealed to her. She no longer fit *them*. Aly wanted to be all the woman Nick could ever want.

Laughing, she started tossing petticoats, dresses and all the other feminine finery Nick had bought her onto the bed. Critical of each one, she couldn't determine which would flatter her the most.

For the first time in her life, she felt totally female and desperately in love.

After putting on the dress of her choice, she opened the first drawer and pulled out Ophelia's gift. Aly trembled, sensing that whatever she found inside might somehow alter her life. "Just get on with it," she told herself, lifting the chain from around her neck to place the key into the lock. With a twist of her hand, the box opened. Two envelopes lay inside—one marked with Aly's name, the other with Nick's.

Temptation to know what was inside the letter to Nick coursed through Alewine. She turned his envelope over and discovered it had been sealed. *Not that I'd read it anyway*, she tried to convince herself.

"Madre Santissima, amiga!" Connie came rushing into the room, her face flushed, worry widening her eyes. "I went to check on *Ninita* . . . Jezlynn, but could not find her there. Then I noticed the little colt standing at the corral gate, neighing for his mother. The mare is gone. Ninita must have taken Troublemaker and followed Nick to town!"

"She's too little for a horse that big!" Aly returned the box to the drawer. She put the letter in her pocket. Reading it would have to wait until later . . . when Jezlynn was safe.

When they reached town, Aly suggested they split up. Too much time had already been spent making sure Jezlynn had not fallen from the horse and been left afoot. Confident that a riderless Troublemaker would have passed them on her way back to her colt, Aly felt certain Jezlynn had made it to town. "She's smart enough to know I'd follow when I found her missing. I'll check the saloon. You look in the livery and see if you can spot Troublemaker. Stop by the bank, too. I wouldn't put it past her to take advantage of you and Sullivan being gone."

"Ninita is only six years old." Connie commanded her horse to turn toward the livery. "How much trouble can such a small one be?"

Worry took voice within Aly. "She's got you and me hauling hooves, don't she?"

"Si, amiga." Connie laughed to ease Aly's worry. "I forget which six-year-old we speak of."

"If you don't find her before I do, meet me at the saloon. If it's the other way around, I'll find you."

Chapter Eighteen

Nick studied the three men playing poker with him at the saloon. He could tell Banker Sullivan didn't have a decent hand for five-card stud. The man's moustache twitched slightly, revealing irritation with the cards.

The blacksmith, Daniel Tyler, must have played often enough to know a professional gambler watched for such ticks to clue him in on his opponent's luck . . . or lack of it. The behemoth-sized man looked as if he were carved from stone. Big-knuckled fingers, stained black from working iron, gripped his cards in a solid pack. They left no smudges on the cards for the black was thickly embedded in his skin. Had he fanned his cards, Nick could have guessed how many of them were worth saving or needed culling.

A man who worked all day polishing metal to a fine sheen tended to rub anything of value he held. He wasn't stroking the outermost card, making Tyler's hand unreadable. All Nick could determine was that he didn't want to be on the receiving end of any punch the blacksmith threw.

The third player Nick knew too well. Driscoll had a decent hand and let every man know it.

"You fellows are going to have a hard time beating this hand." Driscoll drummed his fingers on the table and grinned at Nick. "Can't win them all, can you, Turner? The odds are against you."

Nick tired of the bragging. "I'd say the odds are against any of us adding more to the pot if you really have that good of a hand. Might want to temper that enthusiasm if you want someone to up the ante."

"Let me go!" a familiar voice yelled. "I'll kick you, I tell you. He said I can play poker, and I'm gonna."

Nick rose just as the curtain that divided the private gaming room from the main saloon jerked to one side. The burly-looking bartender who'd served them earlier held Jezlynn by the scruff of the neck.

"This belong to you?" The bartender frowned, his handlebar moustache drooping even more than usual.

Exasperated, Nick claimed his daughter. "She's mine."

"Boss don't allow kids in the saloon." The bartender let go of her and pointed to the bench against the windowed wall.

He didn't have to say another word. Jezlynn obeyed and sat on the bench.

"I'll get to the bottom of this and see that she leaves quickly. Can I pay you for your troubles?"

The bartender glared at Jezlynn. "No, but make sure she stays behind this curtain. Don't want no customers finding a kid in my saloon. Makes for bad business." The man yanked the curtain closed.

"He's a big one, ain't—"

Nick didn't let her finish speaking. "Where's Aly,

and what are you doing here, young lady? It's impolite to interrupt these gentlemen's poker game."

"You said you'd teach me how to play." Jezlynn ignored his questions, tilting her chin defiantly. "Aly said you was gonna play poker today, and you didn't take me with you. How come?"

"Like the bartender said, Miss Turner . . ." Irritation echoed in Driscoll's voice as he glared at Jezlynn. "A saloon is no place for a child. Neither is a poker game."

The banker and blacksmith remained silent, but their discomfort with the child in their midst was clearly visible. As much as Nick hated to agree with Driscoll on anything, the Valiant businessman was right this time. Still, he wouldn't allow him to use that tone with Jezlynn. "Bridle that temper, Driscoll, if you want to walk out of here on your own two feet. She's a child."

Jezlynn stuck her tongue out at the man. When Nick's brows knitted in disapproval, her dark lashes dipped in embarrassment. Her lower lip pouted. "I just want to learn how to play. You promised."

"Anyone object if she watches the round?" Surely, Aly would show up soon. "My wife should be here any minute. She'll take Jez off our hands."

It sounded like all hell broke loose in the saloon's main room.

Nick shoved his chair aside and reached for the knife he kept hidden in his boot. The other men bolted to their feet as well. A known poker game and the need for money in this town could easily draw interest from outlaws.

"Move out of my way, mister! You should've told me there was a back room the first time."

"Out of mine, too, senor!"

191

Nick recognized the voices giving the bartender fits. He slipped the knife back into its sheath then waited for Aly and Consuela to join them.

A second later, the curtain whooshed to one side. Aly halted in a rustle of petticoats, her eyes glaring hard at Jezlynn, then filling with apology when they moved to Nick.

Before anyone could speak, Nick motioned to the two women. "Gentlemen, I think most of you know my wife, Aly, and her friend, Consuela Calhoun."

"Ladies." The blacksmith's thumb raised above his head as if he were about to tip a hat at them, but no hat covered his head.

The man had taken it off earlier and raked his winnings into the crown, then set it on the floor next to his chair. They'd been playing little more than an hour, so there was no way for Nick to determine the quality of the man's game. So far, Tyler held his own against Nick's skill.

"Back off, bartender." Aly glared at the burly mixologist standing in the doorway. "You saw me poke my head over the doors. I asked you if you saw a little girl run through here. Even told you what she looked like." She shot the man a look so hard it could have left bruises. "If it weren't for Connie coming along when she did, I wouldn't have known about the back room."

"Females aren't allowed in the saloon. Leastways, not your kind," the bartender bellowed. "Boss's rule, not mine."

Nick held up one palm to quiet Aly. "Point taken, sir, and they won't be in here long, I guarantee it. But as you can see, my wife insists on having her say." He shared a glance with Aly. "Whatever that is. Please allow them to take a seat, and we'll work this out as quickly as possible."

"You got five minutes."

Nick waited as the barkeep left. The women sat down, sandwiching Jezlynn between them. He would bet all the money in the room his daughter had been up to something other than disturbing a poker game. Aly would never break her pledge to give him a day on his own so Jezlynn must have done something serious.

He needed to get the game under way and keep the promise he'd made. "The men have all agreed I can explain the game to Jez. It shouldn't take too long to play out one hand."

"Half-Pint has some explaining of her own to do."

Aly's remark caused Jezlynn to scoot closer to Connie.

The game resumed.

Jezlynn raised her hand as if she were a student in class. "Can I see what everybody has?"

Banker Sullivan frowned but conceded to her request. "All right, if you sit down afterward and not say a single word to anybody. If you tell what our cards are, the game is void." He looked at each man. "Agreed?"

The blacksmith nodded. Driscoll smirked. "Fine by me. Kid needs to see my hand anyway, so she'll know what to look for."

"Be quick about it, Jezlynn." Nick decided to be more careful what he promised in the future.

She circled the table, stopping at each hand. Just as she moved toward the blacksmith, Jezlynn stumbled. "Uh-oh!"

Tyler reached to help her up. "You all right, girl?"

She nodded and laid a coin on the table. "Yessir. But I knocked this out of your hat by accident."

"Thank you kindly, miss."

"Can I see your cards, too?"

Tyler fanned them and gave her time to study, then

193

pushed them into a single pack again. Jezlynn returned to her seat between Aly and the bookkeeper, tucking her hands into her pockets and acting as if she were in a prayer meeting. Nick was proud of her. She had the makings of a fine gambler, if history repeated itself.

"Here's where the fun begins." Nick examined his cards one last time. Hearts—ace, king, jack. Excitement rushed through him at the possibility. Maybe Aly and Jez would bring him luck. He willed his voice to remain calm, offering no hint of the cards held in his hand. Nick threw down the culls. "Each man gets rid of the cards he doesn't want. I'll take two, Driscoll."

The blond man grinned slightly and dealt two cards. Nick left them face down.

Driscoll moved on to the next player. "How many for you, Sullivan?"

The banker sighed with disgust and slapped the table with most of his cards. "Give me four. Anything would be better than what I've got."

"Tyler?" Driscoll waited for the big man to answer.

The blacksmith's eyes locked with Nick's. "Let 'em stand."

Driscoll's grin faded as he set the remainder of the deck aside, his confidence obviously shaken. "None for me, either."

Tension layered the room. Jez scooted to the edge of her chair, craning to see more. "Whatcha doing now?"

"They're trying to outsmart each other," Aly whispered, caught up in the suspense.

Connie fanned herself, reminding Nick of the heat of the day. He still wore his coat, while the other men had stripped off theirs and rolled up their sleeves. The heat of the challenge thrived in Nick, making him feel at ease when other men began to sweat. He never bet more than he could lose, which automatically made him a winner. Winning the wager became an added victory.

"My compliments, daughter," Nick offered, using the time to make Driscoll perspire more and give Tyler a moment to have second thoughts. "I appreciate you being quiet."

"Being quiet can save your life, Ninita. Aly saved my life once when she kept *me* from talking." Connie frowned at Driscoll when he waved a hand of dismissal at her. Her chin lifted in indignation. "Si, she did. A gang of outlaws meant to rob the stage I had booked passage on. They fired into the air, frightening the team. Alewine had been riding shotgun with the driver and decided to get a better bead on the robbers by climbing over to the luggage boot."

Connie's body started swaying back and forth like a pendulum. "The coach teetered one way, then another. The team left the trail only to find the path more dangerous." She exhaled a deep breath. "Later, Aly told me she'd swung into the open window because she didn't want to be thrown off." Connie touched her forehead, drawing the sign of the cross. "A wise decision, I soon learned. The driver was crushed beneath the stage."

"Let's get back to the game," Driscoll grumbled.

"What were they after?" Curiosity filled Jezlynn's voice. "Were you hauling bank money?"

Just what she needs to hear. Nick scowled at Mrs. Calhoun. *The tale of a successful robbery. Then again, maybe I'm being unfair. Connie has no way of knowing my daughter's misguided aspiration.*

"No, amiga. This happened long before I worked for Senor Sullivan."

"An interesting story left for another time, Jez." Nick tried to steer the conversation away from less dangerous avenues. "I'll bet Mrs. Calhoun will be delighted to tell you about other experiences she and Aly have shared, but after these fine gentleman and I—"

"Let the lovely lady finish her story. The cards'll hold for the moment."

Connie flashed the blacksmith a smile that could have melted iron into a molten puddle. "One of the robbers wanted to see if we women were still alive. To . . ." Her gaze slanted to the child. *"Take liberties.* But Alewine whispered to play dead. I said nothing."

"If you know Connie at all . . ." Aly winked at them. "You'd know what a great sacrifice it was for her."

"I do." Connie's gaze darted at the blacksmith. "It is one of the many uses for a mouth, si?"

"Connie!" Aly's elbow shot out to jab her friend, accidently glancing Jezlynn's arm before connecting with her true target. "There's a youngun present. Remember?"

Jezlynn glared at Aly and rubbed her arm. "Yeah, and you remember it, too."

Nick's eyes met Aly's. Both were recalling the other uses Connie implied. He rather liked the way his wife's cheeks darkened with a rosy blush. God, would he ever get enough of seeing her, touching her? Though he'd yearned for this day away from responsibilities, no poker game on earth would be worth losing a night with Alewine.

"Did you fool 'em?" Jez ignored the adults' laughter.

Connie shook her head. "No, but Aly did. She was wearing buckskins and covered with traildust. Thinking she was dead, they turned their backs on her and tried to drag me kicking and screaming. She was able to grab their pistols before they knew it."

Jezlynn's mouth gaped as she stared up at her substitute mother. "Did you shoot 'em?"

Nick could almost see Aly's mind evaluating how much she should tell a would-be robber. Her eyes silently asked him to determine how she should answer. In the end, he shrugged, leaving it up to her own wisdom.

"Let's just say, they've got some mighty sore feet. They won't be chasing anybody anytime soon. Best way to stop a thief is to take something away from him and let him know how it feels. That shows him you mean business."

Jezlynn shifted in her seat, scooting closer to Connie.

"Let's show 'em." Driscoll fanned his cards. "A flush, king high." The pause that followed swept away his uneasiness and made him more daring. Driscoll grinned, his face beaming with triumph.

Banker Sullivan threw his cards down without showing them. "Beats me all to hell and back." Suddenly, he remembered the women's presence. "Pardon me, ladies."

"Guess that leaves you and me, Tyler." Nick eyed the blacksmith's cards. "You want to go first, or shall I?"

"You." Tyler studied Nick. "I hear a good gambler can still pull the right card to beat any other hand on the table. From what I've heard about you in town, you're one of the best. I'll show my hand last."

Nick laid the three hearts he held down for all to see. "There's still two down. I haven't seen."

The women stood and moved closer, everyone leaning in to see the cards he'd been dealt.

Lady Luck danced an invisible jig with Nick. "Anyone care to up the ante?"

"No one's that lucky." Tyler bent down and grabbed money from his hat. He paused, then slowly raised and tossed in five more gold pieces. "I raise you a hundred dollars."

197

Chink. Chink. Chink, chink, chink. Driscoll's coins landed on top of Tyler's. "I think you're both bluffing me."

"Can I come over and touch your cards?" Jez asked. "For luck?"

Nick eyed the other men. "Have any problem with that, gents?"

"As long as she keeps her hands where we can see them." Tyler watched Jezlynn move to her father's side.

Nick placed his cards in order in front of him. "Now what do I need to turn over to win the game?"

"A ten of hearts and a lady of hearts." Glancing up, Jezlynn grinned. "Johnny Johnson's been teaching me how to play some. I just want to know how to play *good.*" Jezlynn tapped the cards seven times. "Seven is my favorite number. Uh-oh . . ." Her mouth rounded in horror. "You don't suppose one of them will be a seven now, do you?"

"Even if it is, I've already got the ladies of my heart—you and Aly." Nick hugged his daughter and shooed her toward Aly. "Thanks for the luck, Half-Pint."

"Well, don't keep us in suspense," Driscoll ranted. "Show us the cards."

Nick flipped them over.

A loud intake of breath echoed over the room.

The ten and queen of hearts smiled back at Nick.

The women began to clap furiously. Driscoll sank back against his chair, all the spunk sifting from him like a sack of cornmeal with a hole punched in it. Tyler threw down his full house, his mouth a grim line.

Banker Sullivan nodded. "You are, by far, one of the luckiest men I've ever known, Turner. I deliberately set out to see if I could catch you cheating, and I can honestly say you didn't. Someone's taken a shine to you today, that's all I know."

Nick smiled at Aly. "Yes, she has and she's my Lady Luck, it seems."

"You get to keep all of that?" Jezlynn's eyes widened as Nick raked the winnings to his side of the table.

"I'm done." The blacksmith rose. "Gotta save the rest for supplies and take a meal over at the hotel. I should have been back to work a long time ago."

"The same for me." The banker glanced at his pocket watch. "With the lack of luck I'm having this morning, I'd be a wiser man to quit while I'm ahead." Sullivan looked at Connie. "And speaking of work, Mrs. Calhoun, who's minding the bank?"

"Your wife, senor, but I am leaving now." Connie stood.

"It's not Connie's fault she's here," Aly defended her friend. "I . . . um . . . ran into a slight problem this morning. When she came by, I asked her to stay and help me. I'll pay for her time and any loss to the bank."

"What problem?" Nick asked.

Aly shook her head. "We'll talk about it later."

"If you two would like to talk privately, I will take Jezlynn with me to work." Connie held out a hand to the child. Jez grabbed it quickly. "That is, if Senor Sullivan approves."

Jezlynn started bouncing with excitement. "Let me, please, please, please?"

Sullivan laughed. "I wish everyone in town had such enthusiasm to visit the bank. Of course she can go with you. You can even show her the safe and how we do business."

"I've never seen the inside of a safe," Jezlynn whispered in awe.

"She can't go." Aly and Nick said in unison. Both knew giving her ready access to everything in the bank was the last thing Sullivan wanted.

"I mean, Jez has to eat something first. She didn't have breakfast this morning. None of us did." Aly gently grabbed Jezlynn's arm and made her quit bouncing. "She was in such a hurry to get to town."

Nick wondered what had made Aly interrupt his so-called day alone. Now he understood. Jezlynn had been up to some of her antics again. He tossed Aly a few coins then flipped one to Jez. The child caught it. "Go eat something. It's lunch time, but I think the restaurant still serves breakfast at this hour." His gaze leveled on his daughter. "No peppermint candy until afterward. Understand?"

She nodded.

"I'll join you in a while, and we'll all take Connie a hot meal. I have some business to discuss with Silas."

Banker Sullivan struggled into his frock coat and eyed Nick speculatively. "Will you be going with me or do you have another stop to make first?"

"I'm going with you."

Driscoll scowled. "Anyone care to know what I plan to do."

"No," Aly, Nick, Jezlynn, and Connie replied together.

Silas Sullivan placed his hat on his head and thumbed it up. "Mrs. Turner, it's been a pleasure, indeed. Miss Turner, give my regards to your mother. And Mrs. Calhoun . . ."

"Si, senor?"

"My wife has handled business this long, she can do so while you eat. Go enjoy your friends."

"Ahh, shucks," Jezlynn complained loudly. "The bank'll be *closed* by the time *she* stops eating!"

Chapter Nineteen

The mouth-watering aroma of freshly baked bread hit Aly full force as she entered the hotel and guided Jezlynn and Connie toward the dining room. Though the restaurant was small, it didn't lack atmosphere. The planked walls were made of ponderosa pine; the tablecloths were Navajo blankets. Prickly pear cacti served as centerpieces, their pink blossoms lending color.

Aly would have to talk with the hotel owner and see if he had designed the room himself or if he'd had someone do it for him. She'd never thought much about her freight office looking like a tack room, but she decided it could use a bit of dressing up.

Eying the handful of diners, Aly noticed the blacksmith who'd left the poker game. He didn't look very happy at the moment. She chose the table in front of him. "Let's sit here."

"No, let's get that one over there." Jezlynn pointed to the table nearest the kitchen.

Shaking her head, Aly informed the child, "Not this time. The smoke from the kitchen bothers my eyes." Her nose wrinkled. "They ain't changed the grease in a while."

"Then, can I sit here?" Jezlynn plopped down in the chair, her back to the blacksmith.

Aly didn't blame her. That look Tyler gave them could curdle a glass of milk. She waved at the waitress wiping the long counter that divided the dining room from the kitchen.

The woman strolled to their table. "The special today is fried potato cakes and hamhocks. Breakfast is served all day. What'll it be?"

"I want biscuits and gravy and eggs." Jezlynn plopped the coin Nick had given her down on the table.

The waitress smiled. "That'll even cover jelly, with money left over."

"That's okay, I've got plenty." Jezlynn's hand dug into her pocket, then instantly jerked back. "I mean, I can get some more from my pa, if I need it. He just won a whole bunch over at the saloon."

The blacksmith grumbled and said something under his breath.

"What did you say, mister?" Aly craned to look around Jez to the sour-faced man.

Another couple and their children took a seat a few tables away. The waitress looked impatiently at Aly. "Ma'am? What'll it be?"

"Give me breakfast, too, I guess."

"Me, *tres*!"

"That means three in her language," Jezlynn informed, looking smug with her knowledge.

Aly wasn't certain, but she thought the blacksmith's anger might be targeted at Jezlynn. He was sure glaring hard at the child. "Give us milk all around."

"Yes, ma'am," the waitress said and bustled away.

Ma'am. Aly liked the respect the title offered her. "I'm so hungry, I could eat the south end of a buffalo all by myself. I've been wanting some biscuits other than my own . . . or Madeline's. No offense to your roll-making, Connie."

A few minutes later, the waitress approached carrying a huge tray. She gave each of them a glass of milk and a plate of scrambled eggs, then set a bowl of gravy and a platter of biscuits in the middle of the table. She set the dish of jelly next to Jezlynn's plate.

"You gonna pay for the jelly?" Jezlynn scooted the jam closer to Aly.

Aly laughed. "Starting some savings, are you, Skunk Wrangler?"

"Not with her own money she isn't."

Patrons' heads turned at the blacksmith's accusation.

"What do you mean by that, mister?" Aly demanded.

"Ask your daughter." The man pushed back his chair and stood. "That little thief stole some money from me when she pretended to stumble over my hat. You need to teach her better manners."

"Did you do that?" Aly eyed Jezlynn, wishing she didn't have to ask. But the child intended to be a robber some day.

"No!" Tears welled in Jezlynn's eyes. "I promise I didn't."

"Somebody ought to bend you over his knee, little girl." One of Tyler's hands slapped his other palm to demonstrate his meaning.

The blacksmith might look as tough as iron, but she'd be six feet under before he laid a finger on Jez. Aly sought Connie's counsel. "Con, she promises she didn't do it. I can't tolerate no man mean-mouthing my kid."

"Just what do you intend to do about it?" Tyler challenged, his broad shoulders rising.

What could she do? "This!" Aly acted before she could have second thoughts. She grabbed a handful of eggs and threw it at him. Tyler ducked only to raise again and be hit by the biscuit Connie let fly.

"Have another one, senor." Consuela sent more sailing. "And another."

The wad of eggs Jezlynn threw missed the blacksmith and splattered on the waitress's face.

"Watch that aim, Half-Pint!" Aly warned, taking a cold splash of milk from the boy behind her.

"Fight!" the young boy said, startling his parents.

All of sudden, food flew in every direction. If people didn't throw, they ducked. If they didn't duck, they wiped off the mess. Screams of outrage mixed with squeals so loud that several people came running in from the hotel lobby—Nick in the lead.

"What's going on here?"

His demand went unanswered. Nick ducked a glob of mashed potatoes only to have his vest smeared with a dollop of jelly. Fury stained his face. "*Aly* . . ."

"*I* didn't start it . . . exactly." She pointed at the blacksmith. "*He* did. He called Jez a thief and a liar. Said he oughta turn Jez over his knee and spank her. If she was guilty, I reckon that's our duty. But she promised she didn't take none of his money. So I let him have it."

"If you're my daddy and you love me"—Jezlynn lined up behind her dad, handing him a wad of scrambled eggs—"then you can't let him talk bad about me. Here, better hit him with this."

"Put the eggs down, Jezlynn. I have a better way to deal with this. Tyler, care to tell me your version of the story?" Nick listened while the blacksmith said his piece. Then Nick studied his daughter's face. "And you're certain you didn't take any of the man's money?"

Jezlynn shook her head adamantly. "I even gave some back, remember? I *promise* I didn't do it."

With a heavy sigh, Nick began to roll up his sleeves and faced the bigger man. "Well, Tyler, I'm her daddy and I love her. And if she says she isn't guilty, then you and I have a problem. Care to settle it outside?"

Tyler growled. With one blackened hand, Tyler grabbed Nick by the collar, jerking him forward until they were nose to nose. "I'm gonna mop this floor up with you, Turner!"

"Don't!" Jez ran to separate them. "It ain't Papa you're mad at. It's me." She pushed against each man's stomach as if she were holding up the walls of Jericho. She bowed her head. "I kind of took some money from him."

Nick rolled his shoulders, returning the shirt to its normal position. Anger creased his forehead, his eyes turning dark with disappointment. "You lied. To Aly and to me."

"I guess so." She dug one toe into a mess of potatoes beneath her feet, then looked up. "I didn't plan on keeping his ol' money for long." She glared at Connie. "I was gonna put it in the bank for him, but she wanted to come eat."

Aly had never felt so disappointed in Jezlynn. "Connie's not the one to blame here, Jezlynn. I think we all owe Mr. Tyler an apology."

Nick turned his daughter around to face her accuser. "I'm sorry for my daughter's actions, sir. I assure you, it will never happen again. Give the man back his money, Jezlynn."

"I just wanted to fill up the bank. I didn't want it for *me*." Jezlynn's eyes glimmered with tears.

"You went about it all wrong." Nick held her shoulders. "Now you must apologize to Mr. Tyler for the wrong you've done him."

Aly waited, not certain if the child cared enough about Nick to want to please him.

"Sorry, Mr. Tyler." Jez dug into her pocket and handed over the coins. "It was just some of those funny old eagles anyway."

"I'd like to apologize, too, by buying your meal." Aly stared at the mess they'd made of the dining room. It would be a long time before she trusted the child's word again.

"It takes a brave soul to 'fess up when she's wrong, and a smart one to remember that when she gives a promise, it's her word on the line. Don't give it lightly next time, girl." Tyler offered his hand to Jezlynn. She tentatively extended hers, and he shook it. "Apology accepted." He looked at Aly as well. "From everybody."

"I'll pay the waitress for her troubles." Aly called the lady over. When Aly reached into her pocket, she realized she carried no money. All she had was Ophelia's letter! "Uh . . . my husband will have to pay us out. I left my . . . money . . . at home. Sorry about the mess."

Nick quickly settled up for the damages.

As they headed out the door, Nick studied Aly's comical appearance and winked. "I think a bath is in order, don't you?"

Grateful for the release from her disturbing thoughts about Jezlynn, Aly winked back. "Tub or horse trough?"

People strolling down the sidewalk and riding past in the street gaped at the exiting diners. One particular face looked more shocked than any other.

Madeline.

Aly's grin faded. She nudged Nick with her elbow

and nodded toward the buggy that had just pulled up in front of the hotel. "Seems your luck just flew the coop."

A reed-thin woman Aly had never seen before shared a seat with Madeline. The driver secured the reins, then offered a helping hand. Madeline stepped out and waited until he'd aided the mystery woman as well. Both females' mouths looked like grim lines.

"I'm glad to see you're all together." Madeline's eyes studied them with obvious distaste at their appearance. "It seems my sister has come at the most opportune time." She waved a lace hanky in Nick's direction. "You remember Jezlynn's father, Nicodemus." Dabbing the hanky against her nose, she nodded at Connie. "This is the banker's bookkeeper, Consuela Calhoun."

Madeline rested both hands on the handle of her parasol. "And this, my dear, is—"

"Someone worth more than you have time for knowing, I'm sure." Aly didn't like Madeline's habit of addressing her last.

"This is Alewine, my wife." Nick stepped in to finish the introductions. "Aly, this is Madeline's sister, Elmertha Bartholomew of Bartholomew's School for Young Ladies."

Madeline linked her arm with her sister's and urged the woman forward. "Jezlynn, come kiss your aunt hello. I've invited her for a short stay in the event you change your mind about living with your father. I've invited a few friends over for dinner to celebrate her arrival. Please see that you dress properly for the occasion."

Jez took a step backward, melting into Aly's skirt.

"I can see I'm needed here." Elmertha studied her niece, her mouth curving like a down-turned horseshoe.

Chapter Twenty

Frustration rode with Aly as they approached Madeline's main house. There had been little time to do anything more than give herself and Jez a bath, while Nick brushed down the horses, fed them, then hitched them to the wagon. Knowing it would most likely be dark when they returned home, Aly brought lanterns and blankets to ward off the chill of the Arizona desert. Connie had insisted she would meet them at Madeline's after she finished working, saving them the trouble of having to offer her a ride from town.

Both of Ophelia's envelopes rested deeply in the pocket of the pumpkin-colored dress Aly wore. Though practicality warned that she should have left them at home, her curiosity would not be denied an opportunity to tear hers open and read it. Maybe she and Nick could take a walk at some point—like he and Madeline had done during the first dinner party.

"Do I have to go?" Jezlynn squirmed on the seat

beside Aly and Nick. The team came to a halt. The man they'd seen driving Madeline's buggy earlier stood up from the rocker on the front porch and approached.

"Yes." Nick patted Jezlynn's arm. "But remember, you don't have to *stay*."

Aly flashed Nick a look of appreciation. Though he wanted Jezlynn to know how angry he was about her lying, he still realized her need for reassurance. Aly wished someone had cared enough to look beyond her mischief as a youth.

"Good evening, folks." The driver tipped his hat. "Glad you could join Mrs. Gilmore." He pointed to the servant woman standing in front of the opened entryway to the house. "Beth will show you to the parlor where everyone's gathered. I'll see to the horses."

"Thanks." Nick exited the wagon and helped Jezlynn down, then hurried over to Aly. "Ready, Chick?"

She turned and allowed his hands to grip her at the waist. As he helped her disembark, her torso slid a few inches down the hard wall of his chest. Nick's hands caressed the small of her back. He pulled her close and kissed her.

Aly returned his kiss, hungry for the night shadows to envelop them and Elmertha's party to be finished.

"Lovely evening for a party." The driver cleared his throat as he found a seat on the driver's box and took up the reins.

Nick's lips left Aly's, pulling into a smile. "Yes, it certainly is."

The driver tipped his hat. "Mrs. Turner, may I say I've never seen you looking finer."

"She's even prettier than my Mama," Jezlynn announced from the porch steps.

A hot sting of tears erupted in Aly's eyes. Her heart seemed to swell as if it wanted to burst. She'd never felt so wanted, so beautiful, in her entire life. A sniffle betrayed the emotions surging inside her.

"Dang ocotillas." She pretended to swat away the air and wrinkled her nose. "All them weeds riding the breeze makes a body want to sneeze."

Jezlynn giggled. "Sounds like a song."

Aly laughed and started to wipe the tears away with her sleeve, but Nick delved into a pocket inside his frock coat and handed her a hanky.

"Here, Chick. Use this."

"T-thanks. Guess I'm . . ." She refused to make an excuse for feeling female. Those days were gone. "Feeling a bit sentimental tonight."

Nick wrapped his arm around her waist and escorted her to the steps. Once there, he rested his other arm on Jez's shoulder. "Well, family. We're about to enter the lion's den. Everybody ready for the roar?"

Aly nodded and tucked the hanky into her pocket, bumping her fingers against the envelopes. "Only if you promise we can take a walk if it gets too pestersome inside."

"Deal." Nick gave her a gentle squeeze and winked. "I think a stroll in the moonlight would do us both some good."

"Can I go, too?" Jezlynn looked up at the two adults.

The tiniest measure of disappointment dashed through Aly before she finally nodded. "Wherever we go, you go too."

Aly didn't like Elmertha Bartholomew one bit. The woman was a self-righteous, pompous jackass.

Madeline's sister sat at the head of the massive dining table, holding court with the twenty or so people in attendance. "Jezlynn, dear, do sit up. You're slouching and getting your sleeve in the corn." She dabbed her prim mouth with a napkin. "That's an example of what I've been saying about bringing the right element into Prickly Bend." Her smile was patronizing. "The only way to easily draw new people here is for every citizen in the community to abandon the crudeness of a rougher society."

The food Aly had eatened soured in her stomach. She couldn't let the schoolmistress' opinion go unchallenged. "I beg to differ with you."

"Oh?" Elmertha sat back in her chair, her chin tilting slightly. "How so?"

"Well, first of all, take Jez here."

Jezlynn sunk back into her chair so she wouldn't be the focus of attention.

"No need to hide, Jez." Aly checked both of her own sleeves, certain that she had gotten *something* on them during the course of the meal. As luck would have it, she hadn't! Not to be daunted, she studied Madeline a moment and found the exact thing she'd hoped. "We all dirty our sleeves or drop something on our dress, now and then. Take Madeline, for instance . . ."

A look of mortification swept across Madeline's face when Aly's finger lightly touched her own bodice to point out the place where Madeline's was soiled. Their hostess grabbed a napkin and wiped furiously at the revealing stain. "Knowing manners is good, but being friendly and making people feel welcome will draw in a crowd, too. Madeline ain't done anything but what we all have at some point." Aly met every gaze she could. "Does that mean she's not mannered enough to be welcomed in our community?"

"Hear! Hear!" Banker Sullivan raised his glass in salute. Others followed suit, Nick being the first.

Elmertha's expression turned to ice as she reluctantly joined the toast. After everyone returned the glasses to the table, the woman cleared her throat. "Point well-taken, Mrs. Turner. However, I ask if what you imply is for us to invite in . . . shall we say . . . more of the uncouth among us?"

Nick's hand gently rubbed Aly's thigh beneath the table. Had she been in a less irritated mood, she'd have rubbed his right back and really given Elmertha something to raise her brows about. As it was, Nick's effort to halt the anger caused her right leg to bounce. She appreciated his effort, but she intended to have her say. Aly put her hand over Nick's and squeezed it to reassure him. When his fingers eased beneath hers, she scooted them off.

"What's uncouth to some, ain't to others," Aly continued. "Take me, for example. I'm rough as a week-old beard and quick-tempered as a badger. But I've been thinking of transferring some of my money from Valiant to Mr. Sullivan's bank. You gonna turn my money away because I ain't couth enough?"

Elmertha's eyes darkened to jade. Her hawklike nose twitched, making it look more pronounced. "Please continue. I'm not sure I fully understand your point."

"The point is . . ." Aly placed her hand on Nick's shoulder. "My husband, here, is a member of one of the town's founding families. Families that built this place and wanted it to grow. He took a roughhouser like me and gentled me up, showed me how to be more than I gave myself credit for. Shouldn't we offer that to others? Give them a helping hand in getting or becoming what they show promise for?"

Jezlynn raised her hand.

Elmertha acknowledged her niece's wish to be included. "You have something to say about all this, child?"

The girl nodded. "If everybody is welcome in town,

maybe we can even get some outlaws. They'll have plenty of money to put in the bank."

Laughter echoed over the table, Aly's and Nick's the loudest.

Elmertha's eyes rolled in their sockets. "My point exactly. Do you want to draw in *that* element?"

" 'Course not." Aly twisted the handkerchief laying across her lap, wishing it was Elmertha's neck instead. "But, most folks are law-abiding, hardworking, everyday kind of people. We have to go about doing things, speaking, conducting ourselves according to what's going on at the time. If I'm fussing with one of my mule skinners, do you think he'd listen if I said, 'I must say, Pug, I'm very disappointed in you?' "

Nick laughed and Aly flashed him a grateful grin. "No. I gotta go toe-to-toe, nose-to-nose, curse-to . . . Well, you get my meaning."

Chuckles rippled across the room.

"Ask Banker Sullivan there. I bet plenty of the higher bred folk in town ain't been able to save money, either."

Several guests' cheeks turned red.

"That's not said to belittle anyone." Sincerity echoed in Aly's apology. "It just goes to show you everybody has hard times. *Everybody.* And I don't know a man or woman alive who wouldn't be grateful to a community that offered them a place to repair their hard luck." Aly's eyes focused directly on Elmertha. "Maybe by giving a little, you'll get back more."

"Giving *in* is what you suggest." Elmertha attempted too outstare Aly, but lost. She smiled indulgently. "I realize that since Prickly Bend is not my home, *my* opinion should have no real influence."

The woman's digging her spurs into me, Aly realized, reminding the guests that she was an outsider as well.

"But I would be remiss if I did not encourage you to consider how other communities have risen from impoverishment to become thriving townships."

"We value your educated opinion, sister." Madeline dabbed her lips with a napkin. "And, I might add, particularly since you've expressed an interest in building a branch of your school here."

Approval echoed through the room. "What are your plans, Miss Bartholomew?" The possibility of profit gleamed in the banker's eyes.

"How much space will you need?" The landlady of the boardinghouse sat up straighter. "My house may just be what you're looking for—plenty of bedrooms and a study that could be turned into a classroom. The parlor is huge and the kitchen separate from the main house."

Madeline shook her head. "Sara, dear. We're trying to bring more business in, not replace old ones. We'll need somewhere more than the hotel for people to spend the night while they're determining where they want to live."

"Should I decide to expand my business enterprises to Prickly Bend, I shall have my ladies home *built*." Elmertha looked smugly at Aly and ignored the look of surprise on her sister's face. "Financing one's own enterprise is wonderfully gratifying."

Nick lay down his fork and stood, his jaw set in stone.

"I won't have you sticking your nose in the air at my wife, Elmertha. You forget I knew you when you used to hang in the trees to watch Silas walk by."

Dismayed, Elmertha's hands tented over her bosom. Banker Sullivan coughed, initiating Mrs. Sullivan's study of the guest of honor.

"Don't think for one moment that Aly hasn't earned every penny she's made through her freighting business." Nick glared hard at Jezlynn's aunt. "No one gave her anything."

Aly gently tugged on his sleeve. "Sit down, Nick. She's not saying I came by my money the easy way." Aly waited until he returned to his chair. "Fact is, she's attacking *you*."

Aly looked at the guests, then focused on Elmertha. "You can believe what you want. But let me tell you one thing, Miss Bartholomew. Nick wouldn't hesitate to give me all his earnings and more if I'd asked him to help me. But I didn't ask him. And Nick's not a cheat. He plays the game fair and square and still manages to make his living in a way few others can."

"I did not mean to imply any ill will toward Nicodemus." Elmertha attempted to cool the rising tension. "I merely stated that hard work and its results have allowed me to look for another location to expand my business."

Madeline spoke up. "I think we should have a party. A real one where the whole town is invited. Everyone can reacquaint themselves with my sister and get to know Nick and Alewine better."

Wanting no part of such a gathering, Aly shook her head. "Ain't got—"

"It will be such fun," Madeline insisted, not letting her finish. "In fact, Nick could host it at his place. That would give everyone a reason to bring a housewarming gift." The back of her hand gently pressed her forehead. "I've been remiss in arranging more of a welcome for you." Her hand trembled on its way back to her side. "Unfortunately, I just haven't felt up to it."

Several women commented that they would help as well.

Madeline's dark curls bounced as she swung around to level her emerald gaze on Aly. "I would be happy to finance the party, if you approve"

Wonder what you'd say if you knew I could buy your home ten times over? Aly didn't flaunt her money to anyone, but with Madeline she just might make an exception. The woman was issuing a challenge, and Aly refused to back off. Which would be worse, leaving Nick to Madeline's connivings or trying to match the vixen's hospitality and cooking skills?

A party would take time and trouble. Aly knew she would have to cook a heck of a lot better than she'd done so far. Folks usually wanted something out of the ordinary when they paid a call at somebody else's supper table. Maybe she could fire up the kettles outside and cook over a spit like she did when she was hauling freight. Aly couldn't remember a time she'd ever had to bury anything she'd cooked on the trail.

Unwilling to let Madeline think she'd intimidated her, Aly accepted the challenge. "On one condition."

She waited for Madeline to quit smiling. Connie flashed Aly an "I'll help you" expression. "Keep your money and plan to sit back and enjoy yourself. I'm the hostess for the party, not you."

Silence ensued as the two women took measure of each other.

After a few moments, Nick rose again. "If you'll excuse us? My family and I will be leaving a bit earlier than expected. We'll have a lot of planning to do between now and Sunday. Let's set the time for two o'clock. That will allow everyone to chat after church, then ride out to our place. The afternoon should be enough time to enjoy each other's company and still get home before dark." He offered a hand to his wife and daughter. "Aly, Jez, shall we be off?"

After laying down her napkin, Aly placed one hand in his. "You set a fine table, Madeline. I'll do my best to see you enjoy mine. Elmertha, welcome to Prickly Bend."

Elmertha offered a fake smile and an even phonier reply. "I'll look forward to sharing another meal with you, Mrs. Turner."

"Yeah, it was good food, Mama." Jezlynn frowned at her aunt. "Hope we don't keep you away from Boston too long."

A giggle rose within Aly, but she managed to contain it.

"Shall I have your team brought around?" Madeline rang a small handbell near her glass.

"No need to trouble your servant." Nick waved her away. "Aly, I suspect, is in the mood for handling some reins tonight."

Minutes later, they headed home. Grateful that Nick understood how much she needed to leave the party and do something totally commonplace, she eyed the gambler with new affection. He was beginning to read her like a day-old trail, picking up on what contented her.

Aly glanced back at Jezlynn to make sure she was comfortable. The child lay on the wagon bed, wrapped in quilts to ease the bounce of the roadway. Aly swung back around and flashed Nick a look of appreciation. "Thanks for going when you did. I don't think I could've taken one more word of snobbery from those two."

"I couldn't either, Chick, but something's bothering me about what they said."

Alewine concentrated on the road again. The moon lit the trail well, and the lanterns gave her a good view of the immediate countryside. But dark shadows still loomed in the distance. She rethought what had been said and wondered what had put him in such a stew. "They didn't say anything worth fretting about."

Nick's sigh sounded years-deep. "That's where you're wrong, Chick. They're right about one thing. I

217

can't possibly take care of you and Jez on what I earn at the poker table. It wouldn't be fair to ask you to live on something as unpredictable as my winnings."

"I have a little money put back." Aly said it before she'd really thought how it might sound to him. Then she realized she'd insinuated the very thing Elmertha implied. "What I mean is, most folks expect us to share our money, them not knowing we ain't married."

Nick checked on his daughter. "She's asleep. I figured she would be before we got home. It's been quite a day." Nick faced the front again and continued the conversation they'd been having. "I appreciate your offer, Chick, but I have to find a way to take care of the two of you. I won't be satisfied till I do. Gambling's a way I lived my life before. Isolating myself seemed the best way to put my past behind me and learn to read a crowd."

"You aren't happy with who you are?" Aly wasn't sure why she was surprised by that fact. Maybe because he'd never complained about his choices or mentioned what else he'd like to do. In light of the conversation at tonight's supper table, Aly saw the irony of it all. While she'd defended everyone's right to be who they are, Nick wanted to be something other than himself.

"That's not what I'm saying. I just want to be more of what you and Jez need. I can't see gambling as a permanent means to achieve that. One of these days, I'm going to run up against someone with a better game. Or, more than likely, someone who accuses me of cheating and is fast with a gun."

"Why won't you carry a gun, Nick?" Aly hoped his talkative mood would finally open up his past a little more for her. She wanted to know everything about the man she loved.

"Long story, best saved for another day."

His eyes slanted to Jezlynn, making Aly understand that it was not a story he wanted told in front of his daughter.

"Just give me your top effort, Nick. That's all Jez and me ask. You can be a gambler, a preacher, a side-walk-sweeper for all we care. Whatever you are, we'll stick by you."

"I know that. That's why it's got to be the best life I can provide for you. You two deserve all a man can offer."

I love you. Aly's heart beat the words strongly, but she held them back. Something inside her wanted Nick to say he loved her, too. Not just promise to provide for her well. She could do that on her own. She didn't need him for that reason.

The envelopes seemed to burn a hole in her pocket, reminding her that she'd confessed once again to loving him. "I . . . uh . . . opened the box Ophelia gave me before we left home. There were two envelopes in it, one for me and the other for you. If you'll hold the reins a minute, I'll dig yours out. You can read it, if you like."

"A letter?" Nick grabbed the reins. "There may not be enough light to read by."

Quickly checking her left pocket, she grabbed the envelopes. Aly squinted and tried to decipher the name on each. In frustration, she handed him both. "Here, I can't see well enough to tell which is which."

Nick took the missives and returned the reins. "And I'm letting you drive? When we go to town next time, I want you to check in with the doctor for some spectacles."

"No need." Aly shook her head. "I've already got some. Back in Valiant."

Nick's laughter didn't last long. He selected one of the envelopes and handed the other back to Aly. "Is your heart still set on returning to Valiant so soon?"

219

Chapter Twenty-one

A sudden gust of chilly wind whipped around the corral and tugged at Aly's skirts, flickering the flame in the lantern she held. She shivered and quickly shooed the colt inside the barn. Though she always watched the weather with a healthy dose of respect, they had not lived in Arizona long enough for her to be sure how quickly it might turn bad. Maybe getting to know Prickly Bend better was all that had spurred Nick's earlier question about returning to Valiant. Had he decided to make Arizona his home again rather than Texas?

Aly had dismissed the question by saying she intended to stay as long as he needed her. When he said nothing more for the rest of the ride, then offered to carry Jezlynn inside the house while she put away the horses, Aly thought she had misread his meaning and made more of the question than she should have.

The colt found its mother, and Aly opened the

stall's gate to let him pass through. All the necessary tasks were now completed. The time had come to read Ophelia's letter.

Hanging the lantern high on a peg to shed more light, Aly sat on a bale of hay. She retrieved the letter from her pocket and unfolded the paper. The familiar handwriting sent a wave of homesickness through her.

A glance in the direction of the house only deepened the homesickness, knowing that Nick and Jezlynn would be her family only for a while longer. The days were passing swiftly. Tears stung Aly's eyes as she wondered if Nick's question meant he didn't believe they'd convinced Madeline enough to let him have total custody. Elmertha's arrival seemed to confirm the need for a better plan.

The lantern light flickered again, wind rattling the paper in Aly's hand. She blinked back the tears and began to read.

Aly,

If you opened this envelope, I assume you have admitted to yourself that you are deeply in love with Nick. Frankly, I hoped that by knowing your own heart you might be more willing to believe what I have done is truly in your best interest.

Apprehension swept through Aly. Ophelia rarely apologized, making sure she was right before she committed to anything. Could the saloon keeper have dealt Nick the better cards, like Aly first suspected— hoping to win the side bets she'd placed?

I couldn't be happier for you, Aly. I knew from the first moment you couldn't throw Nicodemus out of your wagon that he was the man for you.

Your growing friendship only served to convince me more. When Lady Luck shined on Nick with a winning hand, I saw destiny stepping in to bring you together. I just gave her a little help. (No, I did not rig the cards.) But I do ask your forgiveness and understanding for what I did do.

I am a woman in love with a man who does not trust his heart well enough to trust in love. I couldn't watch you travel that same road, my friend. The ceremony was real. You are truly Mrs. Nicodemus Turner. If I'm guilty of anything, it's that I've played matchmaker to two stubbornheaded mules who don't have enough sense to know they love each other.

Aly's heart raced like a thoroughbred's heading for the finish line. Elation pumped in her bloodstream. "I'm really Mrs. Nick Turner." She now knew what it felt like to be a woman, to be the mother of the orneriest, yet most precious child God had ever put on this earth, and to be desperately in love with her husband. Her dreams had never seemed more real.

"Yeehawww!" Aly shouted, throwing her hands into the air and rocking backward. When she nearly slid off the bale, she instantly planted her heels on the floor and steadied herself. The horses protested, whinnying.

"Easy now, I didn't mean to raise a ruckus." She had to get a handle on herself and make sure this wasn't just some practical joke Ophelia had played on her. Aly continued reading.

I'm sure you've noticed there is an envelope for Nick. Please see that he receives it . . . unopened. Write and let me know whether to congratulate you or to take on a bodyguard for protection when you return to town. Either way, I will never regret my actions. You deserve happiness.

Ophelia

"That's it?" Aly flipped the page to see if more had been written. Nothing. All she got was a *"by the way, you're really hitched and hand this letter to Nick?"* What kind of enough was that?

Questions rampaged through Aly's mind. Had Ophelia told Nick the same thing? If so, Nick must not have read the letter yet, or he'd be out here having his say.

Elation turned instantly to dread. What if Ophelia expected *her* to tell him, and Nick's letter said something else? A vile possibility darkened Aly's thoughts. Suddenly, her stomach cramped as if someone had thrown a punch at her. What if Nick *knew* the truth? Would he think she and Ophelia had deliberately set him up?

Recalling the events of her last day back home, Aly groaned. The conversation she and Ophelia had shared at the bar could have *looked* as if they'd been scheming against him.

Aly promised herself that when the time came to return to Valiant and end the charade, she would make things easy for Nick. She knew just how big a mistake marrying for the wrong reasons could be, because she'd watched her mother maneuver her stepfather into marriage. The two were never happy again. Aly had suffered the calamity of a home without devotion. She would settle for nothing less than love.

Aly read the note one more time to make sure she hadn't missed anything, then placed it back in her pocket. "I should be happy," she told the horses. "I'm in love with my husband and now I'm really married to him. So why do I feel so mixed up?"

All of a sudden, the letter's true impact hit Aly hard. No longer did she have to dream of what she wanted. It was there, within her reach.

Faced with the reality, Aly felt her brain and her heart compete in a taffy pull. Her heart said, *Yes, this is all you've dreamed of.* Her brain countered with, *But is this what you really want?*

Aly attemped to decipher the battle raging within. She'd been a successful businesswoman. She'd made a life on her own without anyone's help. She didn't need to be a wife to be proud of herself. So why then did the reality of being truly married scare the heck out of her?

"Because you got what you wanted, fool." Aly voiced the fear aloud. "Like the old saying goes, be careful what you wish for, you might get it."

What was she afraid of—more burnt meals? Having to be accountable to someone? Learning how to love someone as deeply as she'd dreamed of being loved? It was all those things and more. Being Nick's wife meant she could never return to their former friendship unchanged. *Could* she be all Nick wanted and still remain the woman she'd worked hard to become?

"You better hope you have to worry about it," Aly voiced her qualms aloud. She needed two routes to travel in case he was ready to send her back on the next stage.

Lord, but it was harder to make up her mind what to do since she'd become female!

The thought made Aly giggle. She laughed from the pure joy of having a friend like Ophelia who obviously knew her better than she knew herself. She laughed from the joy of being so in love, she didn't make a lick of sense. She laughed almost hysterically, realizing Nick had finally played the biggest joke of all on her. Her fate now rested in his hands. Would he hold the hand Ophelia dealt them and hope for a win, or would he fold and take a loss?

This wasn't a bluff. This was her happiness, the rest of her life, her dreams, stampeding here. Aly couldn't sit back and give circumstances their rein. If she did nothing, she'd be left for dead. Joining the stampede and turning the bull that led the death rush was the only answer. But how could she convince Nick to keep her as his wife?

Maybe she ought to welcome Clay Driscoll's visit instead of turning him away. Maybe the gambler would stake his shaky claim a little stronger.

If things didn't work out, there was always the option of divorce. Not that she ever wanted to separate herself completely from Nick. She just didn't know if she had enough in her to be the best wife and mother for Nick and Jez. Anybody could playact the part, but she wanted to be really good at it.

Aly had always thought she'd ride that trail slow and pick her way through until she felt comfortable with the scenery. But Lady Luck and Ophelia Finck had sent her galloping hellbent for leather into her future. It was time to choose which fork in the road to take.

It doesn't have to be done tonight, Aly reminded herself. Best to wait and see how Nick felt about the news.

By the time he won custody, Aly promised to make a decision about taking on the responsibilities that went along with her dreams. It had been easy all these years blaming her mother for being less than loving. Though Aly would never forget her mother's lack of affection, she might finally be able to forgive the woman. Maybe being somebody's wife and mother required something that had somehow been left out of her own mother's making. Maybe, too, the desire to be those things just wasn't enough.

A noise behind her captured Aly's attention. She swung around to find Nick leaning against the door-jamb, his arms crossed. When he didn't say anything for a minute but kept studying her, Aly smoothed back the wisps of curls that brushed her cheeks. "Whatcha looking at me like that for?"

"You continue to amaze me, Chick."

"About what?" Aly tried to appear unaffected by his tone. The truth was, it thrilled her and made her want to hear more. Who did she think she was fooling? She wanted to be his wife, every night for the rest of her life. "You've seen me take care of a team before."

Nick licked a finger and held it out in the wind. "Storm tonight. We'll definitely have some rain and maybe some hail with it." He dried the weather gauge on his pant leg. "Probably nothing worse than the rumble it took to get Jez to go to bed."

He smiled at Aly, an infectious, mischievous smile that shifted the lines on his face and made deep indentations on either side of his mouth.

Aly's heart began to pound violently. How could she ever think of wanting to give up *that*? Nick was all the man she'd ever dreamed of loving, all the friend she hoped to find in a husband.

She leaned back against the stall to steady the rush of desire that engulfed her. Desperately, Aly fought to regain control of her breath and racing pulse, wiping her palms against her skirt. But her blood still ran like fire in her veins, burning for his touch.

"Do you feel like taking a walk, Mrs. Turner?" Nick strolled over and offered his arm.

"Is that all we're gonna do, Mr. Turner?" Aly linked her arm with his.

"For starters." Nick motioned her out of the barn

and into the night. "Depends on the weather."

The hint of rain drifted with the breeze. Aly snuggled closer to him.

"Cold?" He moved away for a moment and took off his coat then draped it around Aly's shoulders. "There, is that better?"

The warmth and scent of his body still lingered in the material's folds. Aly inhaled deeply and nodded. Let him think she shivered from the coming chill. She knew her body trembled because Nick had touched her.

Nick pulled Aly to him, his arms firm around her. Aly closed her eyes and waited for his kiss. When nothing happened, she opened them and realized that he was staring down at her. "W-what are you doing?" she asked in confusion.

"Warming you up, Chick." He smiled again. "Let's dance."

"I'm a little rusty at it." Lord, how long had it been—thirteen, fourteen years since she'd suffered those first attempts at putting one foot in front of the other without tripping? "I was voted the worst dancer in Mrs. Wanamaker's class, you know. None of the boys at the socials wanted to dance with me, anyway. I could beat the tar out of them, and they knew it."

"Well, that still may be the case, but I'll take my chances tonight." Nick chuckled, guiding her through a few steps.

Pleased that she hadn't forgotten the lessons entirely, Aly discovered she could hold her own with Nick. She floated through the steps easily, feeling quick and light on her feet. "Guess I finally shed all that gangliness. I was just a hank of legs and arms at one time, you know. And I didn't have much control over how well they moved."

"You move *perfectly* now, Chick."

Her heart sped up as his mouth·claimed hers, his tongue gently prodding her lips apart. The taste of him proved her undoing. Aly answered his hunger with her own, an unspeakable sweetness engulfing her.

"Nick." His name escaped her lips in a breathless plea. He pressed a trail of kisses down the long column of her throat, murmuring endearments. The warmth of his palm covered her breast and caressed her gently.

"Let me love you. Here. Now."

Rain sprinkled Aly's face. "The rain's here."

"I like you wet, Chick. Remember?"

Yes, she remembered. Every detail of the bath had branded itself into her memory. A warning went off in Aly's head even as her body reacted with urgency to his seduction. Her nipples hardened and thrusted upward at his touch. A warm wave of desire flowed over her, causing her hips to move provocatively against him.

"Please," she said, needing to regain control so she could think clearly. The questions she'd asked herself earlier must be weighed against what she agreed to from now on. But thinking seemed too bewildering at the moment when all she wanted to do was feel.

Aly willed herself to push away from him. "Please, Nick. There's something I have to know first."

Nick let go of her and took a step backward. "What's so important it can't wait?"

Hugging herself to ward off the chill and to shield herself from his passion-filled gaze, Aly mentally nestled deeper into his coat. The warmth was reassuring. "Did you read Ophelia's letter?"

He stared at the house, then back at Aly. "Did *you*?"

"Don't answer my question with a question, Gambler." His evasive reply disturbed Aly. He didn't want to make a commitment until she did, which meant he

228

didn't want to disappoint her, which probably meant he disapproved of Ophelia's actions. "I want a yes or a no."

"Yes, I read it." He stood there, looking like a man bracing himself for a hanging.

"What did it say?"

"What did yours say?"

Aly sighed in exasperation. "Why don't we tell each other at the same time? I think she told us both the same thing, and we're each trying to see how the other one is gonna react. Whatever it is, I'm not going to be angry with you, if that's what you're thinking. If it's something you might be mad at me about, then at least give me a chance to explain."

"Deal." Nick took a deep breath and gently grabbed Aly by her shoulders. "She told me—"

"That we are truly married," Aly said the words in unison with him. *Say you love me*, she pleaded silently.

They stood staring, awaiting the other's reaction. The silence lingered. The rain became a drizzle.

"Well . . ." Nick exhaled a heavy sigh and let his hands drop to his sides. "I don't know what I expected, but I didn't expect silence." His eyes raked her from her damp hair to her sodden hem. "Are you happy about what she did? Or do you plan to skin her when you go home?"

"I think Ophelia had good intentions." He hadn't said he loved her. He hadn't asked her to stay. He obviously considered Valiant *her* home or he wouldn't have asked what she planned to do when she returned to Texas. Misery settled deeply into Aly's bones. She sought safer ground, preferring to talk about Ophelia than themselves. "I don't think we should cull her from the herd, do you?"

"She meant well."

"Meaning well can get in the way of the truth sometimes." Anger at his defense of Ophelia drummed inside Aly. He could show a little irritation at the saloon keeper's interference. After all, he wouldn't be saddled with a real wife if Ophelia had minded her own business and let things be.

"I hope you believe that I didn't know anything about it." Aly disliked the fact that she sounded defensive and wanted to blame Ophelia. The real blame was hers and Nick's, for not loving each other enough to make it real and not just on paper. "I just agreed to help you keep Jezlynn."

Holding up his palms, Nick backed away. "No one says you did. When we return to Valiant, we can explain it to the judge and, under the circumstances, I'm sure he'll grant us a quick annulment." His gaze swept over Aly, the embers of passion little more than a spark. "Then again, I guess it's too late for that. We'll have to get a divorce. That wouldn't stain my name any worse, but it will certainly taint yours. Being a divorced woman, you might even lose some business. We don't have to end the marriage. I don't mind you using my name."

"I don't care what anybody else thinks." She just wanted to know what he thought about it. *Guess I got my answer*, Aly acknowledged begrudgingly. Disappointment coursed through her as she took off his coat and handed it back to him. "Here, I'm getting used to the chill."

Aly knew she was being unfair. She'd said that to hurt him, as she was hurting now. If he didn't love her, wouldn't it be better to end it now, than later, after they'd grown attached and she'd failed him in some way?

The drizzle became a downpour, soaking them to the bone. "Thank you kindly for the coat." Aly took off the ring he'd given her and stared at it sadly. "But you need to take back your name. That oughta be an honor given to the gal who spends the rest of her life with you."

Jezlynn stared at Aly from the mirrored dresser that reflected the child's image. "What's wrong? You look real sad."

"Nothing." Aly dabbed a hanky at the puffiness of her eyes. All this week, Nick had escorted her to their bedroom, pretending that nothing had changed between them. But he did little more than lay beside her until he was certain Jezlynn was no longer awake, then he moved into the sewing room. The rain had come and gone, but Aly had cried herself to sleep each night. Whenever anyone asked her why her eyes were so red, she lied and said they were itchy from standing too near the cookfires.

Surprisingly, her idea to use pits and kettles outside as she would on the trail proved she wasn't a total cull at cooking. She'd taken Connie's advice, seasoning the beef with peppers, cumin, and other spices then letting the meat soak for hours to add more flavor. Aly couldn't believe she had created the tantalizing aromas wafting through the house and backyard. She thought she might even eat some of the food herself.

By preparing the food her own way instead of trying to imitate Madeline, she'd managed the main course pretty well. Connie had convinced her to hire every lady in the Ladies Auxiliary to bake a cake or pie, letting Aly off the hook and giving the women an opportunity to feel neighborly. It would take more than a rangy campfire for Aly to master baking.

"You and Papa have been fighting, haven't ya?"

Aly closed the drawer and moved behind Jezlynn. She smiled, not wanting the child to worry about the security of her home. "All husbands and wives argue

231

sometimes. We're two different folks, so we ain't gonna see eye-to-eye on everything."

"Are you gonna mess up things today so he'll look bad?" The child swung around to frown at Aly. "I heard mama say that you'll probably make so many mistakes, you'll ruin my papa's chances. You wouldn't do that, would you, Aly?"

Gently guiding Jez to face the mirror, Aly started to brush Jezlynn's thick, dark curls. The child's hair had grown out from its "runaway cut" and curled softly around her cherubic face. "I can't say I won't make a mistake or two, but I've tried my dang best not to let that happen."

Easily appeased, Jezlynn glanced at Aly's hairdo. "Are you gonna wear your hair like mine?"

Glad for the less disturbing question, Aly nodded. "Connie loaned me some fancy hair bobs to pin it up in a kind of bun. Or, she said I could gather it all at the top of my head and make a bouquet of curls. Or, I could put it up in a bonnet since I'd be hosting outdoors. She called them some kind of pins, but I forget. I tried all three ways. Made me look older, more refined, I'd guess you'd say. And the hair bobs hurt like sin!"

Aly eyed herself critically in the mirror, watching how her hair cascaded down her back. She had pulled the hair away from her temples and tied the strands with a ribbon at her crown. "Refined is the last thing I am, and I ain't scalping myself for no bunch of biddies who judge a body by how she wears her hair."

"Papa doesn't like your hair down."

"He told you so?"

"He didn't have to. He looks real mad every time he catches Mr. Driscoll watching you. I think Papa wishes you looked older and uglier."

Nick? So jealous that his daughter noticed? Isn't that what Aly had hoped for when she'd invited Driscoll to pay a call every day?

Pride kept her from confronting Nick, asking him outright if he loved her. Leave she would, if he never said the words. It didn't matter that she would love him forever or that she would never share with another man what she'd shared with him. Aly refused to beg for acceptance, and she would never burden him with a responsibility he didn't want. She loved him too much for that.

On one hand, his silence disappointed her. On the other hand, she welcomed the delay. As the days passed and Nick refused to make his feelings known, Aly gathered the courage to tell him and her dreams good-bye. Maybe being a lady freighter had some purpose higher than those held in her dreams.

"He thinks you like Mr. Driscoll," Jez suggested.

"If your father says anything about Driscoll, be sure and let me know."

"Okay." Jezlynn shrugged. "All he said so far is that the man won't know what hit him." She got down from the bench in front of the dresser and hurried to the door. "Is Papa planning on hitting Mr. Driscoll?"

The child loved drama. Aly wanted to be sure she wasn't making this up. "When exactly did your father say that?"

"Remember when we came home from Mama's? After the party for Aunt Elmertha?"

Aly nodded.

"Well, Papa carried me into bed while you brushed down the horses. I asked him how come *he* didn't do it, but he said you got real quiet on the way home, so you probably needed some alone time. He knows how much you like the horses, so he said it was his turn to tuck me in. I know you two were fighting, even though you didn't yell at each other."

"We weren't fighting," she assured the child. "I just had something to work out in my head and needed a little time to think."

"Papa said that, too, after he read that letter. Then he said the man won't know what hit him."

Ophelia's letter? Nick never mentioned Ophelia had said anything more than what she'd told Aly.

"Do you know what he did with the letter?" Aly regretted the question the moment she asked it, worried that Jez might let her curiosity slip.

"Uh-uh. Except I know it ain't in your box no more." Alarm swept across Jezlynn's face. "I mean, I don't think he—"

"How did you know where I kept it?" Aly knew the answer before she asked. "You've opened the box, haven't you?"

Jezlynn's chin dipped against her chest.

After the incident with the blacksmith, Aly anticipated another lie from Jezlynn, but the child surprised her.

"I just wanted to see if I could get it open real quiet-like," Jez admitted. "I wanted to see if you could tell I was there."

"Did you use my key?" Aly tried to recall the last time she'd taken it off her neck and couldn't. Jezlynn had left no trail of any sort. The child was good at her would-be craft. Too good.

Jezlynn nodded. "That was the best part—making sure I didn't wake you up."

"Well, it seems I've lost some of my edge." Did Nick know his daughter spied on them during the night and practiced her skills at robbing? "Is there anything else I should know . . . like whether you've read

234

the letters or not?"

"I was real careful and didn't touch them with no dirty hands."

"Do you know what they say?"

"I'm just six. I don't know how to read nothing but printing."

The child had a point, or she was smart enough to save her skin. Grateful for the relief of tension, Aly grinned. "What happened to 'almost seven'?"

"That kind of gets in the way when I'm in trouble."

The sound of more people entering the house echoed up the stairs. Aly needed to hurry. Connie had been forced to chase her away from the cookfires outside long enough to help Jezlynn and herself get dressed. Aly had seen to every detail, checking everything twice, three times. "So you have no idea what either of the letters said?"

"I only had time to open one. Papa's. Then she caught me."

"She—meaning Connie?"

Jez seemed to gauge her answer before finally nodding. "She started to read it, too, then didn't. When she put it back in the box, she made me promise not to tell anyone and said she wouldn't tell, either. I said okay since I would've been telling on me, too."

"I think it's time we take ourselves to a party, don't you?" Aly offered a hand to Jezlynn. "Ready?"

Jezlynn tentatively reached out and threaded her fingers through Aly's. "I'm not in trouble?"

"Can't blame you, or Connie for that matter, for being curious. But next time you ask. I always give one warning. The second time, I won't be so nice about it. That means assigning you chores or taking away a privilege." Aly gathered her skirts so her boots wouldn't accidentally snag the hem when she headed downstairs. "Families don't hide things from each other, and they forgive each other for mistakes—as long as they really are mistakes."

"Is Mrs. Calhoun your family?"

"Why do you ask?" When they reached the lower floor, Aly spotted the bookkeeper moving through the crowd toward the stairs.

" 'Cause you look like you're fixing to tear her head off. Are you gonna give her one warning?"

"Depends on just how much of the letter she read before she decided she'd best put it back."

Chapter Twenty-two

The meal had been quite a success. Earlier food-laden tables covered in checkered cloths now held empty plates and even emptier platters and bowls. The delicious aroma of spices Aly had used to flavor the beef still lingered in the air. Everyone had divided into groups.

The men gathered with Nick at a far table, smoking cigars and sipping the brandy he'd bought just for the occasion. Jez played with the children on the grassy hill under the shade of the pinon trees. Aly and the other ladies chatted at the table stationed as far away from the smoke as possible. Driscoll and Mr. Quackenbush joined them because of their tendency to cough when around smoke.

Nick had watched Aly hold her own today and took special pride in the fact that Madeline could not find fault with his wife's effort. A hoot of laughter urged him to look in the ladies' direction, and he saw Aly nearly falling out of her chair. Nick smiled, loving the way she laughed with everything that was in her. No-Holding-Back Aly is what he should call his bride. No holding back with her friendship. With her joy of life. With her lovemaking.

Nick ached to be near her . . . to touch her. Their distance the past few days ate him up inside. The nights were living hell. He couldn't think, couldn't sleep. He didn't want to eat, and that had nothing to do with Aly's cooking. He'd dunked himself at least a dozen times in the creek to cool off his want of her. But reason demanded that he not let her know his true feelings. He couldn't tell her how much he loved her. Not yet. Not when doing so might sign her death warrant.

The fact that she didn't seem all that enthused about their marriage being real had plagued him. He'd been certain she loved him, but her hesitation forced him to weigh the facts again, but Nick didn't want to show any sign of devotion until the other committed equally. They were friends too much to obligate each other if the feelings weren't mutual.

Banker Sullivan chuckled, puffing on his cigar. "Are you going to keep staring at your wife or join in our discussion?" He shared a glance with the other men sitting at the table. "I think, young Turner, there is too much newlywed to want to talk business today."

Nick started to deny the friendly taunt, but instead he rose from the bench and offered a half-bow. "You're right, Silas. I beg your pardon, but if you had *her*"—he motioned to Aly—"to spend the day with, would you want to sit around with a bunch of men while they ignore everything you have to say?"

"We've listened to you, Turner," Daniel Tyler replied for everyone. "We just don't agree with you, that's all. We're just minding our business the best way we know how."

"My point exactly. It's *your* business. You've made it clear that you prefer it not to be mine." Nick held up his palms and shrugged. "To be fair, it's probably because you think I'm not staying around for long so I shouldn't have a voice in the matter. And to be truthful, I'm not sure that I am, unless I can discover what kind of business I would bring here. I see no point in running a race without a leg to stand on. So, I'll bid you good afternoon and take my insignificant opinion over to join the ladies."

He reached for his hat, which lay on the bench beside him. "When you gents figure out what you want to do, I'd appreciate somebody passing along the decision to me. Despite what you all believe, I am interested in the outcome." Nick settled it on his head, then thumbed up the brim. "Gentlemen, I hope you've enjoyed yourselves today. My bride assures me there is plenty more brandy after those bottles are finished."

Nick noticed Aly's glass was near empty. He stopped halfway down the line of tables to pour a fresh glass of sarsaparilla for her. As he approached the group with the drink, he frowned at the words he overheard.

"But if you're really a married woman now," Clay Driscoll insisted, "shouldn't you be at home, cooking and cleaning and taking care of Jezlynn? You ought to sell your freighting business and spend more time at home with your man. If you do that, why not sell it to me? I know Valiant well, and"—Driscoll smiled at all the ladies—"I like to think I'm finding a second home here. Neither branch would suffer."

"What does he mean *if* you're a married woman?" Curiosity filled Ursilla Quackenbush's face.

Others shared Ursilla's curiosity.

Aly shooed away their concern. "Oh, Driscoll here thinks me and Nick didn't really get married back in

Valiant. He figures we're trying to pull some kind of trick on the town so folks would take bets on whether our hitching could last longer than a few months. Heck, if I was gonna do that, I'd have taken outside bets of my own, 'cause I'd have known how the race ended." She laughed. "But we're about as married as two porcupines can be. The stickers get in the way sometimes, but we still manage to find a way to rub each other the right way."

Ursilla gasped.

No! Nick silently yelled. *Don't be so convincing. You're signing your death warrant with Driscoll.* Nick pretended to laugh so hard he nearly spilled the sarsaparilla. After setting the glass down next to Aly's empty one, Nick stuck one leg, then two over the bench to exact a seat between her and Driscoll. "Pardon me, Clay. Hope you don't mind scooting over." Nick gave Aly a gentle kiss on the cheek, whispering in her ear. "Change the subject . . . now!" For the others' benefit, he added, "Having a good time, Chick?"

Nick wished the rosy hue staining her cheek had resulted from his kiss, but he knew she was boiling mad at his command. He draped his arm around her shoulders and pulled her closer. To her credit, she didn't offer any resistance.

"What brings you to our neck of the woods, husband?" Aly's tone made it clear she didn't care for the interruption.

"Everybody's smoking like a chimney up there." He motioned to the men's table. "I decided Clay and Mr. Quackenbush had the smarter idea." He flashed the other women his sexiest grin on purpose so Driscoll would notice him openly flirting. "How more blessed can a man be than to sit in the company of such beautiful ladies?"

Even Elmertha's face beamed from the compliment.

240

Aly's shoulders stiffened beneath his arm, her back as rigid as a fence post. Nick noticed his wife had focused her attention on Madeline, who sat at the opposite end of the table from Aly. He undraped his arm and deliberately rubbed Aly's thigh to reassure her he felt nothing more than pity for Madeline. No woman would ever compare to Aly and the beauty of her soul.

"You will definitely add a unique voice to the game we were about to play, Nicodemus." Elmertha smiled when everyone turned their attention to her. "It's all the rage back East."

"May I be first?" Ursilla raised her hand.

I wouldn't be so quick to rush into anything Elmertha planned, Nick warned silently. But he couldn't do so aloud without coming across as ungentlemanly.

"I haven't told you what we're playing yet." Elmertha seemed amused by the woman's eagerness.

"That's all right," Ursilla quacked. "I love games of any kind. And I can be quite good at them, if I want to be."

Aly rallied the woman on. "Takes grit to go first, Ursilla. Like cutting a new trail. You're my kind of gal."

Rubbing her gloves together, Ursilla took a deep breath. "All right, let's begin."

A glint in Elmertha's eyes warned Nick he had reason to doubt her playful mood. Madeline's sister was definitely up to no good. Nick had seen that glint a hundred times in his youth and had always regretted the aftermath.

"The game is called Truth or Forfeit." Elmertha lowered her voice so that everyone was forced to lean in closer to hear. She pulled a stack of small pieces of paper from her reticule and passed them to the woman next to her. "Choose one of the numbers, then pass the rest on." She glanced at her sister. "Madeline, did you bring the other set?"

Madeline nodded and set a small purse on the table in front of her. She opened it and left the clasp agape.

"Inside you'll find another set of identical numbers," Elmertha informed. She held up a piece of paper. "I took number one so I could start the game and explain the rules. What I shall do now is pull a number from the purse. Whoever has the chosen number must answer a question asked by the person who drew the number."

Several ladies shifted in their seats.

Elmertha looked pleased. "I assure you it can be both fun and disturbing to participate. When you are asked a question, you can either offer the truth or you must forfeit something."

Ursilla scooted back. "I'd rather not go first then."

Dipping her fingers into the purse, Elmertha pulled out a piece of paper and unfolded it. "Number five."

"I have it!" Connie clasped her hands in front of her, squared her shoulders, and tilted her chin defiantly. "Ask me anything. I am an open book."

Everyone appreciated her playfulness and daring. The ladies relaxed and watched with interest. Elmertha looked displeased that she'd drawn Connie's name.

"Let's see. What shall I ask?"

Nick knew Elmertha deliberately pondered the question to regain the crowd's attention.

Elmertha stared down her nose at the bookkeeper. "How many *legal* husbands have you had, Mrs. Calhoun? What shall it be—truth or forfeit?"

Surprise registered on the crowd's faces. Nick suspected it was just the reaction Elmertha intended.

"Too easy a question, senorita," Connie stressed the

fact that Elmertha had never married, then spread one hand in front of her. "Truth *and* forfeit. I lost one for each finger of this hand." She then curled the fingers under and gave a thumbs-up sign. "But I am looking to get another one under my thumb soon."

Nick laughed along with everyone else.

"Now *you* must choose a number and ask a question." Elmertha smiled reluctantly while her fingers shredded Connie's number into tiny pieces.

Connie chose. "Dos . . . two."

Clay Driscoll shifted in his seat. "I've got it."

"There are two parts to my question, senor. First, why do you try to court Alewine, despite the fact that you know she is already married? Second, do you ask so much about her business because you want it for yourself? Truth or forfeit?"

Shut up, Connie. Aly doesn't know of the threat. Nick had to stop the bookkeeper from saying more. *How did you find out about Driscoll?* "Perhaps those questions are best left for Aly and I to ask him . . . at another time."

Aly shirked off Nick's words and glared at Clay. "I'd like the answer now, Driscoll. And keep it in mind, I've known you long enough to know when you lie to serve your purpose."

"Forfeit."

"I thought so." Disgust hardened Aly's expression.

The man feigned indignation. "But let me say this one thing so the ladies will understand why I didn't choose to tell the truth. First, no matter what I may say, you've implied you would think it is a lie. So why say it? Second, she asked two questions. That means two truths. I'd rather take one forfeit. Third, I came here because I had heard about the need for new business. The town elders do have notices in newspapers from Arizona to the East Coast, do they not?"

Elmertha looked disdainfully at Connie. "Of course they do. I've seen them myself in Boston."

"Then why do you pursue the affections of a woman who is already married, senor, unless of course you believe she is not? And if she is not, you wish to persuade her to turn over her business before it becomes the property of whomever she marries."

Driscoll glared at his accusers. "What's your number, Alewine?"

"Thirteen. Why?"

He dug through the purse and unfolded papers until he found what he was searching for. "Thirteen." He held up the number. "Are you or are you not really married to Nicodemus Turner?"

"Don't answer that, Chick." Nick pressed his hand over the wedding band he'd given her.

"Why not?" Elmertha insisted. "I would certainly like to know that answer."

"You can't just take it upon yourself to choose the number you want, Driscoll. You have to play the game just like everybody else. But you like cheating, don't you?" Nick raised his hand to thump the man's chest with his forefinger, uttering a low warning. "If you try to harm one—"

Aly pushed Nick down, making him sit so she could meet Driscoll eye-to-eye. "I can fight my own battles, husband." Her gaze met every eye staring back at her in curiosity. "Truth. He really is my husband. I've got a preacher and a friend back home to prove it." She shook a warning finger at Driscoll. "Let me make one thing clear, mister . . ."

Nick sat rigidly between them, battling his urge to knock the man's teeth down his throat and throw a rope around Aly to protect her from herself.

"I don't scare." Aly motioned to her dress. "I may look a little softer than you've seen me before. But make no mistake, I can be hard as tack and mean as a rattlesnake if I haveta. You come after me or my business, and you'll wish to God you'd never seen me. Understand?"

"I thought we were friends." Driscoll looked genuinely upset.

Either that, Nick decided, or he was one hell of an actor. Was Ophelia right about the man? The words she'd written in her letter rushed through Nick's mind.

My guess is that whoever follows you to Prickly Bend is probably the man who has been causing trouble for Aly's business and threatening to cut up my girls. Be very careful about letting him know the real status of your marriage.

The follower may even resort to visiting Aly a lot in the hopes of winning her away from you. As her husband, he would instantly gain control of her business. I fear for Aly's life if he ever discovers she is truly wed and that option is no longer available. I know you love her. You know you love her. Now you must protect Aly from herself. She may have become a wife, but she still thinks like a bullbuster when she feels threatened.

I'll leave it to your discretion as to when you should tell Aly.

"We ain't ever been friends, Driscoll," Aly's lips stretched into a grim line. "There's no chance we ever could be if I find out there's one lick of truth to what Connie asked."

Driscoll thumbed up his hat. "I think it's best I leave, Mrs. Turner. Thank you for the lovely meal." The businessman stepped over the bench to the other side and offered his hand. "Nicodemus, it was a pleasure."

Nick refused to shake it.

"Ladies." Driscoll bowed. "Another day perhaps."

"You cannot leave yet, senor."

Connie's command captured everyone's attention. "You still owe a forfeit."

Driscoll halted. "Name it."

Connie glanced at Aly, then Nick. "You must not step foot in Nicodemus's home or Alewine's freighting office for the remainder of their stay in Prickly Bend."

The man's set jaw and his fiery glare could have burned Connie to cinders, but Driscoll finally nodded. "Done."

As he walked away, Madeline cleared her throat and stood. "Really, was it necessary to chase him away? After all, there is no proof that he's guilty of anything Mrs. Calhoun implied. I should think it being Sunday, we could offer more Christian charity. After all, it is only a game."

"Sit down, Madeline." Aly frowned. "If he's guilty, it's far from being a game."

"Since it's no longer a game, I do have a question I would very much like answered." Elmertha's gaze met Nick's. "From Mr. Turner. Is it true that you want guardianship over my niece so that you may gain control of the enormous trust fund left to her? If so, then are you not guilty of the same villainy of which you blame Mr. Driscoll?"

Fury swept through Nick. He pounded the table with one fist, shaking the beverage glasses. "Truth? Hell no, I'm not guilty of such nonsense. I didn't know anything about a trust fund."

Elmertha sneered. "It seems odd that a man who makes his living swindling other men out of their earnings doesn't know of his own daughter's inheritance. My mother and father's will states plainly that Jezlynn's guardian will control the fund until her sixteenth birthday, whereupon the guardian will be given a handsome stipend for the remainder of his or her life. Just as they've given me."

"I won't have you tarnishing my husband's good name, Elmertha." Aly met the gaze of every person at the table. "You came here to take Jezlynn back with you. A body could ask if those are *your* intentions after Madeline's gone and doesn't have control of it anymore. In fact, it seems to me you might think you have a right to that money, what with your parents leaving it to a grandchild instead of their own daughters."

"Madeline." Elmertha stood. "We shall leave now. I'll not stand here and suffer such accusations from such an uninformed source."

"Watch what you say, *senorita*." Consuela moved closer, looming over Elmertha's chair.

Elmertha scooted back and took two steps to the opposite side, nearly stumbling when she bumped the person who had been sitting to her right.

Nick noted that Aly wasn't looking at either of the women. Instead, she was staring at Jezlynn. He sensed Aly's regret, knowing that this quarrel with Madeline's sister would send his custody battle into a retreat. He couldn't let Elmertha take Jez from him. He and Aly loved her far too much to let her go.

"She has a right to be suspicious, Chick." Nick cleared his throat. "Stay, Elmertha. I know your intentions are to protect Jezlynn the best way you know how. I find no blame there, but I demand that you refrain from voicing your opinions about my wife."

Elmertha glared at Connie. Connie then glanced at Aly who, in turn, shrugged. The bookkeeper returned to her seat. Elmertha took up her position next to Madeline. "Very well," she said haughtily, her pointy chin rising in indignation. "I suppose I could have waited until another time to voice my suspicions."

"What? And miss an opportunity to plant a bad seed in everybody's head about Nick?" Aly left the table.

"He did that to himself a long time ago." Elmertha's voice echoed with criticism. "Seven years ago, to be exact."

Aly rushed toward her. The woman held up her hands to ward off the attack. Madeline put her arms around her sister to show a united front.

Aly stopped in front of the sisters, fists rounding on her hips as she braced in a warrior's stance. "You'll wish all I intend to do is hit you. I've got more in store for you than flattening your pointy nose. And Madeline, just try taking that young'un away from Nick or fouling his good name, I'll dig up every bone the two of you've buried and gnaw it to the marrow. Ask yourselves, ladies, what you don't want these fine folks to know. Madeline, ask yourself what secret you'd rather go to your grave with you. That's the one I'm gonna dig up."

Madeline paled considerably.

The party broke up as the weather turned cold. A few people offered to stay and clean, but Aly insisted they were guests and she would accept no one's help. She, Nick, and Jez walked their guests to the buggies that would carry them back home. Nick's arm draped around Aly, while one of hers curled around his waist and the other gently pressed Jez against her left hip.

Aly sighed with contentment. She had actually survived her first party and hadn't made a fool of herself. With the food, at least. Now, the the three of them stood here together, presenting a comfortable family front.

Moisture welled in her eyes. Aly couldn't decide if she wanted to cry because she was so happy or if she mourned the moments like this she might never experience again.

As the guests bid the Turners good-bye, Banker Sullivan doffed his hat to his hosts. "Mighty fine cooking, Mrs. Turner. The men and I were just saying you have a fine flair with a campfire. Using mesquite to smoke the beef added just the right flavor to the meat."

"I can't take all the credit. Connie told me what grew best around here. So I just put it all together." Aly nodded at Connie, who had accepted a ride from the Sullivans so Nick wouldn't have to take her home.

Aly had asked her friend about seeing Nick's letter and whether the questions addressed to Driscoll had anything to do with what she'd read. Connie said that once she realized what she held, she'd folded the paper and returned it to the envelope. Her comments about Driscoll were simply her own suspicions.

Feeling the need to reassure her friend she wasn't angry, Aly offered to visit her soon. "Next time I'm in town, maybe you and I can put our heads together and see if we can come up with something even tastier."

Relief lit Connie's eyes. "Si, amiga. I will look forward to it. And soon."

"Will you consider giving a talk at the next Ladies Auxiliary meeting, Mrs. Turner?" The banker's wife looked for approval from several of the other women. Heads immediately bobbed consent. "I'm sure we'd all benefit from learning the proper construction of an outdoor cookfire such as yours."

"And please bring copies of your recipe for the beef," said one of the other ladies as she frowned at her husband. "Morgan told me it tasted better than mine."

The husband's shoulders shrugged. "I'm an honest man."

"That's what saved you, dear." When everyone chuckled, she added, "Your honesty, and the fact that Mrs. Turner's *is* the best I've ever eaten."

Pleased by the compliments and the discovery that she had something worth teaching these ladies, Aly agreed to the request.

"So it's settled." Mrs. Sullivan raised a hand to wave. "We'll be leaving now so you can get on with your dish-washing."

"It's been a pleasure, folks." Silas Sullivan took his wife's hint and led the line of buggies toward Prickly Bend.

Aly waved good-bye to the children and called out, "Y'all come back soon."

Jezlynn frowned. "Why can't Tinnie Pearl spend the night?"

Nick bent down to his daughter's eye level. "Because Aly's had a full week and a huge day today with all the preparations. And it'll take a while to get the kitchen cleaned up. You can invite Tinnie over in a few days if you like, but not tonight. Besides, I don't think she would appreciate having to wash dishes then go straight to bed."

"Wash dishes? She'd have to wash dishes?" Jez looked horrified.

Nick tapped her nose with his finger. "Yes, just like somebody else I know."

Horror turned to obstinance. "I ain't gonna wash no dishes. Why can't we hire a servant?"

Aly would have burst out laughing at Nick's surprised expression if there hadn't been a serious edge to this conversation. When exasperation made him stand erect, Aly turned Jez around to face her. "We ain't gonna hire a servant, Jez. We take care of each other and see to our needs. Sometimes that's fun, and sometimes it's hard work. We're *all* going to do the dishes."

Jez meant to have the last word. "What can *I* do? I'm little. I'll break something. That's why Mama doesn't want me touching nothing at her house."

"A new dish can be bought in the same store you got the last one." Aly knew what Jez was feeling. She'd once lived in a home where she had to watch everything she touched, every move she made, pronunciation of every word. She'd even had to sit on the edge of a bed or chair when company came so that the material covering the furniture would wrinkle less from the weight of her body. Aly despised that house to this day. Despised the life it showcased. Despised the people who kept a little girl from knowing what a true home felt like.

But this isn't about you, Aly reminded herself. *You've got to help Jez deal with her circumstances.* "It's polite to mind your Mama when you're at her house. But when you're here, you remember that everything inside belongs to you and your pa. If it's partly yours, you have the right to touch it. To enjoy it. To wear it out because you use it so much. As long as you don't waste it or forget to show respect for it. Just remember what I told you about Nick's room."

"I gotta ask permission to go in 'cause of his privates."

A giggle erupted in Aly's throat and nearly exited as a honk from her nose. "Not exactly, but close. His priva*cy*. You'll be disturbing his *privacy.*"

Nick grinned at Jez, his good humor returning. "So what will it be, Half-Pint? Wash, rinse, or dry?"

"Wash," Jez declared. "I did pretty good with the goat."

Aly laughed at the memory of the trouble the goat had caused.

"Cleaning dishes is a lot easier. You're gonna do just fine."

The child took off toward the house. When Aly started to follow, Nick gently gripped her shoulder.

"Wait. Don't go in yet, Chick."

The child halted just inside the front doorway. "Y'all coming? I don't gotta do it by myself, do I?"

Nick motioned her to go ahead. "We'll be right there. We've got one thing more to do before we can go in."

Had they forgotten something? Aly waited until Jezlynn went inside, then she turned to look at Nick. His lips lowered to hers.

The kiss sent banners of desire streaming through Aly, her body swaying like a blade of grass buffeted by a gentle wind. When Nick pulled back, she had to clutch his arms to get her balance. "What was that for?"

"To say thank-you." Nick's thumb traced her lower lip as he studied her eyes. "Thank you for making such a perfect day for all of us. For impressing Madeline and showing that we can give Jez a good home. For trying so hard for my sake."

"My pleasure, gambler." Aly wondered if now was the time to put away the anger that had separated them all week. No matter if they dissolved the marriage, they could still be friends. "I've been thinking a lot about what we said the other night."

"Me, too. There's something I've been wanting to tell you . . . about Clay Driscoll."

Curiosity urged Aly to let him speak first. After he had told her what Ophelia's letter said, Aly suspected Nick held something back. Something that needed more time before the telling. What could it be? "The forfeit worked out for the best then, didn't it? He has to keep his word to stay away or it will prove to folks he's a liar. But I don't trust him. I'll round up some men to keep an eye on him."

"Done that, Chick. A couple of days ago. They were in the crowd today."

Aly moved toward the porch as images of her guests raced to mind. "Well, they blended pretty good. I didn't spot them. Then again, I don't know everyone in town yet." Aly halted and studied Nick. "Why'd you wait to tell me?"

He took several strides to catch up with her. "I knew I'd be around to make sure nothing happened."

She met his gaze. "Where you going, Gambler?"

Nick didn't deny her assumption. "To Tucson. A good friend of mine lives there. I'm going to see if he'd like to either set up a business of his own here or partner up with me on what I have in mind. Name's William Ice."

The thought of Nick leaving sickened Aly. It was bad enough that he'd been sleeping in the sewing room. Now he would be miles away. "How long will you be gone?"

"A few days at best, a week at most."

You've lived plenty of your life without this man underfoot. You can survive another sleepless week. Aly didn't want him to see how upset she felt, so she tried to make him think she worried about other things. "Will he be bringing anyone with him? His wife? Children?" She looked at the upstairs window. "How many beds should I get ready?"

"Will's not married. Give him the sewing room while he's here."

She wanted to read the meaning in his eyes. Invitation darkened them to midnight. "That means *you'll* need somewhere else to sleep."

"I know just the place, if there's still room for me."

Aly put her palm on his chest, loving the way his heart beat strong and warm beneath her fingertips. But she had to make him understand what she didn't understand herself. "It ain't that I don't like playing your wife, or even that Ophelia took it on herself to see we got hitched." Aly would never admit this to another soul. "It's just . . . well . . . I ain't sure I got it in me to be a *good* mama to Jez and the kind of wife you deserve. Maybe all I'm good at is eating traildust and hauling freight."

Nick's hands cupped her face. "Aly, Aly, Aly. You have no clue, do you?"

"About what?"

"You are more woman than any man has a right to dream of. And you *proved* yourself both a wife and a mother today. A wife, because of how proud you made me. A mother, because of your talk just now with Jez about being part of a family. You have it in you, Chick, and sometimes it shines so brightly you couldn't possibly hide it."

"It's those other times that I'm scared of, Nick. Maybe someday the *sometimes* will be more frequent than the *other times*. But until they do, I can't see myself as being the best bride for you. And that's what you deserve."

Chapter Twenty-three

Aly settled Jezlynn on the driver's box next to her, then grabbed the reins. She had gathered the supplies needed to last until Nick returned. There was no further reason to delay.

Smiling halfheartedly, she asked, "You sure you took enough hardtack?"

Nick patted the saddlebag cinched to Troublemaker. "Plenty."

"Did you find that flask of—"

"Thanks for thinking of it, Chick. I'll be glad you did when I bunk down on the trail somewhere." His mount bobbed its head. Nick returned Aly's smile, drawing the horse's reins a little tighter. "Looks like Troublemaker's eager to get going."

"Might be tired of her colt." Jezlynn looked at Aly and shrugged. "Most mamas take off somewhere when they get tired of their kids."

Aly didn't know what to say. She liked being

around Jez, knowing what the imp was up to. "All of us have to take care of business now and again, so we have to go away for a while. I bet she told Little Misery that she'd be back." She shared a look with Nick. "Guess you best be on your way. It's a hard ride between here and Tucson."

"I'll be back as soon as possible." Nick reined the horse half-quarter. "It's important that I go or I wouldn't."

"Take your time," Aly lied. "No need to worry about us." Her eyes slanted to Jez so Nick would know she didn't want to say anything more about Driscoll's threat in front of the child. "In the meantime, me and Jez here, we'll take care of each other at the house. Won't we, Skunk Wrangler?"

Tears welled up in the child's eyes. "I don't want you to go, Papa."

Aly's heart swelled with affection at the sight of Nick dismounting to walk to his daughter's side of the wagon. When he opened his arms, Jez catapulted herself into his embrace.

"There, there, sweetie." He patted her back and smoothed her shorn curls. "I'll be back before you know it, and you and Aly won't even know I'm gone."

"Hurry home, Papa." Jezlynn hiccuped with sobs. "If you don't, I'll have to live with Aunt Elmertha. What if there's Indians out there or some outlaws waiting to ambush you?"

"You heard what Banker Sullivan said," Aly reminded. "The Apache are at peace now. And, as far as outlaws are concerned, Nick can hold his own. Besides, do you think he would let anything keep him from returning home to somebody he loves so much?"

The girl's emerald eyes shimmered with tears. "My mama said he loved her and didn't come back."

Nick gently pushed his daughter away so he could

look at her. "I didn't return a long time ago, because I thought staying away would make things easier for your mother. You're too young for me to explain why now, Jez, but I promise I will when you get a little older. Just know that the reason I'm leaving today and the reason I'll return when I said I would is because I love you so much it hurts. There is no way I'm going to lose you to your aunt. You're *my* daughter, not Elmertha's."

The child hugged him more fiercely. "Promise?"

"You better let him go now." Aly blinked away her own tears. "He needs all the daylight he can get."

After Jezlynn took her proper seat again, Nick went around to the back of the wagon, lingered there for a moment, then moved alongside Aly. "Looks like the load's secure, Chick. You sure you'll be okay on your own for a few days? You two can travel with me."

Aly shook her head, studying his beloved face. "You'll ride faster if you travel alone. Don't worry about us. You go on and take care of business. Me and Jez will see the homestead stays sound."

"Kiss me, Chick. I'll miss you."

Her heart felt like she'd spurred the team into a gallop. "Things haven't changed. I still don't know what I want."

"I hope you will by the time I return. I want us to have a serious talk, even if we have to hire Connie to watch Jez while we go fishing. We'll tell each other everything, all right? Won't hold anything back."

"I'll be ready for that, Nick." Aly reached out and cupped his cheek.

Nick stood on his tiptoes to meet Aly's lips. She pressed them against his warm, sweet mouth. A rush of longing swept through her, making it difficult to keep her balance. She'd never swooned in her life, but

Aly knew now what it felt like to be so in love with someone a body could lose all control of her senses.

Aly tasted Nick deeply, hungry for what they once shared, starving for a settlement of the issues that kept them apart. "Come back to me, Nick," she whispered against his lips, then reluctantly pulled away. "*Completely*."

After watching Nick and Troublemaker disappear over the horizon, she commanded the team to turn and head to the business district of town.

"You crying?" Jezlynn asked, sniffling and wiping her eyes with her sleeve.

"No." Aly echoed the sniffle. "Are you?"

"Uh-uh. I ain't no crybaby."

Tenderness welled inside Alewine. "It's okay to cry when somebody you love leaves. It just means you love them so much you don't want to see them go."

"You mean if I cry when my mama dies, she'll think I'll miss her?"

Aly's heart clutched as she glanced at the child, then returned her attention to the roadway ahead. "She'll know you miss her very much."

"That's good. 'Cause I think I'm gonna cry . . . a lot."

Somehow getting caught up in all the circumstances and scheming that went along with gaining custody of the child, Aly had forgotten the most important consideration of all. A little girl was losing her mother—a mother who acted as if Jez was an inconvenience, a mother who criticized everything Jez did, a mother who withheld love from a tiny heart that only wanted to know it mattered enough to belong—but a mother. All of Aly's recent complaints, irritations, frustrations seemed nothing but pure selfishness held up to what Jezlynn faced.

As much as she knew Nick would yell at her for

putting herself in danger of running into Driscoll, Aly asked, "You want to go see Madeline today? We don't have to go straight home. I've just got to stop at the bank for a minute, then we can take her some cookies or whatever else you'd like to give her and your aunt."

"Okay."

The child's quick acceptance surprised Aly. She'd secretly hoped the mention of Elmertha would change Jez's mind, but she had to leave the decision up to Jez.

"Will Mr. Driscoll be there, too?" the child asked softly.

Aly found Jez's concern for Driscoll's whereabouts even more puzzling. What did she know? "He might be. Why?"

"I just wondered, that's all. I don't like him."

"Then I'll ask him to leave while you're there." Stopping the team in front of the Three Rivers Bank, Aly set the brake, secured the reins and helped Jezlynn down. "Here." Aly pulled some money from her pocket. "Go on over to the mercantile and pick out something to take to your mother. Maybe cookies or something. I'll be right out."

Aly watched Jezlynn cross the sandy thoroughfare easily without getting underfoot of any wagon or horse. Lord, but it took a powerful amount out of a woman to make sure her child remained safe. *Her* child? When had she begun to think of Jez as hers?

When you knew it would be impossible ever to give her up. When Elmertha arrived and threatened to take her away. Taking a deep breath, Aly squared her shoulders. Time to make sure Nick proved himself to Madeline.

She grabbed the knob to the bank's stained-glass door and opened it. The scent of leather welcomed Aly into the place where fortunes had been kept and shed.

A bell rang overhead, announcing her presence to

the employees. A familiar voice behind the teller's cage called out, "Si, I will just be a minute."

Consuela finally turned around to greet Aly, a smile edging her lips upward. "Amiga, I did not expect you today." Her gaze swept over Aly. "Is everything all right? Where's Ninita and Nick?"

The bookkeeper's face looked expectant. Aly was glad Connie hadn't read the letter. Their friendship would have changed considerably if she'd satisfied her curiosity. "Jez is over getting cookies and Nick's headed to Tucson. I came to see if you would like to stay with me while he's out of town. We could talk about old times and, in your case, old beaux. Maybe even try a few recipes."

"Gracias, amiga." Anticipation smoothed the lines on Connie's face. "I will come directly after work."

Aly couldn't wait to spend the evening with her friend. "Besides, I've got something really important to tell you about Clay Driscoll." Aly stared at the door that closed off Silas's office from the teller's cage. "Is he here?"

Connie nodded. "But he can't hear. Senor Sullivan is deaf in one ear."

Aly hurriedly told her what Nick had shared about Ophelia's letter. "So you can see how your questions during Truth or Forfeit hit a raw nerve for Driscoll."

Apology echoed in Connie's tone. "I had no idea, just suspicions. But I think you sensed something about him, yourself, amiga. Remember when you warned him to keep away from you the night you arrived? I think you suspected even then."

"You're right. What bothers me is that Nick knew and didn't tell me for a while. I can't reason out why."

"Perhaps he married you to take you to a new place away from Mr. Driscoll's traps? How could he know the man would follow you here?"

Everything fell into place for Aly. Sure, he'd needed someone to play his wife, but he'd wanted a way to protect her from whomever was out to take her business. Nick could handle both problems in Arizona. How better to keep her safe than to make her go with him! Why would he tell her if the threat remained in Texas? Driscoll had paid court for so long, the gambler'd had no reason to suspect the man of wanting to *harm* her. "Nick promised we'd have a long talk when he returned. It looks like I've got some questions of my own that need answering."

A door opened along the polished wooden wall. "Why, Mrs. Turner, what a pleasure to see you." Banker Sullivan rubbed his protruberant belly. "May I say again how delicious the roasted beef was last Sunday? My wife is looking forward to your sharing the recipe."

"I'll see that she gets it." Aly glanced apologetically to Connie. "If you'll excuse me, Con. I've come to visit with Mr. Sullivan on some business today."

"Of course, amiga." Connie resumed her role of employee, eyeing her boss. "Mrs. Turner to see you, sir."

The banker motioned Aly in. She strode past the rotund man and entered a plush room lined with shelves that contained rows of ledgers. A large mahogany desk took up much of the space with a leather chair stationed on either side of the desk. A huge, iron safe filled one corner. A team of draft horses would work up a sweat hauling it.

When Aly started to sit in the chair meant for guests, Sullivan slid it forward. Aly appreciated his manners. "Thank you kindly, Mr. Sullivan."

"Please call me Silas." The banker took a seat and reached for his cigar. He stopped suddenly and glanced at Aly. "Does smoke bother you, ma'am?"

261

Aly opened the silver box sitting on the edge of his desk and took out a cigar. She sniffed the enticing aroma, then held the cigar to her ear, rolling it in her fingers. "Nicely packed," she complimented, then braced it between her teeth. "Gotta match?"

Sila chuckled as he struck a lucifer and waited until she puffed the cigar to life. "You are definitely your own woman, Mrs. Turner. I envy your husband more than you can imagine."

Well, hell, Aly thought. She'd grabbed the stogie without even thinking. Here she was trying to be the picture of wifehood and she'd already backslid. *Oh, well. No use wasting a good smoke.* "My husband is why I've come today."

All the playfulness between them evaporated. Silas looked suddenly ill at ease. "Now, Mrs. Turner . . . Aly. I wanted to give him the loan. I surely did. But he was asking for a lot of money. A lot more than I have here. In order for me to loan that amount, I had to ask him for collateral. All he had was the homestead, and he wouldn't put that up. Said that it belonged to his brother and Jezlynn as much as it did to him. He wasn't willing to risk the loss for their sake."

Silas took a puff from his own cigar and blew out a heavy sigh. Smoke rose above him like heat coming off the desert. "I told him the only other way my superiors back East would approve of such a loan was if someone with enough assets or cash would back him up. I don't know what he told you, but that's the truth. My hands are tied otherwise."

That's why he had to go to Tucson. He had to have a backer or lose whatever deal he was working on. She leaned over and rested her forearms on his desk, silently reading the sincerity in Silas' face. "You didn't deny him because of his so-called deserting Madeline years ago?"

"Frankly, my dear, I never thought him guilty. She married within a month of his leaving. Had Judge Gilmore's inability to sire children not become common gossip, many of us would have never known that Nick was Jezlynn's true father. I personally felt there couldn't have been much between him and Madeline toward the end of his time in Prickly Bend, if she could so easily take up with another man."

"I wish everyone had the same common sense and fairness about 'em." Aly decided she liked Silas the more they visited. She could trust the man with her money. "Just how much money did Nick ask for?"

Aly dug into her pocket and pulled out the telegram she'd sent to Valiant a week or so ago to have some of her money transferred here. She'd meant it to be used to bankroll the new freighting office for a year, but she could send another wire. She scooted the telegram across the desk. "Is that enough to cover it?"

The banker unfolded the missive, then looked up at Aly in surprise. "You are an astonishing woman. Do you honestly have this kind of money?"

"More. Ever heard of Ebenezer Jones in—"

"*The* Ebenezer Milford Jones? Rum magnate of the Carribean? Who hasn't? But he's dead, isn't he?"

"Since 'seventy-two, when I was eight. He was my father. He left me his entire holdings."

Compassion softened Silas' features. "My regrets, my dear. I had no idea you were from that kind of money."

Aly shrugged. "I don't parade around and tell folks, so there's no way for them to know. In fact, Nick doesn't know about it."

"You haven't told him?" Silas looked puzzled. "Then again, I suppose you haven't, or he wouldn't be in here asking for a loan."

Irritation sparked inside Aly, although Silas was

263

simply reasoning out the obvious. "Nick wouldn't take my money if I offered it. Just like I don't squander my pa's. I make my own way, and anything I borrow from the inheritance, I pay back when my business is doing well enough. Nick wouldn't want others thinking he was living off my inheritance, either. Gambler's got too much pride in him for that."

"So why *are* you here, Aly?" Silas glanced at the amount and whistled again. "If people around here knew . . ."

Snatching back the telegram, Aly returned it to her pocket. "That's just it. I don't want nobody but you knowing what I'm fixing to offer. Especially not Nick. Can I trust you to keep it secret?"

Banker Sullivan leaned forward. "Are you going to be his silent backer?"

Approval rushed through her despite her irritation. The man was quick on his thinking trigger. "I'll put up the money with the condition that Nick is never told."

"His plans will bring a lot of commerce to the city. Nicodemus sincerely wants to make amends for his past."

Aly couldn't take the suspense any more. "Just what did my husband do that was so horrible? No one will tell me."

Banker Sullivan shook his head. "And neither will I, Aly. I only heard one side of the story. He hasn't told me his. That's something he's got to tell you himself."

Chapter Twenty-four

"You must go to the sheriff, amiga. Your life may be in danger." Connie held the two spliced ends of the rope that raised the water bucket from the well. "This was deliberately cut, and the other *accidents* make no sense."

Aly studied the rope. Nick had replaced it when they first moved in, not wanting to trust one that had been hanging in the weather for seven years. The corral gate had been left open, the damper closed in the chimney, and a spoke on one of the wagon wheels loosened. Yes, somebody was definitely setting traps around the place.

"I told you, nobody's gonna run me out of here. I can handle anything that comes along. I just wish Driscoll would show his face. I can't go to the law until I'm sure it's him."

"You fear too little, amiga. I think we should stay in town where there will be a crowd. Si, that is what we must do. Many people have come to celebrate Founder's Day tomorrow. Driscoll would dare not molest you in a crowd."

Aly scanned the perimeters of the property, finding everything quiet. Jezlynn played near the house with a yellow-striped kitten Silas had given her. "Could be it ain't Driscoll at all."

"Who else here wants to run you out of town?"

"Madeline, that's who." Aly glanced at Jez to make sure she was too far away to hear the conversation. Still, she didn't want to take any chances, so she lowered her voice. "Don't look so surprised. She's got the means to do it and plenty of fools willing enough to want to please her. Poor Mrs. Gilmore is not as sickly as everybody thinks she is. She's been spending too much time entertaining Driscoll to be that sick. I figure those two are in cahoots with each other."

"Just be careful, my friend." Connie draped the rope over the edge of the well's circular stone wall. "Driscoll has reason to hate you now. I fear he will make his move soon."

Aly patted her shirt pocket. "I dug out the derringer I won in the first poker game I ever played with Nick. Thought I'd taken his personal gun, then I discovered he doesn't tote one."

A column of dust rose in the horizon. "Riders coming," Aly announced.

Two men rode toward the homestead. Shading her eyes with a palm, Aly peered into the distance and attempted to discern the men's identity. From this far away, she couldn't be certain. No need to be too trusting.

"Get Jez and take cover inside the house," she ordered. "May be no trouble at all coming, but don't run. They'll know we spotted them if you do."

Connie met Aly's gaze. Aly felt compelled to reassure her friend. "Don't panic. We'll do what we have to."

"Are you coming inside, too?" Connie walked backward, edging toward Jez while pretending to continue the conversation.

"No." Aly checked to make sure the tiny gun had not shifted; the handle would be the first thing she'd touch. "You'll find a rifle just inside the door. If they get through me." *Two shots, two men.* "Use it. Understand?"

"Si."

· A shout from the approaching riders swung Aly around. She expected them to be spurring their horses into a ground-eating gallop to overcome her and Connie before they barricaded themselves inside the house. Instead, the pair's horses maintained a steady trot. One of the men began to wave broadly.

"Hello the house!"

"Nick!" Aly yelled, recognizing his voice before his features became clear to her. She ran toward him, every ounce of blood in her veins pumping with excitement. God, how she'd missed him!

She brushed a juniper tree. Her hem caught on one of the roots. Aly began to fall. Just as she saw the earth rushing up to meet her, a light flashed in the distance. A whoosh of air warned she'd nearly been winged by a bullet. A rifle retort echoed across the countryside, confirming her theory. Grateful that her stumbling had kept her from being killed, she wiped away the sting of scratching her face on the roots she'd tripped over.

More shots rang out. Aly watched in horror as Nick crumpled against Troublemaker's neck. She took cover behind one side of the house, watching as the blond-haired rider grabbed Nick's reins. He spurred his mount into a gallop, forcing Troublemaker to follow behind. Suddenly, the blond twisted halfway around to return the volley of gunfire.

New shots echoed from the house. Aly glanced at the upper floor. Connie was returning fire, giving the men a chance to reach safety.

When they made it to the yard, the stranger jumped from his horse without even stopping. He swatted the animal and yelled, "Heyaah!" and sent it running.

As Troublemaker passed by, the big-shouldered man grabbed Nick and pulled him off into the dirt. Aly ran over and dropped to her knee to lift the gambler. "Nick!"

"Get him inside, ma'am." He moved to block her and Nick from the bullets blasting into the dirt all around them. Gunsmoke rose like a mist above him as he continued to fire.

Nick didn't move.

With no concern for the gunfire, she braced her shoulder beneath his and pulled with all her might, glad for the strength she'd gained from freighting. He moaned. She'd have to drag him inside. "Come on, Nick. You can make it."

His boots slid backward. Nick dug in his heels to stand. He took one step, two. Aly held him tightly, silently thanking God for His mercy and Nick for his sense of survival.

"Keep firing, Connie," Aly shouted as they entered the house. She spotted the child trying to open the locked gun cabinet. "We'll have to bust it open in a minute, Jez. Grab your kitten and go upstairs with Connie. Stay there until I tell you it's safe to come down. And stay low. Don't walk in front of a window."

She dragged Nick through the parlor and lay him on the davenport. A quick grab of his feet lined him up with the furniture's length. She scanned him for a bullet wound, but no blood stained his clothing. He'd taken a lick on his chin, though. A lump the size of a hickory nut swelled the flesh beneath his jaw and had already started turning an ugly color.

"Hang on, Gambler. I'll be back to check on you. Gotta get your friend inside and safe."

The big man backed into the house, his guns blazing. He kicked the door shut and spun around. "Get them shutters closed, and give me all the rifles and ammunition you've got." He grabbed the wooden bar sitting next to the window closest to him, closed the shutters and slammed the bar down to form a blockade. Bullets hit the door and the window he'd just barricaded. "Whoever the hell it is means business."

Aly grabbed the fireplace stoker and pried the gun cabinet loose. She flung open the doors and found an arsenal, giving a low whistle. "Looks like there's been trouble before. But everything's rusty."

"Hand me that Winchester. We'll make them think we've got more guns than we do."

Aly did as she was told, then opened the first drawer below the gun rack, hoping for the impossible. Though there was ammunition enough to hold off an army, it had lost its potency through the years. "All we got is the rifle upstairs and some ammo for the derringer I carry. That won't hold them off for long."

"They've quit shooting," he said, nestling the rifle barrel between the junction of the two straight lines that formed a cross on the windows.

The firing had stopped upstairs, too.

The silence struck fear in Aly. "Connie, are you all right up there?"

The redhead came rushing downstairs. "Si, I barred the windows and . . ." Her mouth gaped as she caught sight of the six-foot-tall stranger in their midst.

Aly paid attention to his looks for the first time. His blond hair hung to his shoulders, his bronzed skin the mark of an outdoorsman. Though he had the squint of a man who stared too often into the sun, the color of his cornflower-blue eyes revealed themselves when he returned Connie's stare. The pistols strapped to each leg made him dangerously more compelling.

The bookkeeper blinked once. "Holy Mary Mother of God, I have died and gone to heaven." She crossed herself. *"Gracias a Dios. Gracias."*

"I know you said it happens in the heat of the moment, Con—" Aly watched seduction ooze from every pore of her friend's body and noted the delight on the stranger's face. That's what picking up the scent of a willing woman meant, she supposed. "—But this is one time you need to keep it on simmer . . . at least until we're all safe."

The stranger laughed. "Pleased to meet you, too, ma'am. Name's Ice. William Ice. Take a position at one of the windows."

"Si, senor."

"Good, I'll watch from the front." He glanced at Aly. "See what you can do for your husband. I don't think he took a deathmaker. But hurry. Don't know if they're gone or just stalling."

Aly rushed to Nick who was attempting to sit up on his own. "Hold on there, Gambler. I'll help you. Reckon we can get you upstairs? It might be safer up there, and I'd like someone with Jez." She left, "in case it isn't," unsaid.

"Give me a hand." Nick stood, a grim line of pain stretching his mouth.

"Where are you bleeding?" Aly checked his shirt and pants. Nothing.

"I'm not much. Shot me out of the saddle . . . literally. I think I was only grazed in the butt."

Aly linked her shoulder beneath his armpit and giggled.

"It's not funny," Nick grumbled. He rubbed the lump under his chin. "Damn fool hit me so unexpectedly, I crumpled over and nearly knocked myself out busting my chin on the saddlehorn."

Every step upward caused him to flinch and Aly to giggle. "You're enjoying this way too much, Chick."

"Oh now, darlin', you don't think I enjoy seeing you the butt of—"

"Any joke?" he finished for her. "You're not supposed to take advantage of a man when he's down."

Aly winked at him. "I don't know. I've had a pretty good time taking advantage of you recently when you were down."

The look Nick gave her made Aly's toes curl. Yes, she definitely was a willing woman. He had no idea *how* willing!

"Papa!" Jezlynn rushed to meet him and threw her arms around Nick.

"Ouch!"

The child took a step backward, apology changing her expression into one of concern. "Are you hurt?"

"A little." Nick leaned down and ruffled her hair. "Are you okay?"

Jezlynn nodded. "I slid some bars to Connie so she could close the shutters."

"That's my girl." Despite the pain, Nick bent. "Now give me a hug so I'll feel better. I've missed you, Half-Pint."

Aly tugged on his shirt. "Where do you want me to station you? I've got to get back down there."

"Our room. It's got some surprises in it for just such an occasion. I haven't found the need to show you them until now."

"Good." Aly pointed to their room. "Jez, I'm counting on you to stay with your father, okay? No matter what. I don't care what you think you hear going on downstairs, whatever you do, don't leave Nick. Promise me?"

"I promise." Jezlynn's eyes widened in excitement. "Does that mean I get to shoot a gun?"

Nick shared a glance with Aly, then shook his head solemnly before replying, "No, sweetheart. You're too little for that. Papa will do any shooting that needs done."

Aly offered him the derringer.

Nick's eyes locked with hers. His fingers flexed, yet his hand refused to move. His flesh felt cold, clammy, foreign to him.

"Take it, Nick." Aly grabbed his hand and thrust the derringer into his palm. "You *have* no choice."

His finger shook as it curled around the trigger. "It seems history does repeat itself," he whispered.

Chapter Twenty-five

No one had fired for at least an hour. Stranger still, Connie had not uttered a word. Aly glanced at her friend who obviously liked what she was looking at—the backside of the man defending them. Ice maintained his station at the front window nearest the door.

"Buggy coming. A balding, stout fellow's driving. A businessman is my guess."

"Sounds like her boss." Aly deliberately urged Nick's friend to swing around and take a look at Connie. Hell, why not play matchmaker? She couldn't give the man any better thank-you than introducing him to his future wife. From the looks of her, Connie had already set her hat for him. "Connie works for the banker in town, Silas Sullivan. Oh . . . I forgot, there wasn't time for me to introduce you two. This is my friend, Consuela . . ." Aly started to recite all her husbands' last names, then decided that might scare this man off. "Calhoun. We call her Connie."

"It's a pleasure to meet you, Consuela."

Connie sighed. "Si, it is most definitely." Her cheeks reddened. "I mean, it is my pleasure as well, senor."

Ice took another look through the cross. "The man's pulling up out front."

"If it's the banker, let him in. He could be killed."

"Let me see." Connie rushed to stand in front of Ice, stepping on her tiptoes to match his vantage point. "Yes, it is my boss."

"Doesn't look like he's in any danger," Nick's friend said. "But we still want to be careful. The shooters may be waiting to see if we'll take the bait and open the door."

Ice grabbed the handle and moved the door ajar only a crack. Aly shouted, "Come in quick, Silas. We've had some trouble."

Sullivan appeared in the doorway instantly, his rotund body demanding the door to widen more. Still, no shots.

The banker gaped at the bullet holes and the arsenal of weapons lining the room. "How long have you been under attack?"

"Long enough." Ice's gaze met Silas'. "What brings you out, Mr. Sullivan?"

Silas pointed to the stranger. "Who is this man, Aly? How does he know me?"

"A friend of Nick's," Ice answered for himself. "And you know me, if you think about it. Now why did you just happen by at this particular moment?"

"I thought I saw Nick pass through town. Thought it would be a good time to give him some good news."

Aly frowned and held a finger to her lips to silence him. She nodded to indicate someone stood behind her. "He's home. But, as you've already seen, we've got guests. Maybe the two of you can meet tomorrow."

"The man took the time to come out here." William motioned to the stairs. "We can't let him leave until we're sure this thing is over. Let him talk to Nick."

Aly didn't like being ordered around, but William's reasoning was sound.

"Ice?" Silas rubbed his chin in thought. "There used to be a couple named Ice who lived here years ago. You wouldn't be related, would you?"

"To the bone. They were my grandfather and grandmother. Raised me and one of my cousins."

Recognition lit Silas' eyes. "Why, it's Little Bill. You were always so full of spit and vinegar. Remember the time you shot the bell out of the steeple? I tell you, I never saw a finer marksman. Cut the rope clean in half."

"It's William now."

"He's going to back my enterprise," Nick announced from the top of the stairway, Jezlynn beside him.

Aly rushed to him. "You should be in bed. You still look a little pale from that lick you took."

Nick's knuckle gently traced the dried blood along her high cheekbone. "It looks like we both got grazed cheeks today."

"I came to see how things had changed." William eyed Connie, but spoke to the banker. "To see if there's been enough improvements to want to make my home here again. Nicky's pretty convincing."

Silas looked pained. "Does that mean you'll be withdrawing your money, Aly?"

Aly's jaw tightened as she glared at him. "Why should I? I plan to use it to fund my freighting operation for a while." *Get my meaning?*

"I, uh . . . yes, that's very good." Silas tried to change the subject by focusing his attention on Ice. "I'll look forward to dealing with you, sir."

Nick descended slowly. "You came out here to tell me I got the loan, didn't you, Silas?"

The banker's gaze locked with Aly's. She knew the man would lie to keep his word, but she couldn't put him in that position now that Nick suspected the truth. "I asked him to."

Disappointment, or something worse, darted across Nick's face as he glared at her. "You didn't trust me to find a way on my own?"

"I have money, Nick. More than what you might think. I was afraid you'd be too stubborn to ask *me* for help. But when you said you might go in with a friend"—she motioned toward Ice—"I figured why not let me help you instead?"

"What do you mean, more than what I might think?" Nick probed.

"She's the daughter of Ebenezer Jones, the—"

"I know who the man is," Nick interrupted the banker. The gambler began to chuckle, low, his mirth rising in volume as the others watched. He shook his head and wagged a finger at Aly. "And to think, I worried about every pot I ever won from you. Every pot you threw of Ophelia's that had to be replaced. Why, you could pay for this town, lock, stock, and barrel and call it spending change."

Nick rubbed a hand through the hair at his temples and glanced at William. "Seems I made you ride all this way for nothing. My bride's gonna back me."

Aly breathed a heavy sigh of relief. She'd worried every night since making the deal with Silas that Nick would find out the truth and resent her for the deceit. She gave him a hug.

"Easy there, Chick." Nick pulled her closer despite his words. "I'm an injured man."

"Looks to me like you've got things well in hand here, Nicodemus." Banker Sullivan nodded to Connie and Jezlynn who had come to see what was happening, then to William. "Stay for the celebration tomorrow. Who knows?" His eyes turned to his bookkeeper. "Perhaps you'll find something of interest to keep you here in Prickly Bend. Oh, Connie, I've decided to close the bank tomorrow completely. It is Founder's Day. You may have the entire day off."

"Gracias." Connie curtsied and smiled at William. "I hope to spend it with new friends."

Aly grinned, knowing exactly which friend Consuela meant. "I think you ought to show Mr. Ice around town, Connie. Nick and I will have to stay here and watch the homestead. Whoever's out there may decide to come back."

"Don't you think it's wise for Nick to attend the festival?" Silas tugged on the lapels of his coat and rocked back on his heels. "I'm sure everyone will be abuzz when they learn about what Nick intends to do. The celebration is the ideal place to inform the community of his plans and seek their participation as well."

"William . . . Senor Ice . . . and I could stay here so that you may attend." Connie moved closer to the handsome man. "Unless he prefers a crowd. *No?* Good." To Aly and Nick, she insisted, "You should show a united family so the people will know you all plan to stay. And . . ." She held out her hand to Nick's friend. "That would give Senor William and me a chance to become better acquainted."

Ice bent and pressed a kiss lightly against the back of her hand. "I'll look forward to it, senorita."

"Senora," Connie corrected, her lashes dipping demurely against her cheeks. "I am a widow, you see."

Aly saw all right. Although she wanted to stay out of Cupid's way, they would be taking a big chance leaving. "What if the shooters are still out there? They'll hit us on the trail to town."

The banker foolishly opened the door and swung it wide.

"Don't!" everyone else yelled at once, freezing in their positions.

Startled, Sullivan slammed the door and backed away. Silence reigned as everyone awaited the sound of gunfire.

"See? They're gone. No more danger." The banker grabbed the handkerchief from his coat pocket and mopped his brow. "I saw no one along the road from town. They may have been gone before I arrived." A frown creased his brow. "Come to think of it, I passed Madeline's buggy along the way."

"Are you sure it was hers?" Anger echoed in Nick's tone.

Aly didn't like the turn of the conversation. "Jez-lynn, go on back upstairs and decide what you want to wear for tomorrow. We'll ride back with Silas so he doesn't have to go alone."

"Did my mama do something wrong?"

She was too little and had suffered too much heart-break already to know the truth. Yet, Aly had to pre-pare her for the worst. "Probably just a coincidence she was out this way. Now run on up and get ready. We'll spend the night at the office."

"I insist you be guests in my home."

"Mighty kind of you," Aly told the banker, waiting for Jez to disappear. When she was sure the child was out of earshot, Aly turned back to Silas. "Now, are you sure it was Madeline?"

"I can't be certain. It may have been Elmertha or a servant she sent to town to fetch something. Whoever it was sat too far back into the seat for me to see her clearly."

"Madeline may have hired some shooters or is out

here doing the job herself." Aly frowned. "She does everything else well, why not shooting?"

Silas' face turned to stone. "I find that hard to believe, Mrs. Turner. Gentlemen, ladies, please excuse me. I must insist on going back to town now. The missus will want to know of the added company before you get there. Supper is served at six."

Nick approached the doorway cautiously. "I can't let you go alone, Silas."

"I'm in no danger, and I *insist*." Stubbornness echoed in the banker's tone.

"What are you doing?" Aly asked.

"If he must leave, then I'm gonna make sure he can." Nick grabbed the rifle Connie had leaned against one shutter. "Stand away. I'll stick this barrel out the door and see if anybody fires back." When he cracked the door open, Nick showed a great deal of rifle, then fired.

No return fire came.

Nick stepped out into the daylight. "Looks like it's safe, Silas."

The banker hurried to his buggy and grabbed the reins, nodding politely at the gambler. "Nick." He tipped his hat to Aly. *"Mrs. Turner."* He urged the team into a trot down the same road it had come.

"He's madder than a rattlesnake at me." Aly thought she and Silas had been getting along well. "Maybe Madeline's a prickly subject for the man."

"You could not have known, amiga." Connie halted beside her. "Senor Sullivan has been in love with Madeline for a very long time. He only married his wife after Nick left and Madeline gave her hand in marriage to Judge Gilmore." Compassion echoed in Connie's voice. "He told me so himself, when I found him crying after one of Mrs. Gilmore's visits."

* * *

The Founder's Day celebration was a rousing success. Even Madeline and Elmertha appeared to be having a wonderful time. Nick quit rowing and let the canoe glide through the water. He glanced at the rafts and boats riding the current with them.

Madeline had asked Driscoll to join her and Elmertha on the special raft she had built for just this occasion. She made it bigger than anyone else's and more elaborate. While others sat on hard benches or on their knees in a canoe, Madeline offered comfortable-looking chairs for each of her guests as well as a table set with linen and a silver tea service. Not exactly what the founder of Prickly Bend, Thomas Wayne, had in mind when he'd started the tradition of the picnic on the river, Nick was sure.

Wayne had found the junction of waters while rafting downriver to Tucson. Knowing how rare such a place would be in this desert environment, he'd determined it to be the ideal place to build a town, pulled to the bank and staked his claim. The first anniversary of his docking, the settlers had celebrated by having a picnic *on* the river. The tradition remained to this day.

Canoes and rafts had been decorated festively, some of them shaded by leftover tarpaulins from the Conestogas that had brought settlers here. Desert flowers, even cookfires, adorned several of the rafts. Families worked all year on their floats, trying to impress the neighbors with artistry or oddity.

A musicians' raft had been built, sturdy enough to hold a makeshift band that serenaded the crowd with lively tunes. A kaleidoscope of parasols warded off the afternoon sun for the ladies as the flotilla glided along the current.

Nick didn't relish the idea of sitting in a canoe all day. Though he'd only been grazed, his rear end was still sore. In fact, he'd delayed the boat ride by talking with Silas about the loan. "I'm sorry I took so long at the bank. There were a lot of details to discuss."

Aly had waited patiently for them to finish, but Jez inspected every cranny of the establishment. Being cooped up all day had made her cranky.

Not that Jez minded where she'd been cooped up. Silas let her study the safe. Nick paddled, nearly choking again as he had on his coffee earlier, when he stared at Jez who sat between him and Aly. "I still can't believe you actually had the gumption to ask him for a rope so you could measure the safe."

"I'm surprised you didn't con the man out of the combination." Aly laughed and rumpled Jez's hair.

"I did," Jez stated matter-of-factly. "When you and Papa went over to the hotel to bring us back some breakfast."

"Hey, canoes. Having a good time?" Driscoll waved at the gathering of crafts riding alongside Nick and Aly.

"Watch where you're headed, Driscoll," Nick warned. "That will get away from you if you aren't careful."

Driscoll stood at the post that held the large rowing oar used to guide Madeline's raft and jerked backward on the oar, giving it a hard yank.

"I'm doing fine." Driscoll frowned at Nick. "I can handle this." His eyes lit with appreciation as he studied Aly. "You're looking mighty fine, Alewine. I don't think I've ever seen your hair up like that."

Aly's hand pressed against the back of her neck. Nick had never seen her wear it twisted up off her shoulders. "I haven't, either."

She shrugged. "Thought it would be cooler. Tried to do the same to Jez's." Aly urged Jezlynn to turn around and show Nick the back of her head.

Curls stuck out everywhere. When the child faced him again, and he saw the expectation in her eyes, Nick didn't have the heart to disappoint her or Aly. "That's one mighty fine hairdo, Half-Pint. Makes you look grown up, sophisticated."

"Older, he means," Aly grumbled despite his effort. "Which is good for you, but doesn't say much for me." She patted the uptwist of her own hair once again. "I'd take out these hair bobs and let everything hang, but it was too hard getting them in there the first time. I'm afraid if I take 'em out, they'll leave a bunch of holes and all my brains'll seep out."

Jezlynn giggled.

"Those are hatpins, Chick. Not hairpins," Nick informed her, laughing. "No wonder they hurt."

All of a sudden, the canoe shuddered and pitched. Madeline's raft had collided with their boat!

"Hang on," Nick yelled and lurched for Aly and his daughter. The canoe turned sideways. Aly leaned a hard right to correct the position. The abrupt shifting sent Nick over the brink.

He plunged several feet into the water before he managed to gather his wits about him and head for air. A glance at the underbelly of the crafts showed the larger of the two had not pulled away. He broke the surface and sputtered in anger. "Watch where you're going, Driscoll! Back up!"

Driscoll no longer stood at the oar. He floundered in the river beside the raft.

"Serves you right," Aly shouted, shaking her fist at the man. "You did that on purpose."

"It was an accident," Madeline insisted. "But it proves Jezlynn should ride on a more stable craft." She motioned to the empty chair beside her. "Jezlynn, as soon as we get this a bit closer, climb aboard."

"I don't want to," Jezlynn wailed and sank back against Aly.

"I didn't ask if you wanted to. Now be ready." Madeline moved toward the oar rest. "Elmertha, come help."

"Don't let her go," Aly insisted, wrapping her arms around Jez to keep her there.

"What are you going to do, sister?" Surprise filled Elmertha's face as she rose and followed Madeline.

"We have to get back to shore someway." She stared disdainfully at Driscoll. "It doesn't seem I can trust Clay to keep us safe, so we are going back to shore ourselves."

"*We're* going to row?" Elmertha looked as if Madeline had asked her to swim the length of the Mississippi.

Nick doubted the two women had done any hard labor in their entire lives. It would be worth it to leave them stranded, but he couldn't, for Jez's sake. Or Aly's. He needed to make sure Jez was safe all the way around. "Come closer and let Jez and Aly join you. I'll man the oar and get you back to the bank, provided you drop Jez off at my place when you head toward home. Connie's there. She won't mind taking care of Jez until we get back."

Aly waited until Jez got onto the raft, then offered Nick a hand.

When he accepted it, his weight rocked the canoe. He tried to throw his leg over the side to keep from going under again, but his backside wouldn't cooperate.

The canoe dipped, spilling Aly into the river with him. She came up sputtering.

"That's just great, Gambler!" She shook her hair like a dog shedding the water from its latest bath. All of a sudden a smile replaced the irritation bracketing her mouth. "Say . . . these hat pins work. There ain't"—she glared at Elmertha, defying her to say a word—"a hair out of place."

"Hey, what about me?" Driscoll treaded water with his arms.

"A little cooling off is a fitting punishment for putting our lives in danger." Madeline waited until Nick and Aly managed to climb onto the raft.

"You'll regret making me a laughingstock." Driscoll shook his fist at Madeline, then swam toward Nick's overturned canoe. "All of you."

Nick gave the canoe a resounding kick, sending it bobbing toward the river's edge. "You touch a hair on anyone's head here, Driscoll, and I'll personally drown you myself."

Chapter Twenty-six

A copse of trees shielded the slough where Nick and Aly swam a short ways down the river. After he'd seen Jez off with Madeline and Elmertha, Nick asked Silas to keep Driscoll busy while he retrieved their canoe and used it to show Aly the place he wanted to build the hotel. When she'd seen it, Aly shucked everything but her chemise and pantaloons and dived into the water. Nick shed his clothes and joined her.

"Oohhh, this feels so good. The hot springs that feed it will make this a place everyone will want to visit." Aly ducked her head beneath the surface, then burst through the water, shaking it from her face. "I can't wait till Jez gets to see it."

"She will soon, I promise." After they frolicked, splashing each other and stealing wet kisses, Nick reluctantly suggested, "Want to dry off so we can have our talk? I'm not sure how long Silas can keep

Driscoll occupied. He'll do his best. He knows you and I haven't had any privacy since I came home."

They swam to the riverbank and, hand in hand, waded to shore. Both lay on the sand and caught their breaths. After a peaceful silence of staring up at the occasional puffy white clouds and listening to the sound of Aly's steady breathing, he wondered if she'd gone to sleep. "Are you awake, Chick?"

"What do you expect with you laying naked next to me?"

Nick laughed and rolled over to hug her. "Is that all you're thinking about?"

"No." Her honey-colored gaze softened. "That we have a lot to say to each other, and this sure is a nice place to say it."

Nick sat up. She did the same. "You want to go first or do you want me to?" He waited, hoping she would so he could watch her for a while, sitting there like a fair-haired goddess rising from the shore.

"I'd like to, if you don't mind." Aly took his hand and squeezed it. "I haven't ever told anybody some of what I'm gonna tell you, and I may bust if I don't get it said."

"By all means, love. You go first."

Something sparked in her eyes when he whispered the endearment. She unbound the lace that held her chemise in place and handed it to him.

"Me and Glory—you remember, I told you she's my half-sister, were sent to a boarding school that tried to mold us into one of the Madelines of the world." Aly stood and stepped out of her pantaloons.

He stood with her, taking the garments and placing them over a branch where her dress had been draped.

"Glory fit those shoes pretty good and was even happy wearing 'em." She started to take down her hair, then didn't. She'd worn her hair this way when she left the others at the picnic. They'd expect her to come back looking the same way. "But then you have to understand, Glory was everyone's favorite. Particularly my stepfather's. She could do no wrong in his eyes."

Nick caressed the slope of her neck. *So soft.* "But you were like Jez."

Aly stood naked in all her beauty, as if only they alone lived in this part of the world. Had this been what Adam felt when he saw Eve the first time? Faint strains of music, someone singing and children squealing reminded him that this was not Eden, and they were not alone. Someone was bound to find them soon.

"I made sure I had everyone's attention so I wouldn't be ignored." Aly's fingertips traced a trail across his shoulders, urging his arms to lock themselves about her waist. "Even if it meant I had to cause trouble to get noticed."

Nick's gaze swept over her, admiring every treasured curve and fullness. Desire rushed to harden him. "You've got my attention."

He wondered what had made her choose a freighter's life. Nick pulled her to him, staring at her mouth as if it were a plump apple and he were in need of fruit. "Is that why you came to Valiant?"

"Partly. I couldn't see myself prissing around in some petticoat and living by standards that ain't fair most of the time. I guess you noticed I backslide a bit on my pontifications."

"Is that what brought you to Texas? A need to talk any way you were big enough to defend?" Nick teased.

Her chin dropped, and she hesitated. He curled a finger under it and gently raised her face to his. "There's nothing you've done that would make me love you any less, Chick."

"You love me?" Tears shimmered in her eyes as her voice lowered. "You honest-to-goodness, with all your heart, for now and forever love me?"

"Yes, Aly." Nick smiled from the depths of his heart. "With everything I am and all I ever hope to be."

Aly threw back her head and shouted, throwing her arms around him. "Well, why'd it take you so dang long to say so!"

Nick kissed her long and hard, his hands playing over her body, exploring the wet, hard length of her. She clung to him, wordlessly begging him for more. When the kiss ended, her tongue traced hot circles along his jawline, down his neck, setting fire to his flesh.

"Glory got into trouble with the law. On a dare, she stole a brooch from Mrs. Wanamaker's desk. There had been a rash of thefts at the school, so everyone knew whoever got caught would be branded a thief. Glory feared she would be forced to flee West to hide her shame," Aly whispered hotly against his skin. "I knew she couldn't make it out here on her own. She was delicate and pampered more than most. I knew everyone would think I was guilty of theft or that I was only trying to make Glory take the blame for me. I'd wanted to go West all my life, so I took the blame."

Nick finally understood. His hands caressed, worshipped her. "So you can't show your face back East."

"Let's just say, as hot as it gets in Texas, it's hotter for me in Savannah. When I confessed to the theft, they thought it would tie things up easy if they blamed me for everything. And don't go thinking I'm being a martyr—I knew if I took the blame, Glory would have to grow up after that. I wouldn't be around the second time to be her scapegoat. My stepfather loved it, of course. He spit me out of his life like a bad seed."

"And your mother?" Nick gently pushed her away to arm's length so he could read her eyes.

"She knew I could take care of myself."

The lack of emotion he found there made him hurt for Aly. "Do you hate her?"

"Does Jezlynn hate Madeline?"

"She doesn't like her very much."

"Strange thing about being a kid." Her golden eyes began to shimmer. "You ain't had your heart broke so many times you stop wishing to find even a little bit of good in people. When you get older, you come to realize some folks are just mean. No matter how much you want them not to be."

Aly sighed and stepped back into his embrace. "Maybe that's why I rebelled so much. I wanted to break out of the role everyone expected of me. I wanted to toughen up so I didn't hurt no more."

She pressed kisses along his collarbone. "But I've got some gentle seasons left in me, Nick. A whole crop of love and laughter to offer if you'll look past the weeds."

Their bodies began to sway, like they had done out in the rain. There was something about Aly and water—the critter-wash, the trough, dancing in the rain . . . today. He suspected he would never see fishing the same way again.

"Make love to me, Nick," she half-whispered, half-moaned. "Make love to me so I know you mean it."

"Here?"

"Now." Her body folded, drawing him down with her.

"You're a dangerous woman."

"Let me show you how much."

As Nick's legs straightened atop hers, pain stabbed through him from his injury. He groaned, but nothing could keep him from making love to Aly.

Aly pressed a finger to his lower lip. "I'll move for both of us."

Determination broke into beads upon his brow. "Through pain and pleasure, sickness and in health, till death parts us, Chick, I promise to love you without restraint. You will always have a home with me."

He was lost the moment she opened to him, welcomed him, and met his driving thrusts. Higher and higher they climbed toward release.

"You're mine," she entreated against his lips. "Tell me you belong to me."

"For always, Aly." Nick buried himself completely one last time. She began to shudder, her golden eyes looking up at him with complete trust and love. Aly clung to him, crying out his name. His own shout of ecstasy blended with hers as his world spun out of control. His promise became a vow. "We belong to each other forever."

Chapter Twenty-seven

"Your turn." Aly grinned, trying to ease her ragged breathing.

Nick looked down at her and laughed. "Again?"

Aly meant for him to think she could make love forever, but they'd spent far too long away from the others. She pressed a kiss upon his lips, then urged him to turn over.

When Nick moved Aly sat up. "I meant it's your turn to tell me all about you. I want to know everything, Nick. Why you won't carry a gun, what you did in Prickly Bend that was so bad you had to leave, and why you've hesitated to tell me that you really love me. I have a good guess at the last answer. I think I figured that out just before you came back from Tucson."

Nick rose and strolled to the tree to fetch their clothing.

Aly shook her head. "Let's go rinse off. If somebody finds us, we ought to look like we've been swimming. Our hair should be wet."

They ran hand-in-hand to the water and dove in. Aly laughed from the pure joy of being on God's good earth—well, His soothing waters—and knowing that the man she adored returned her love.

She broke the surface and giggled when something pinched her bottom. "Ow!" she complained teasingly when Nick burst through the water. "I could do the same to you, Gambler."

His palms raised to ward off her attack. "Now, Aly, remember it's sore."

"You should have thought of that before you pinched."

She backed him up until his hips cleared the water and he stood there in all his magnificent nakedness. "God, but you're beautiful, Nick."

"I love you too, Chick."

She moved toward him, never wanting to let anything part them again. A thrill coursed through her when he wrapped his arm about her waist and waded with her to the shore.

"Much as I don't want to leave, we'd better get dressed." Nick kissed her. "We look convincing now, but if this keeps up, we'll be dry in a flash."

"If what keeps up?" Aly stared at him boldly. A husky chuckle said he'd known exactly what she was asking.

"You are going to be one long adventure, aren't you, Mrs. Turner?"

"Yes." She laughed gloriously. "And you're coming along for the ride."

"Like I said." Nick tapped her nose. "If you keep looking at me like that, the heat you're stirring up is going to dry us to the bone."

They shared another passionate kiss, then Nick headed for their clothes. Aly accepted the chemise and pantaloons and began to dress. "You didn't answer me a few minutes ago. I want to know all about you as a man. Now . . . before we have to go back and become part of the community."

Nick dressed hurriedly.

"Is it that bad?" Aly reached out and touched his arm.

"No." The gambler left the buttons of his shirt unfastened. "Yes."

Aly smiled and pressed a palm against his right cheek. "Nick, I love you, and the Almighty knows I've never been perfect. So, there's nothing you could have done that would make me love you any less."

"Let's finish dressing and get in the canoe. I'll tell you while we're paddling back."

Aly hurried, ready to learn what disturbed him. When the canoe swept past the bend in the river that kept the slough from view, Aly looked at Nick. "It's time."

His muscular arms flexed beneath his shirt as his body bent forward, then back to paddle. "Remind me not to go canoeing the next time I get shot out of a saddle."

"Quit stalling." Aly didn't laugh, knowing he meant the delay.

Nick let the craft glide for a minute and sighed. "All right. I'll tell you." The humor that had lit his eyes disappeared. He seemed to focus on something directly behind her. "I shot my father. Killed him. That's why I don't carry a gun."

Aly drew in a deep breath, surprised by his blunt confession. He stared at her . . . hard, obviously waiting on her to react. *I told you that you could tell me anything.* She would have to see it with her own eyes to believe Nick capable of being a murderer. "It had to be an accident." She reached out to console him. "Or self-defense. You're not an evil man."

His eyes locked with hers, gratitude warming their dark depths. "It was in defense of my mother. She had asked him for a divorce, and he went loco—aimed a gun at her. Mother said she refused to let him ruin the rest of her life, so she tried to wrestle the gun away from him."

The gambler rolled his shoulders as if he were shaking off an unwelcome coat. "Aly, I was seventeen, scared and watching my mother and father in a death struggle. I meant to grab the gun away from both of them. But . . . before I knew what happened, the gun went off. He fell." Anguish echoed in Nick's tone. "You know, to this day I don't know who pulled the trigger—me or her? But I told everyone I did."

"And your mother, what did she say?" Aly hadn't realized how alike their pasts had been. She had headed west to protect Glory. He, to Texas and to safeguard his mother.

"She took to her bed after that . . . laid there, dying a little bit at a time. I begged her not to leave me, Aly." Tears fell unchecked down his cheeks. "I told her I didn't want to be alone." He wiped his eyes with one sleeve. "Do you know what she said?"

When Aly moved closer to cup his cheek in her palm, Nick turned and pressed a kiss into it. "She said we're all alone in this world unless we're really lucky." Nick exhaled a sigh soul-deep. "That's why I became a gambler, Chick. I wanted to control my own luck."

Then anger blazed in Nick's eyes. "My father was a greatly respected man here in Prickly Bend, an elder of the church, town councilman. Everyone felt he'd married beneath him. My mother had not gone to finishing school, didn't speak as well as she wrote. She was a mail-order bride. She'd married to be provided for, not loved."

Understanding swept through Aly. "So the people of Prickly Bend thought the two of you deliberately killed your father."

"He was a great benefactor to the town. They had no idea he constantly belittled Mother, called her low-class, beneath his station. When she asked for the divorce, he said she would not diminish his reputation. He would rather see her dead than set her free." Nick's teeth gritted as his jaw set. "He signed his own death warrant."

Aly reached to smoothe the hair hanging over his brow. "It was an accident. You didn't set out to kill him. Either of you."

"I've told myself that a thousand times. But when I dream at night, I remember all the times I yelled at him and told him I hated him. That I wished he was dead." An unbidden tear trickled down his cheek. "And, I may have actually pulled the trigger. I certainly can't cast the blame elsewhere. Not on my mother, God rest her soul."

"No, but the burden shouldn't rest on your head, either. He might have killed her. Or you," Aly reminded.

Nick straightened his shoulders and blinked back the tears that shimmered in his eyes. He let out a long breath and dipped the paddle into the water. "So that's the story."

"How does Madeline fit in? Why was everyone angry about the way you left her if no one knew she was carrying Jez at the time?"

"Same reason. They thought I'd deliberately set out to find a wealthy girl, tell her I loved her, then break her heart. Like mother, like son—right?"

"But you said once that you asked her to leave with you."

"I begged her. At the time, I was deeply in love with her. Or thought I was. But Madeline laughed and said there was no way she'd leave what she had here. She threw Judge Gilmore's name in my face, and the banker's. It seemed she had a string of wealthy lovers, and I was too besotted to know it."

Nick dug the paddle deeper into the water. "When you asked me a long time ago if I thought Jezlynn was mine, I told you it didn't matter. If she carried my name, then I claim her." Nick's gaze locked with Aly's. "I mean that with everything that I am. I'll not leave that baby alone in this world to wonder where she belongs. She'll at least have one person she can count on."

"Two," Aly whispered, throwing herself into his arms. "She has two now."

Nick's body tensed.

She pulled back to see why.

"Paddle as hard as you can," he commanded, handing her the second oar just as shouts rang over the countryside.

Aly carefully faced the opposite direction and discovered the other canoes and rafts swung toward shore, as if someone had fired a starting gun for a race. People on shore had left their picnic blankets and chairs behind, rushing toward town. Black plumes of smoke rose in the distance.

"A fire!" Aly exclaimed.

"Pull ashore here." Nick's oar cut deeply into the water. "It'll be faster to run on foot."

Minutes ticked by as the canoe shot through the river. A painful grunt blended with Nick's labored breathing. *The injury.* "Let me have both paddles. You rest," Aly insisted. "That can't be easy on you."

"I'm fine, Chick. But I'm not sure whatever is on fire will be if we don't get there as quick as we can. I'll keep paddling, too."

Finally, they neared land. Paddling one last time, they sent the canoe sliding onto the shore. "Don't moor it," Aly insisted, climbing out of the canoe. She lay her paddle inside the craft. "We'll come back for it later."

They joined the tide of people rushing to help.

"The bank's on fire!" Silas pointed to his establishment. "We need a bucket brigade!"

The crowd divided, everyone grabbing anything that could hold water. Aly ran to the front of the line with the men. Grateful, once again, for the strength her job had afforded her, she took her place and waited for the buckets to be transferred.

Huge flames shot high into the sky, and smoke roiled out of shattered glass doors. A prayer of thanks swept through her thoughts before she voiced them aloud. "Thank God Jez is home."

All of a sudden, William Ice moved up beside Aly. Then she saw Connie joining them in line. Jez wasn't with them. "Where's Jez, Consuela?"

Connie's brows arched. "I thought she was with you."

"Madeline and Elmertha didn't drop her off to you this afternoon?" Panic erupted in Aly.

"I have not seen them, *amiga*. We have only just arrived. It was so quiet there, Will and I thought it would be safe to leave for a while. We only left about twenty minutes ago."

Aly stared at the bank in horror, her thoughts too concerned to voice the fear that consumed her. *Skunk Wrangler has no reason to be inside*, she reminded herself.

"Jezlynn!" Nick fought his way to the shattered glass, dodging the flames that licked out. "Isn't that one of your hatpins, Aly? Like the ones you put her hair up with today?"

At the sight of one of Jezlynn's hair pins laying on the first step leading into the bank, Aly almost lost her lunch. It took everything she had to yank him back. "It's too far gone. If she's . . . no one could survive in there. You can't save her, and you'll be killed. Besides, you saw how badly I pinned up her hair. Remember?" Aly tried to reassure herself as much as she hoped to give Nick hope. "I bet that one came loose when we were here earlier. I bet she's lost several over the day."

"Aly, that's my daughter. I left her alone. I left her alone, and now she's . . ." Nick buried his face in her bosom and sobbed.

She lifted his head. Tears streamed down her cheeks. "I'm going to Madeline's right now and find out why she didn't do as you asked. You stay here. They need every man available so the fire doesn't spread. I'll be bringing Jez back with me." *Please God, let this be truth, not forfeit.*

"Bring her back to me, Chick." Nick took a deep breath and returned to his place in line again. "Bring her back to me."

Aly raced down the line to the river, looking for Banker Sullivan. When she found him, her fear became reality. "Where's Driscoll?" she asked. "He's supposed to be with you."

Silas' face flushed red. "I kept him busy for part of the day, I surely did. But he decided he should apologize to Madeline for the incident with the raft. I thought it was a good idea."

Dread and determination coursed through Aly. "How long ago did he leave?"

"An hour, maybe two."

"If I'm not back in an hour with Jezlynn, tell Nick to come looking for me . . . and to bring a gun."

Aly rushed through Madeline's front door and met silence. "Jezlynn?" she yelled at the top of her lungs. "If you're here, answer me."

No one answered.

Checking each room, Aly methodically made her way upstairs. Madeline's bedroom and Jez's old room were empty. Aly opened the door to the room she and Nick had shared. The sight before her confirmed her worst fears.

Elmertha had been gagged and bound by sheets to the rocking chair. The woman's eyes widened at the sight of Aly, and she began to struggle against her bindings.

"Where's Jez?" Aly demanded, rushing to the closet to see if the child had been hidden from view.

Elmertha mumbled. Then Aly realized she should take the time to at least loosen the spinster's hands. She quickly unfastened the knot that bound them. "You'll have to do the rest. I've got to find Jez."

Elmertha quickly removed the gag. "That brat will pay when I get my hands on her. The very audacity of tying up her own aunt! Hey! Where are you going?"

"When I find Jez, I'll come back for you and let you free."

"Come back here this minute. Do you have any idea who you're—"

"Sorry." Aly raced through the remainder of the rooms, then headed out back.

"You can't get out." The sound of the precious voice she'd grown to love made Aly race to the spring-house. "Not until the sheriff comes. No way!"

Several crates had been piled in front of it. Jezlynn

stood on a crate, desperately bracing herself against the shelter's barred door.

"Damn kid," Clay Driscoll's voice sounded from the other side of the door. "When I get out of here, you're gonna wish you never laid eyes on me." A loud thud against the wooden panel punctuated his anger.

"Jezlynn, don't let him out." Madeline's command echoed with dark promise. "He'll hurt you, darling. No matter what he says, don't let him out."

"Shut the hell up, Madeline." Driscoll cursed louder. "Since when did you decide to play mother instead of dead? You're in on this, too, so don't go acting like you aren't. Open this door, brat. Now!"

"Aly!" The word barreled from Jez's throat in a hoarse whisper as Aly joined her. "I can't hold them back."

"Why are they shut inside?" Aly demanded quietly, wondering how long Jez thought she could keep two adults at bay with nothing but her small back to brace the door. The wooden bar stretching through the two metal rings to barricade the door didn't look solid enough to withstand much pressure without giving.

" 'Cause Mr. Driscoll tried to shoot me." Jez's green eyes narrowed. "And 'cause I'm saving them for the sheriff. They broke the law."

"Shoot you?" Aly hesitated, wondering how much of the story was real and how much part of the child's imagination. If the man had a gun, he'd have already fired through the door. Still, Jez had locked up her mother, as well. Caution seemed the wiser choice at the moment. Aly lent her back to the task. "For what reason?"

" 'Cause I said I was gonna turn him in for robbing the bank. Mama helped him. I seen 'em hiding the money in the springhouse. But when he came out, he must've seen me too. He had a big ol' gun in his hand. She got real mad when he pointed it at me."

Something close to pride lit Jez's eyes. "She flew into him like a wildcat. Scratched his eyes and knocked the gun out of his hand. It went flying and landed somewhere in the grass over there."

The tiny head motioned to the left. "She must've hurt him real bad, 'cause he couldn't see very good for a minute. He grabbed her by the hair and pushed her into the springhouse. He told her to get his share of the money out of the bags and he'd leave her with me, if that's what she wanted. Mama told him to get it himself. Then he said for her to get some water to wipe the blood out of his eyes. She wouldn't do that neither."

A frown creased Jez's forehead. "Next thing I know, I heard a loud smack, then Mr. Driscoll said some bad words. He said she better watch who she was kicking, and she said he better not lay a finger on me when he got up from there. She said she'd tell *you* all about something I didn't understand. Something about him wanting to pay your daddy back for stealing his family's money. Did your daddy steal money from people, Aly?"

"I don't honestly know." In her heart, Aly refused to believe such of the man she'd loved so deeply. "I'd like to think he didn't." Her father had run rum ships from the Caribbean to the States. Some folks had said he made so much money by pirating, but Alewine thought he'd paid his crew well and dealt honest with his customers. He had more business than merchants with a hundred more ships to their fleets.

"Mr. Driscoll must think so. When Mama said she was gonna tell you about him trying to get your money, the next thing I heard was the two of them fighting again. That's when I did this."

"Did what?" Aly locked her knees to give her more leverage against the wooden door. Her eyes scanned the ground to see if she could spot a gun. Nothing.

Driscoll threw his weight again, splintering the wood and warning Aly that she couldn't chance the time to look for the weapon. Jezlynn would never be able to hold them back.

"I slammed the door and almost didn't get that big old stick slid into the loops in time." Jez's shoulders bounced off the wood when Driscoll gave another resounding kick. She glanced down at one of the crates she'd obviously slid over to stand on. "I ain't big enough to hold 'em back."

"I hear you out there! Let us out, Turner, or you and that kid are gonna wish you'd never seen me." Driscoll's threat echoed with malice.

Madeline's voice answered. "I told you, you are not going to lay a hand on my daughter, Clay. She's got nothing to do with—"

"Fine time to think like a mother, Madeline. That kid was supposed to be our hostage, how else are we going to insure our way out of the territory? This is about as wrong as it gets."

"You promised she wouldn't be harmed." Madeline shrieked.

"Would you quit fighting me, woman, and help me get us the hell out of here? We can be long gone from here, if you'll lend a foot and kick this door down. That woman and girl are no match for the two of us, and they already know you're involved. You think they're gonna let you go free just because you suddenly dug up a little motherly instinct?"

Up to now, Aly had been willing to give the woman the benefit of the doubt, but her teeth jarred as Madeline showed her guilt by making a choice. Both criminals threw their weight against the door.

"You set fire to the bank while everybody was out on the lake, didn't you?" Aly realized the pair had been trying to cover their tracks. Everyone would think the money burned up in the fire.

"They wouldn't let me help, neither. They said I was too little." Jez's lips pouted. The criminals slammed against the door again, pitching the child forward. She quickly regained her position. "At first I was mad 'cause they wouldn't let me help. Then I remembered what you said—that families help each other for *good* reasons. Burning down the bank would be a bad thing to do. So I didn't want to no more. That's when I decided I'd be the sheriff."

"Is that why you tied up your Aunt Elmertha?" Aly heard Madeline gasp.

Aly laughed nervously. Her shoulders began to tremble from the strain of holding back the door.

The door rocked with another blow. "It's all your fault, Aly." Rage bellowed from Driscoll's voice. "I paid you every social call you'd allow, and every man in town laughed at me because I had the guts to court you proper. I actually came to love you. But you only had eyes for that gambler. Your inheritance money is mine, not Turner's. My father lost his fortune to your father. Left my mother and I destitute. She's ill and needs special care. Before he died, I promised him I'd get it back any way I had to and see that she was properly taken care of. And I meant it, Alewine. Even if it meant marrying a no-good thieving bullwhip of a lady freighter."

"My business was never your true aim, was it?" Aly knew Nick had been led to believe a ruse. "Why did you spread such a lie? Why threaten to cut Ophelia's girls?"

Driscoll laughed harshly. "Scare tactics to make you turn to me for help. You couldn't watch your back *and* run a business. I thought by providing the heroics, you'd take my affections for you a bit more seriously. Then Turner returned to town and decided to ride to your rescue by marrying you. Or so he wants everyone to believe—"

"We really are married, Driscoll!" Aly's teeth clenched as she held off another blow. The door wouldn't be able to withstand them much longer, even with her weight bolstering it.

She glanced at Jez. The child's body shook with every impact of fist or foot against door. Aly had to send her for help, give her time to regain her strength.

Did she dare ask Jez to search for the gun? Aly could hold them off if she had the weapon. No . . . the thought of Jez handling a gun frightened Aly more than the possibility of having to fight Driscoll with her own two fists. She couldn't put Jez through what her father had suffered as a child. What if the gun went off and killed someone?

She prayed Nick would get there in time—but just in case, she'd send Jez to reach him. "Run, Jez. Run as fast as you can and tell Nick to grab a gun. Tell him what all has happened. If no one believes you, tell them to come ask me. I can verify it. And hurry, Jez. *Hurry!*"

Jez raced ahead.

"Take my horse. It's already saddled," Aly yelled.

A fist broke through the door. She dodged it, wishing for the knife normally sheathed in her boot. All these frills and flounces didn't do a woman a lick of good when in the thick of trouble. She needed something sharp to jab back at Driscoll.

The hatpins. She yanked a pin from her head and poked it at his hand, like she was a woodpecker carving at wood.

* * *

Nick rushed toward Aly just as Driscoll broke through the springhouse door. Instead of trampling her, the Valiant businessman darted to the left.

Panic gripped Aly as she realized his intent. "He's trying to get his gun. In the grass!" she shouted, stumbling to regain her footing.

"Connie and the stage, Aly!" Nick yelled. "Connie and the stage."

Play dead. Aly collapsed on the ground and rolled to her knees. When she looked up, she saw Driscoll and Nick diving at the same time toward a clump of thick grass. The gun!

Nick's hand reached it first. He batted it away. A struggle between the two men ensued. Just as Driscoll seemed to get the upper hand and reach for the weapon, Banker Sullivan yelled, "Hold it right there, Clay! Unless you want to die where you lay."

Driscoll's fingers clutched desperately.

Sullivan's bullet shattered the gun's handle, sending pieces of the weapon flying. "I'll not give another warning. One more inch and you're a dead man."

Driscoll's body slumped in defeat. He buried his face in the grass and beat his fists against the ground.

While Nick struggled to his feet, Sullivan motioned several men to take Driscoll prisoner.

Nick rushed toward Aly. "Are you all right, Chick? I hurried as fast as I could."

"Grab Madeline!" Aly yelled, pointing to the woman who was attempting to sneak away—skirting the outer edges of the crowd, trying not to be seen. "She helped Driscoll rob the bank and set fire to it."

"Yeah, Sullivan," Driscoll taunted as the men pulled him to his feet and tied his hands behind him. "Sweet Madeline's in on this, too. She set fire to your bank. Are you gonna shoot *her?*"

The sound of a hammer being cocked stopped Madeline in her tracks.

Madeline stared at the banker in astonishment. "Surely you don't take the word of such a scoundrel? Can't you see he took me prisoner? I was forced to help him. He made me do it. He said he would take Jezlynn hostage if I didn't. I had no choice."

"You liar!" Driscoll struggled against his binds. "I'm not taking this blame on my own." He glared at Silas. "Quit lusting for her long enough to see the truth, Banker. I'm paying for half the crime, but not all of it."

"It's over, Madeline." Silas exhaled a sigh that was years in coming. "Time to give up the game."

Nick motioned to the rest of the crowd. "Jez told us what she overheard, and Driscoll just confirmed it."

"Silas. *Friend*. Don't make me go to prison." Madeline's face lost all color. She swayed as if she were a pine that was about to topple. "You know I'm not a well woman."

"I'll always be your friend, Maddy." Banker Sullivan found his wife in the crowd and smiled at her. "But I'll no longer be your fool. My wife and I'll help you find a way back into society when you get out of prison. That's a promise."

Aly watched tears brim in the corpulent man's eyes as he took his childhood flame into custody. She'd known only one man braver in her entire life—Nick. Aly locked her arms around her husband's neck, staring into his beloved eyes. "You would have used that gun if you'd been forced to?"

"A man has to face his demons sometime, Chick, or live the hell that might follow if he doesn't."

Aly kissed Nick, mindless of all who stood around them.

"It's all your fault," Madeline hissed at her daughter. "You've been nothing but trouble to me since you were born."

"I advise you to shut your mouth, Madeline." Aly pulled away from Nick. "While you still have one."

"Why? I'm going to jail anyway. What more can you possibly do to me?" the woman taunted. "In fact, you're doing me a favor. I sent Nick the letter so he would take her off my hands."

Fury blazed through Aly. "You aren't really sick, are you? You never have been. Planning to head back East during your last days, were you? So no one would know you survived?"

Tiny fingers tapped Aly's fist. She opened her fingers to clasp Jez's hand with her own.

"I promise I'll be a good daughter if I can live with you and Papa for a long time."

Aly hugged her fiercely. "You already are, Skunk Wrangler. All you need is someone to believe in you. Love you. Nick and me, well, we're plumb loco about you. Ain't no way anybody's ever gonna take you away from us again." Aly swung around to face the crowd. "Ain't that right, folks?"

Though the crowd still seemed divided in loyalties, the following for Nick and Aly had grown considerably.

Pleased that some of the community agreed Nick was a better parent for Jez, Aly glared at Madeline. "I want to know why you hitched your team to Driscoll's wagon."

"I wanted your money. Nick told me how much you're worth. That it was your money in the bank. Your *daddy's* money. It seemed a fair trade."

Greed filled Madeline's face, making Aly hold Jezlynn closer.

"You got Nick and, along with him, control of Jezlynn's inheritance. That money should have been mine." Madeline glared at Jez. "My own father and

307

mother cared more for her than they did Elmertha
and me. Why shouldn't I take that money from the
bank, cash you won't even miss to begin my new
life?"

"Mama?"

The crowd silenced.

Madeline took a deep breath and glared at each of
the men who had her arms locked in an inescapable
vice of power, then focused her anger on Silas. She
seemed incapable of staring at her child.

"Thank you for not letting Mr. Driscoll shoot me."
Jezlynn leaned back against Aly. "Maybe when you
get out of prison, things will be different. I promise to
cry a whole bunch for you." For the first time, Madeline cracked. Her shoulders slumped and she looked
away.

Overwhelmed by the courage it took for Jezlynn to
accept life as it was, no matter how cruel, Aly swept
the child into her arms. Jez had a love and a forgivness
wiser than someone twenty times her age. "You're one
special little Skunk Wrangler, you know it? None of us
are gonna cry anymore. You and your Papa and me are
going to be happy all the rest of our days. That is, if he
answers the last question."

"What question?" Jez asked.

Suddenly Nick took Jezlynn from Aly's arms and
handed her to Connie. Then he pulled Aly close. "She
wants to know why it took me so long to tell her I
loved her." He grinned, his glance encompassing them
all. "And I do love her, folks, make no mistake."

Aly grinned. "Go on, Gambler. Spit it out."

Just as Nick started to say something, a high-
pitched shriek echoed from the house.

"Uh-oh." Jezlynn hid behind Aly's skirts. "Aunt
Elmertha's gonna be really mad at me."

Elmertha stood in the doorway of the house. When she spotted all in attendance, the back of the woman's hand pressed against her brow and she fainted.

"Better see if you can help her." Nick motioned a couple of men to check on the spinster.

"Now, back to the answer my wife has waited so patiently for." Nick's hand rubbed Aly's cheek where it had been grazed. "I believed that if Driscoll thought we were truly married, he would seek revenge on you. He had spent a lot of time courting you, apparently in the hopes of winning your fortune. I, on the other hand, knew nothing about your treasure and thought it had to do with him wanting your business."

Alewine looked up at him. "I planned to talk about my finances the next time we go fishing."

Nick and Aly shared a private laugh, then she sobered. "So you didn't tell me you loved me because you feared Driscoll would hurt me if he thought I was really and truly yours?"

"That, and I wasn't sure you knew what you really wanted, Chick. I couldn't force you to stay married if you didn't want to."

Now, Aly understood completely. He didn't want her to be a captive, like his mother. "I have to know just one more thing, Gambler."

"Name it."

"When exactly did you fall in love with me?"

Nick's teeth flashed broadly against his bronzed skin. "The day you walked down the street in those silly feathers and molasses, that's when. I knew it would be one hell of a ride taming a woman like you."

"I did when you climbed out on that tree and nearly fell," Jezlynn spoke up. At Nick's look of surprise, his daughter shrugged. "Well, we both gotta love her, don't we, if we're supposed to be happy?"

Everyone laughed.

Aly offered a playful wink. "Hang on, you two. I still got a few wild seasons before you gentle me up completely."

Nick dug into his pocket and took out the wedding ring he'd given her in Valiant. After he placed it on her finger once again, Nick's lips halted a breath from her own. "I'm counting on it, Love. 'Cause you're a sure bet."

DIA HUNTER
THE BEHOLDING

Tess Harper should hate Luke Reeves. He enters her life with the news that her husband is dead—and he is the one who killed him. But despite the bounty hunter's cold expression and scarred face, despite his quick draw that makes men fear him, the young widow hopes against all hope that he will lead her out of her lonely life and make her forget her checkered past.

___4321-1 $4.99 US/$5.99 CAN

Dorchester Publishing Co., Inc.
P.O. Box 6640
Wayne, PA 19087-8640

Please add $1.75 for shipping and handling for the first book and $.50 for each book thereafter. NY, NYC, and PA residents, please add appropriate sales tax. No cash, stamps, or C.O.D.s. All orders shipped within 6 weeks via postal service book rate. Canadian orders require $2.00 extra postage and must be paid in U.S. dollars through a U.S. banking facility.

Name_____
Address_____
City_____State_____Zip_____
I have enclosed $_____ in payment for the checked book(s).
Payment <u>must</u> accompany all orders. ❏ Please send a free catalog.

HALF-BREED'S

Lady

BOBBI SMITH

To artist Glynna Williams, Texas is a land of wild beauty, carved by God's hand, untouched as yet by man's. And the most exciting part of it is the fierce, bare-chested half-breed who saves her from a rampaging bull. As she spends the days sketching his magnificent body, she dreams of spending the nights in his arms.

___4436-6 $5.99 US/$6.99 CAN

Dorchester Publishing Co., Inc.
P.O. Box 6640
Wayne, PA 19087-8640

Please add $1.75 for shipping and handling for the first book and $.50 for each book thereafter. NY, NYC, and PA residents, please add appropriate sales tax. No cash, stamps, or C.O.D.s. All orders shipped within 6 weeks via postal service book rate. Canadian orders require $2.00 extra postage and must be paid in U.S. dollars through a U.S. banking facility.

Name_____
Address_____
City_____ State_____ Zip_____
I have enclosed $_____ in payment for the checked book(s).
Payment <u>must</u> accompany all orders. ❑ Please send a free catalog.
CHECK OUT OUR WEBSITE! www.dorchesterpub.com

WESTON'S Lady
BOBBI SMITH

There are Cowboys and Indians, trick riding, thrills and excitement for everyone. And if Liberty Jones has anything to say about it, she will be a part of the Wild West show, too. She has demonstrated her expertise with a gun by shooting a card out of Reed Weston's hand at thirty paces, but the arrogant owner of the Stampede won't even give her a chance. Disguising herself as a boy, Libby wangles herself a job with the show, and before she knows it Reed is firing at her—in front of an audience. It seems an emotional showdown is inevitable whenever they come together, but Libby has set her sights on Reed's heart and she vows she will prove her love is every bit as true as her aim.

___4512-5 $5.99 US/$6.99 CAN

BOBBI SMITH

THE LADY & THE TEXAN

"A fine storyteller!"—*Romantic Times*

A firebrand since the day she was born, Amanda Taylor always stands up for what she believes in. She won't let any man control her—especially a man like gunslinger Jack Logan. Even though Jack knows Amanda is trouble, her defiant spirit only spurs his hunger for her. He discovers that keeping the dark-haired tigress at bay is a lot harder than outsmarting the outlaws after his hide—and surrendering to her sweet fury is a heck of a lot riskier.

___4319-X $5.99 US/$6.99 CAN

BRIDES OF DURANGO: ELISE
BOBBI SMITH

Elise Martin will do anything for a story—even stage a fake marriage to catch a thief. Dressed in a white lace gown, she looks every bit the bride, but when her "fiancé" fails to show, she offers ten dollars to the handsome gentleman who just stepped off the stage to pose as the groom. As a fake fiancé, he is all right, but when he turns out to be Gabriel West, the new owner of her paper, the *Durango Star*, Elise wants to turn tail and run. But she can't forget the passion his unexpected kiss at their "wedding" aroused, and she starts to wonder if there is more to Gabriel West than meets the eye. For the more time they spend together, the more Elise wonders if the next time she says, "I do" she just might mean it.

___4575-3 $5.99 US/$6.99 CAN

Dorchester Publishing Co., Inc.
P.O. Box 6640
Wayne, PA 19087-8640

Linda Jones

On A Wicked Wind

Hurled into the Caribbean and swept back in time, Sabrina Steele finds herself abruptly aroused in the arms of the dashing pirate captain Antonio Rafael de Zamora. There, on his tropical island, Rafael teaches her to crest the waves of passion and sail the seas of ecstasy. But the handsome rogue has a tortured past, and in order to consummate a love that called her through time, the headstrong beauty seeks to uncover the pirate's true buried treasure—his heart.

___52251-9 $5.99 US/$6.99 CAN

Jackie & The Giant

LINDA JONES

It isn't a castle, but Cloudmont is close: The enormous estate houses everything Jacqueline Beresford needs to quit her life of crime. But climbing up to the window, Jackie gets a shock. The gorgeous giant of an owner is awake—and he is a greater treasure than she ever imagined. It hardly surprises Rory Donovan that the beautiful burglar is not what she claims, but capturing the feisty felon offers an excellent opportunity. He was searching for a governess for his son, and against all logic, he feels Jackie is perfect for the role—and for many others. But he knows that she broke into his home to rob him of his wealth—for what reason did she steal his heart?

___52333-7 $5.99 US/$6.99 CAN

Dorchester Publishing Co., Inc.
P.O. Box 6640
Wayne, PA 19087-8640

Please add $1.75 for shipping and handling for the first book and $.50 for each book thereafter. NY, NYC, and PA residents, please add appropriate sales tax. No cash, stamps, or C.O.D.s. All orders shipped within 6 weeks via postal service book rate. Canadian orders require $2.00 extra postage and must be paid in U.S. dollars through a U.S. banking facility.

Name_____
Address_____
City_____State_____Zip_____
I have enclosed $_____ in payment for the checked book(s).
Payment <u>must</u> accompany all orders. ☐ Please send a free catalog.
CHECK OUT OUR WEBSITE! www.dorchesterpub.com

TEXAS EMPIRES:
Lone Star
EVELYN ROGERS

The Lone Star State is as forthright and independent as the women who brave the rugged land, and sunset-haired Kate Calloway is as feisty an example as Cord has ever seen. A Texas woman. He has not dealt with one in a long time, but he recognizes the gumption in her blue eyes. He would be a fool to question the threat behind the shotgun leveled at his chest. He would be still more a fool to give in to the urge to take her right there on the hard, dusty ground. For though he senses they are two halves of one whole, Kate belongs to the man he's come to destroy. That they will meet again is certain; the only question is: how long can he wait before making her his?

___4533-8 $5.99 US/$6.99 CAN

BETRAYAL Evelyn Rogers

By the Bestselling Author of
The Forever Bride

If there is anything that gets Conn O'Brien's Irish up, it is a lady in trouble–especially one he has fallen in love with at first sight. So after the Texas horseman saves Crystal Braden from an overly amorous lout, he doesn't waste a second declaring his intentions to make an honest woman of her. But they have barely been declared man and wife before Conn learns that his new bride is hiding a devastating secret that can destroy him.

The plan is simple: To ensure the safety of her mother and young brother, Crystal agrees to play the damsel in distress. The innocent beauty has no idea how dangerously charming the virile stranger can be–nor how much she longs to surrender to the tender passion in his kiss. And when Conn discovers her ruse, she vows to blaze a trail of desire that will convince him that her deception has been an error of the heart and not a ruthless betrayal.

___4262-2 $5.99 US/$6.99 CAN

Dorchester Publishing Co., Inc.
P.O. Box 6640
Wayne, PA 19087-8640

Please add $1.75 for shipping and handling for the first book and $.50 for each book thereafter. NY, NYC, and PA residents, please add appropriate sales tax. No cash, stamps, or C.O.D.s. All orders shipped within 6 weeks via postal service book rate. Canadian orders require $2.00 extra postage and must be paid in U.S. dollars through a U.S. banking facility.

Name_____
Address _____
City_____State _____Zip_____
I have enclosed $_____ in payment for the checked book(s).
Payment <u>must</u> accompany all orders. ❑ Please send a free catalog.